Pauline McLynn gr..... ....cting
while studying Histo.... ....layed
many stage roles, b.. ... .table
Mrs Doyle in Fathe.. .... Her other television work
includes *Aristocrats* and *Bremner, Bird and Fortune*.
Pauline has read several *Books at Bedtime* and her
appearances on cinema screens include *Angela's
Ashes*, *Quills* and *An Everlasting Piece*. Pauline has
contributed to several short story collections, as well
as writing three extremely successful and highly praised
comic novels featuring Dublin private detective Leo
Street. When *The Woman on the Bus* was first
published it shot straight on to *The Irish Times* best-
seller list where it remained in the Top 5 for seven
weeks.

Praise for *The Woman on the Bus*:

'It is her new novel, *The Woman on the Bus* – upbeat,
witty and with a cracking plot – that is going to mark
Pauline as a writer of substance. The Irish community
is evoked in wonderfully lyrical passages and the
dialogue is impossible to read without hearing lilting
Irish accents . . . she is a gifted storyteller as well as an
exceptional comic actress' *Sunday Express*

THE WOMAN ON THE BUS

PAULINE McLYNN

review

First published in 2004
by HEADLINE BOOK PUBLISHING

First published in paperback in 2005
by HEADLINE BOOK PUBLISHING

A REVIEW paperback

10 9 8 7 6 5 4 3 2 1

ISBN 0 7472 6782 0

Typeset in New Caledonia by
Palimpsest Book Production Limited, Polmont, Stirlingshire
Printed and bound in Great Britain by
Clays Ltd St Ives plc
Headline's policy is to use papers that are natural, renewable and
recyclable products and made from wood grown in
sustainable forests. The logging and manufacturing processes
are expected to conform to the environmental
regulations of the country of origin.

HEADLINE BOOK PUBLISHING
A division of Hodder Headline PLC
338 Euston Road
London NW1 3BH
www.reviewbooks.co.uk
www.hodderheadline.com

For Richard,
at long last

One

Cathy Long waited by the wall as the bus inched along its route. She closed her eyes and felt new freckles burst onto her face in the late evening sun. Maybe if she got enough of them they'd join up to form a tan. At least then she'd have something to show for this endless drag of a summer. Normally she had company but her dog, Dennis, had died and had been buried earlier that day in a patch by the apple trees reserved for family pets, past, present and future. As the bus edged by Cathy gave three short barks, in honour of the late Dennis, and waved to the driver. He gave a grumpy shake of his head and went back to looking poisonously at the swaying rumps of the cows blocking his way. A voice called from the Long house.

'Cathy, time to go into town and get your father. Tell him his dinner is on the table.'

There might have been an argument another time, but Cathy was missing the dog and little inclined to add to her present mood by rowing with her mother. She broke into a loose run, all bouncing curls and adolescent lengthening of legs, overtook the bus without breaking a sweat and left it to ponder her dust as she headed for the least favourite part of her day.

Ozzy O'Reilly sat on the graveyard wall watching the bus through his binoculars. Best bloody present he'd ever bought himself. His watch, another treat with, as he endlessly told all who'd listen, more dials than the old phone service, called the time at 19.05. Fourteen minutes late already and two miles yet to go. It was the new driver again, a young Dublin fella, too cautious by half on the country roads. Not like Ozzy who tore up that tarmac in his red Ford Capri; a vintage motor for a classy guy. He was a small man with a big interest in transport. And some other things. He let the binocs roam at will. The Marrs had the washing out on the line. Nothing much to see since herself had got the circular job. Now she put all the underwear on the inside, to hide the state of it, and the even bigger garments on the outside. They waved to him in the breeze. Further on, Bert Fahy was marching through his fields kicking the stones and rocks as he went. Temper, temper, Bert. Ozzy could've taken a good guess as to why Bert was so disposed. And he knew what would cure him too. In fact, Ozzy knew a lot more than he usually shared with anyone in the town. Wasn't information power, and all that? His gaze drifted to the bus again as it wound over and back the tortuous route leading to Kilbrody. At this rate of going it would be at least half an hour late into town. That young fella had a long night ahead of him getting out and on to Limerick. Ozzy chuckled. Nothing more amusing than another man's misfortune. Then he began to laugh out loud. No one to hear but the dead, and they didn't seem to mind, having had their fair share of misery.

'Sure you have to laugh,' he told them. 'If we didn't laugh we'd cry and then where would we be?'

Jack Cunningham swore to himself as he ground the bus to a halt behind the herd of cows ambling home to be milked. Picture-postcard Ireland full of moo cows and red-faced farmers and dogs and mountains and tourists and potholes and delays. He hated this route above all others. He should never have given his boss lip over that Friday pint a fortnight ago. Now he was on the punishment shift: Dublin to Limerick via Kilbrody, County Clare; one hundred and seventy miles of hell. Then a shitty overnight in McDonagh's Bed and Breakfast with a nymphomaniac landlady the size of an articulated lorry. And a smell of bacon and cabbage off everything, including her. Back again the following day to Dublin via Kilfeckinbrody. No doubt about it, everything west, south and north of Dublin was a toilet and the tourists were welcome to it. As well as the culchees, of course. Savages, the lot of them. Cute hoors trying to take the eye out of yer head without you noticing, and even then their left hand not letting on to the right what it was up to. There was the crazy kid on the wall, as usual. No dog though. Maybe it was dead, or arrested for harassing motorists. Could dogs actually be banged up for that? Now she was legging it ahead of him into town. Was there no justice in the world at all any more? He needed a career break, he thought, as he picked his nose and chewed on the harvest. And a good ride; clear the blood a bit. Maybe he should shag the McDonagh woman. He shuddered. Ah now, lads, stall on. He must really be losing it if he was contemplating that. Imagine her bouncing up and down on top of him, folds of overripe flesh quivering long after he'd done with her, orange lipstick smeared across those crooked teeth; all the better to eat you with, my dear. That wasn't an image to dwell on either. And while he was at it, if he found one more orange mouth print on his tea cup in the morning he was going to say something. He was. Definitely. And move B & Bs, if he could afford it.

He checked on the passengers in the rear-view mirror. Usual lot of tossers and losers. A few Germans in search of the 'real' Ireland, and a load of bumpkins back from a day out in the Big Smoke. He could hardly understand a word any of them said with the big aul bog accents on them. That went for the Irish too. If he hadn't been so far gone he'd have laughed at his own joke, but stopping every quarter of a bleedin' mile to deliver the locals to their bloody doors had his heart broken. This evening there was only one item of exotica on display: a woman on the back row who'd slept all the way from Dublin. As he looked at her the woman stirred and opened her eyes. She caught her reflection in the bus window as the hedgerows passed gently by. Recognising no one, she drifted off again. Bit of a looker, thought Jack, and a bit drunk too, if the shape of her when she was buying her ticket was anything to go by. Maybe she'd need a cure when she woke up. Maybe she'd missed her stop along the way and he could show her a good time in Limerick later. If it was humanly possible to find a good time in that shithole. He needed cheering up, no mistake. And anything was better than ploughing into the Widow McDonagh. The cows decided to take a right into a field that looked like any other to his eyes. Dumb animals. He eased the bus forward past them then cut loose along the potholed road to the town of Kilbrody. That should jolt a bit of life into all concerned. They'd be forty-five minutes late arriving.

As if he gave a flying fuck.

Charlie Finn was beginning to think that it was a bad idea to have the dartboard so close to the toilet door, as a missile thudded into the outermost ring of the target. Luckily, the latest exitee of the gents was a bare five foot one and walked with a natural stoop, well below the arc of the arrow so violently flung by a drunken neighbour. No rancour involved, just a lot of alcohol fuelling the vehemence; the importance of being seen to be Still Totally In Control. A typical Tuesday evening, then.

A tiny nod from a customer signalled the pulling of another pint. Charlie reached for the glass and three-quarters filled it with a hush of liquid, the waves of effervescent foam settling and separating into a handsome division of black topped by a creamy head. He could almost taste its smooth, bitter darkness.

'The bus is in,' Old Mikey Byrne observed.

The stragglers at the bar nodded at the wisdom and sheer accuracy of the statement.

'At last,' Charlie rejoined, to more accord from the barflies.

'We'll have reinforcements so,' Mikey continued, in time-honoured tradition. 'And, please God, plenty of them, sez you,' he directed graciously to Charlie, landlord of the establishment.

'Please God,' Charlie acknowledged, reaching for the waiting pints of stout to finish them off, slowly and lovingly, under the watchful gaze of the experts lining the counter. Ritual was everything.

Old Mikey's gnarled and hairy paw engulfed the glass and he lowered a good half of the pint before declaring, ''Tis thirsty work all the same.' He met with no argument and nodded his head of startled grey hair like the dog on the back shelf of a car always agreeing with life.

Cathy Long exploded through the door, spilling the late sunlight in her wake across the dull, stone floor. The codgers at the bar instinctively turned their backs lest the light dissolve them from their dreamlike vampire existence, shielding their precious pints from an unwelcome, and most likely hostile, outside world.

'Where is he?' Cathy asked Charlie.

He nodded towards the usual corner. Her dad was involved in a convoluted argument with the Whinge O'Brien, who was threatening to run for the local County Council after planning permission was denied him for an ugly bungalow his wife had wanted built nearer than was allowed to the main road.

'Discrimination, pure and simple,' insisted the Whinge. 'It's nothing but punishment for doing well. But sure anyway weren't they always a mean shower of shites, them lot, and doesn't every dog and divil walking the street know that?'

Tom Long had reached a point well past inebriation where he was thinking almost cogently again, but more or less unable to articulate his responses. It was the stage of the day he loved and the one his daughter detested: he was anaesthetised, she saw a drunk.

'Ah, it's my own darling girl,' he declared, for all to hear.

Cathy doubled over on herself to make her presence as small as possible. She hated the attention. She hated this place. She hated her dad.

'Dinner,' she growled. 'And I'm not waiting for you.'

Though of course she did, outside.

The bus was disgorging its cargo.

'Kilbrody,' roared Jack the driver.

He shook his head at the child-like delight of the tourists, excited at being amongst the natives. Gobdaws, the lot of them. What was there here to please them so much? An uppity two-horse town with a rake of pubs, a chemist, a few hucksters' shops and a grotty café. He didn't 'get' the Clare thing. Beyond the towns and villages was nothing but rock and scutch, and eventually the sea. The famous Burren was supposed to have rare plants and the like but he never saw any of it, and anyway *so what*? All there was by way of nightlife was a few hairy aul fellas banging on bodhrans and sawing away at fiddles with mad diddlyidle music. No clubs, no babes, no action. No thanks.

The woman on the back row shook herself upright and headed for the door.

'Are you sure, love?' he asked her. 'You could stay on with me and we'll have a mad night of it in Limerick.'

For a moment, he almost believed that any or all of that last statement was possible. She looked through him and out onto the main street. Across the road a large sign over a door said 'Finn's' and, seeming satisfied that this was where she'd wanted all along, she crossed the road and went through the door.

'Bitch,' Jack muttered to anyone who chose to hear. He slammed the bus into gear and tried to take off with a movie-like screech of tyres. The vehicle hulked and baulked, then sluggishly picked up a pace and headed for the nearby hills. Jack glanced in the rear-view mirror along the near empty aisle. Silently watching him from the back seat was a handbag.

Oops, he thought, smiling. Someone's forgotten her bag. Too bad I didn't notice it till we got to Limerick.

Charlie consulted the pub clock, prominent above the empty fireplace. Eight o'clock. Dear Jesus, another three and a half hours to go. That was if he managed to shift everyone out on time, and there was precious little chance of that. Might as well call it another five hours and be done. He reached for a packet of dry-roasted peanuts and poured himself a lemonade; no point in letting his sugar levels plummet him into a worse place than where he was headed. This was his twilight zone, the terrible hours when he switched to auto-pilot and his mind fevered the same old questions. Why had he come home at all, really? Or, more importantly, why had he stayed on then when his immediate business was done? And what had he come back to? A place where he'd always be known as 'Young Finn' in spite of his forty-three years. Aul lads marking his card with that name and their seniority, like cats spraying territory: 'Sure I remember you when you were in nappies . . .' Oh, the punters called him Charlie or Charles while in the pub, but it's what they call you behind your back that matters and defines you, in their eyes. And that would always be Young Finn.

Tom Long got to his feet, leaving the Whinge in mid-complaint. He nodded to Charlie on his exit and announced to the gathering that the War Department had summoned him. They threw their eyes to heaven in acknowledgement of a universal situation. The door opened, light made a brief, unsuccessful foray then the usual torpor settled itself once more. Even the Whinge was silenced.

Standing sentinel at the bar, Charlie knew there were other matters lurking in a particular darkness of his mind. It was best not to let them surface because there was no telling what the consequences might be. They were hard to shake tonight. Why? And then, as a tiny gesture indicated another pint was to be poured, it hit him: he was bored. Very, very bored. Bored almost to death.

And that's when the woman from the bus came through his door.

TWO

She drank brandy, sat with her back to the pub crowd, idly playing with a newspaper. It seemed not to bother her that it was in French, having been abandoned by a tourist earlier in the day. Every so often she would squint and take in her surroundings. Then she would rustle a hand in her jacket pocket and produce a note for more drink. Her voice was so low as she ordered that Charlie could not detect her accent. She was of unremarkable height, being neither short nor tall. Her shoulder-length hair was a mid-brown with well-applied blond highlights. Her clothes were casual and crumpled: a white linen blouse, beige pants and light jacket. Her face was pleasant and troubled, and in the dim interior of the pub Charlie was sure he could see that her eyes were tired with crying.

Now and again one of the regulars would try to put the chat on her, but she simply ignored them, without glancing at the source of the voice or registering its sound; a very effective system, and soon they gave up and abandoned her to her thoughts, shrugging their eyebrows to show they had an odd one here, a bit of a loulah. When the newspaper finally lost its odd charm she began to shred beer mats. This was a slow, precise activity which involved piling the debris in a small mountain on the table. She obviously doesn't smoke, Charlie thought, or she'd have been through a pack and a half by now.

After her third squint and puzzled look round the joint he knew she was drinking to be drunk and staving off reality each time it tried to impinge. Each to her own.

'Come ON, Daddy,' Cathy implored.

This walk was taking forever. It always did. If she had a sister or brother she could share the burden but there was only her. Just her bloody luck. And now he was singing; one of his nonsense ditties with no tune but plenty of words, and all about her.

'She loves a song, our Cathy Long, she's never wrong, not Cathy Long. She's very strong, is Cathy Long, she doesn't pong, she's Cathy Long.' Drink made him even more foolish than usual. Cathy couldn't wait to be sixteen, then she could legally leave school and this awful place and her parents. But although she had a birthday coming soon, she would still only be thirteen and it was intolerable to think that she had another three long years before her escape.

They had just reached the boundary of the front garden when her father started clicking his tongue for the dog.

'Dennis,' click-click-click. 'Where's the Denny? Dennis?' Click-click-click. 'Here, Denny-den.'

Tears stung Cathy's eyes. Stupid bastard couldn't even remember that the dog was dead. Dead and buried. As she felt salt liquid burn her cheeks, Cathy let out a muted 'FUUUCK' and ran for the house.

The night brought a steady dribble of punters to Finn's. Grizzled, mountainy types still smelling of livestock and their few acres of bog and reed. Some of the town's smarter set were in attendance also, including Carol Kelly, one of the few eligible women of Charlie's age in the area, and her friend Linda. The former was chasing him with a view to marriage and the latter, unbeknownst to her friend, was shagging him on a regular basis. Linda's husband was not aware of this arrangement either. Charlie sighed contentedly; he hadn't lost it yet. And with the arrival of the cuckolded spouse he had the added frisson of deciding whether to take Linda out back for a quickie or relax and let her deal with the mess that was her marriage.

The women added a sweet, synthetic perfume to the pub air but, as Charlie knew, the smells of the night before often brought unwelcome memories and a lot of laundry. In spite of a nationwide smoking ban in public places, and a stonker of an air conditioning system, he still reeked after a day's work. Partly, it was because the law round these parts smoked and liked to drink in Finn's, so the ban was flouted royally when the Sergeant was 'in the house'. In retrospect, as it always is, it was inconceivable to Charlie that the stinking clothes worn the previous night could signify a good time. In fact, in the bad old days, after he hit his first thirty euro bill for three dry-cleaned items, he switched to natural fibres ripe for the twin tub and some ironing, at five euro an hour à la Mrs Daly next door. This was robbery according to the national average wage but, as no one was kicking up, a neighbourly consensus materialised with uninjured parties and even a little satisfaction, if truth be told. He finally invested in a front-loading machine and dryer and still enjoyed using them. Was he that easily pleased now? Well, he still loathed ironing and though some might say he had little else to occupy his down time, he'd prefer to remove his own kidneys with a blunt spoon. Memories of his earlier years tried to butt in and he knew if he let them take hold, he couldn't guarantee where he'd end up. He set about collecting empties with the vigour of a man possessed.

Bert Fahy came through the door, looking as if he'd bring the frame with him. He was a large, handsome farmer with an equally large and handsome portfolio of land and assets. He hung his head low, the mark of a painfully shy man. All he was short of was a stutter to complete the stigma; what a companion piece that would make for the poor divil, Charlie thought. Linda nudged Carol and gestured towards the new customer. They both giggled softly. That settled it for the landlord; she was not getting the ride this evening.

'Evening, Bert,' Linda called.

If the earth could have swallowed Bert Fahy he would have been grateful and paid it a tip for its trouble. Still, he wanted every opportunity to speak to Carol and if this was one, he had to grasp it. Bert, for all his shyness, loved women, and battled gamely with his condition when they were in his orbit.

He reddened and said, 'Ladies. Ye're looking lovely this evening.' They let him squirm so he continued with, 'Can I get ye anything?'

'You're grand,' Carol said. 'We're sorted.' Bert was so crestfallen she added, 'Maybe later?'

He nodded energetically. 'Later, yes,' he said. 'That'd be great. Let me know when.'

He moved over to join the Whinge who took up where he'd left off with Tom Long earlier.

The woman from the bus ordered another brandy.

Cathy Long lay sprawled across her bed, cheek to cheek with Britney Spears, courtesy of her matching duvet cover and pillowcase set. The dreaded dinner hour was approaching with its endless questions and annoyances. He'd be slopping food on the table and himself. Her mother would pretend not to notice, probably. Unless it was a night when she decided to make a stand; those were nearly worse than ignoring the situation. Cathy could hear her parents shuffle around the kitchen.

'Ah, Tom,' her mother was saying. 'Would you look at the cut of you. Clean yourself up till we have a meal in reasonable peace and quiet. CATHY! Come on. Dinner.'

Cathy dragged herself through the rooms and to the table, every fibre wanting to stay in her sanctuary, even if it meant starving to death.

'So, young lady, tell us how your day was.'

Cathy gave a shrug of the shoulder and left it at that. She was nearly a teenager now and had to act like one. It came quite naturally, she noticed, delighted.

'You went swimming? How was it?'

'OK.'

Her mother rose to the lack of details. Why couldn't she just let it go?

'Cathy went to Lahinch with a few others for a day out at the beach, Tom. Didn't you, Cathy?'

She tried another shrug.

'Well?' her mother wanted to know.

'Yeah, it was good.' Then she stuffed as much of her meal into her face as possible and settled back in her chair to chew on it. Full mouth equals no more conversation. End of episode. PLEASE.

Tom Long looked into his daughter's eyes and for a moment he grabbed at lucidity. He winked and asked,

'Is no one allowed to have their own life around here without having to explain every last thing?'

Cathy looked at her plate, not wanting to be sided with him of all people, the root, no the square root, of all their problems. Her mother forged on.

'Ah, come on, Cathy, how was it? That's hardly asking you a deep secret, is it?'

'It was fine,' she mumbled. 'Nothing major.' Which was true.

'Was Fiona there?'

Fiona was supposed to be Cathy's best friend of the moment but was always accusing her of 'going all weird'.

'Did ye go back to her place?'

'Yeah.'

'Well, maybe she'd like to come here next time?'

There, *there* was the crux of it: how could she ask Fiona over when no one ever knew what state *he'd* be in? And was she supposed to bring Fiona along with her later too when she went to get him from Finn's like she had to do most days? No wonder she couldn't have lots of friends, and didn't want them.

There was a late flurry as official closing time approached, though Charlie knew that none of the locals involved had any intention of leaving before one in the morning. It helped their cause that the local Sergeant was propping up the bar and his underling, a rookie called McGowan, wouldn't dream of raiding the place with his boss inside.

Bad enough that he'd ticketed every last uninsured car in the district on his first day and nearly earned himself a transfer to an even more remote outpost of the Irish Republic. No, McGowan had learned a valuable lesson and the Sergeant was pleased with him, especially as once the fines were issued he told the locals he couldn't undo them, so the station was looking efficient in the eyes of his commanding super and the rabble temporarily back in line. Life was sweet and so was the Guinness.

'You've a grand crowd in for a Tuesday,' he told Charlie.

'I do. Though you can't rely on it, that's the trouble with this game.'

'Oh yes, yes, sure don't I know.'

'You'll have a wee something on the house?'

'Well, I suppose I might. And I was wondering if you'd like to sponsor the box of oranges for the under-thirteens soccer match on Sunday.'

This was an order and not a request, as Charlie well knew. And no matter how many of these 'favours' were done, you could never expect one in return. He'd got sure proof of that when the Sergeant searched the place for drugs six months after Charlie took over, found a small lump of hash and threatened him with jail. From there on out Charlie took all the 'hail fellow well met' with a kilo of salt.

'No problem at all,' he told the law.

✿   ✿   ✿

Cathy snuggled under her duvet with her torch and a book. Britney lay over her and kept her safe. She couldn't concentrate. Next door her mother was trying to talk some sense to her father.

'Why can't you even try to give it up? Why don't you go to a meeting or something? It's tearing us all apart, you know.'

Cathy heard a stifled sob. She didn't know why her mother bothered any more. The tears never worked. The silences had no effect. Throw him out, was the only way. Or escape. She heard a gentle snore escape from her father and the discussion was at an end. Thing was, he'd be up and out to deal with the livestock and all the other farm business at cock crow. He never let the work suffer. But when it was all seen to and afternoon came, it was off into Finn's and that was the end of that for the day. Every day. Cathy rolled onto her side. She missed Dennis. The tears came freely and soon she too was snoring gently into a wet pillow.

She was the last to leave. In fact, she didn't look like she was going anywhere.

'Sorry, Miss,' Charlie said. 'We're all done for the night. Time to go home.'

She met his gaze with drooping green eyes and struggled to her feet. He noticed a red mark on her cheek, like a touch of sunburn.

'Wherem I?' she wanted to know.

'You're in Finn's of Kilbrody.'

This seemed to draw a blank.

'Wherezat?' A reasonable question, actually, and frequently asked. The arse end of the planet, he might have tried, but settled for the truth.

'County Clare,' he said.

'Rilly?' She tried to make sense of it. 'My s'posed be here?'

'Well, I couldn't tell you that.'

'Jye know you?'

'No.'

'Oh.' She seemed confused. 'You 'specting me?'

'Definitely not.'

She thought about that too. 'Then I'va problem.'

Charlie believed that she did. 'I don't suppose you have a place to stay,' he said.

'Donthing so.'

Her speech grew more halting and sibilant as impossible new information confronted her and she began to close down. Charlie made the only decision available to him.

'Right,' he said. 'You can stay here and we'll deal with this after a good night's sleep.'

She began to check in her pockets, hands emerging with the loose change he'd given for the brandies. Then she searched under the table and the stools.

'Musdava bag.'

'I didn't see one.'

She looked at the few coins left to her.

'S'all I have to pay for accom . . . acc . . . accom . . . idayshun.'

Now she was swaying and incomprehension was only a syllable away. She was just about asleep on her feet. Or semi-conscious, to be more precise.

'Don't worry about that,' Charlie told her. 'You can work off the debt.'

He made for the door at the back of the pub, which led upstairs to the living quarters. He turned to beckon her and was astonished. The woman was naked. Here, amongst fag ash and the certainty of a blocked gents toilet, he approached a luminous figure, whose vulnerability lit up the smoky darkness. And it touched him. He wanted to help. He did.

'Oh no, no,' he told her. 'Not like that. You can do some bar work to pay me.'

He almost laughed at the absurdity of the situation and, above all, that he was refusing sex with a fine woman. This would not look good alongside his legendary reputation for conquest. Nevertheless, he went to wrestle her back into her bits and pieces. Although Charlie was a man who knew his way around women's lingerie as easily as a homing pigeon found its base, he settled for simply draping her jacket around her shoulders and helped her up the narrow stairs.

'You arrived on the bus, so that's maybe where your bag is. We'll check on all of that tomorrow.'

'Tomorrow,' she slurred.

But in fact that particular tomorrow never came for her. It was almost two days before she woke.

Three

It was Deborah from the chemist who suggested the baby monitor. When the woman from the bus didn't wake the next morning and seemed to have no intention of doing so in a hurry, Charlie found himself without adequate cover to run the bar or a body who could be trusted to sit with, well, the sleeping body. And Charlie was needed downstairs. Business was booming with word of the strange arrival and, as the rumours and falsities made their way around the town and onwards, pilgrims came to hear of his curiosity woman from the horse's own mouth.

'You'll be able to keep tabs on her,' Deborah explained. 'The last thing you want is for her to wake up and wander out onto those stairs. She could fall and break her neck.'

Card schools sprang up to while away the long hours as the sentries waited for word of consciousness. The monitor sat amongst the rarely opened bottles of vermouth and Pimms lining the shelves by the cash register. Occasionally a sigh would bring a hush to the gambling, then the sound of sleep once more.

In the meantime Ozzy O'Reilly narrowly missed losing his life to a dart thrown by the Whinge. It was generally accepted that he would have died if the Whinge had been even half a glass of Guinness less drunk. Feeling ran high over the banned bungalow and Ozzy was a member of the County Council. The attempted murder cleared a little of the venom from the Whinge and he settled for relieving Ozzy of a hundred and fifty euro. A betting man would have predicted the money would yo-yo between them over the next week, and the betting man would have been correct.

The Whinge was an undefined hulk of man, with a fleshy, disappointed face and a soft, under-used body. He was overfed and had almost returned to that baby stage where human children have limbs but no joints, where arm meets hand and decides to form a wrist later. He looked allergic to sunshine. In contrast, Ozzy was a tanned, wire terrier with pinched features and a yappy personality. He could never shake the idea that the town was dragging him down into its festering gloom; but better to be the big fish in this claggy, ornamental pond than a minnow a few miles down the road. Ozzy ran a turf accountants cum internet café called Surf 'n' Turf and was constantly dismayed by the community's reluctance to embrace his empire. Tweenies were a whizz on the computers but legally barred from placing bets on dogs, horses or other sporting events, whereas the oldsters just wanted a smoke and the traditional pencil and paper of a bookie's business. And now they weren't allowed to smoke on the premises, so times were slow.

The O'Reillys were new men who fumbled in the greasy till of Irish commerce and local politics, whereas the Whinge was of ancient agricultural stock. In his day, the Whinge's father drank half the O'Brien family farm but died of a heart attack before he could finish the job. His son never forgave Old Mikey for taking advantage of the O'Briens' need and buying the acres sacrificed by his daddy. He didn't dislike Old Mikey, just couldn't forgive him. And that was understood by all.

'Sure, weren't they miserable enough fields?' Mikey would often ask in mitigation.

But in a country where land was Land, this rang hollow as a defence, and no one knew it better than himself.

They called her the woman on the bus, because that was indeed how she had arrived in their lives. The local quack, Gilhooley, said she had to be left till she was ready to return, and that there was nothing much to worry about as long as she was kept hydrated. Charlie thought about that a while, aware that Gilhooley was of the old school, who would examine a woman's breasts to determine pregnancy rather than use a new-fangled and ninety-nine per cent accurate tester. But there was something in the woman's situation that triggered recognition in him and he was happy to wait until she decided to waken, while spooning her water on the hour and half-hour. And, as Mikey pointed out, if she woke before her time she'd be 'as sick as a small hospital with the hangover she'd have on her'. They let her be.

Cathy Long wanted a bra for her thirteenth birthday.

'Are you sure?' her mother asked, regarding her daughter's flat chest. 'Isn't there enough time for one of those? And besides, won't you have to wear one long enough?'

The speech was always the same and Cathy had zoned out before her mother got to the part where she assured her that she was speaking from experience and that Cathy would look back some day and be sorry that she'd wished her life away. Life wasn't happening quarter fast enough in Cathy's opinion. It was a wonder to her that adults could be so out of touch. Did they pass the age of eighteen and lose all cop on?

Cathy remained adamant. What her mother did not know was that she already had a share in a bra. It was a body-hugging thrill of a secret. She and Fiona owned a white AA-cup which, it had to be admitted, her friend filled somewhat better than Cathy. The exhilaration of feeling the Lycra and elastic against her flesh far outweighed the fact that it did absolutely nothing for her figure, real or imaginary. It was also beginning to lose a little of its sparkle as they had not been able to sneak it into either household's laundry and makeshift washing in the sea or local river wasn't quite doing the job.

Cathy had decided on a nice pretty one of her own for her birthday, with matching knickers. Pink would be lovely but it would probably clash with her red hair; admired by all, hated by Cathy. So maybe white with little flowers would be a better bet. They would travel to Ennis and shop for it there. It would be better than Christmas.

The journey to collect her father from the pub was more exciting today because word had it that a strange woman had got off Tuesday's bus and was now passed out from drink upstairs in Charlie Finn's bedroom. The town was buzzing with theories as to her identity and predicament and Cathy, no more than the next, was dying for a look at her and maybe, even, her story first-hand.

Along the hedgerows berries thickened and drooped. A grey film of exhaust fumes and dust clung to the boughs, dulling the burgeoning harvest. What they needed, Cathy knew, was a few days of rain, to wash the pollution and dirt away. Then the birds would harvest nature's bounty and all would be well for another season. She would get her berries from further into the fields and lie in the long grass, pressing them into her mouth and relishing the abandon of juice and privacy. Later she would carry full cans home to her mother for jam and pies. She sighed to think of it; sometimes life just broke your heart with beauty. But mostly it just broke your heart.

At the pub the news was that there was no news. The woman off the bus was still out cold. And her father was still a drunk.

They managed to keep word of the stranger from the Sergeant for less than a day. Although there were dark mutterings of squealing, no Kilbrodian had broken ranks to tell him. Rather, he had a call from the Limerick lost property office alerting him to the fact that a drunken woman had alighted from the bus on Tuesday and crossed the road to enter an unidentified pub, leaving behind her bag. The Sergeant was no flat and it didn't take long to do the maths. He had once been a bright light amongst the Garda recruits at Templemore, but placements in one hick town after another had ground any great ambition out of him and he had settled into a life of hard-boiled detective novels and as little work as possible. As the years passed, his resentment levelled into a mean application of the law, ruling by tough talk and the odd thrashing. Now he had revolution in the ranks and he was not pleased. It also confirmed his notion that Young Finn was a maggot in the barrel of pastoral rivalry that was Kilbrody and the Sergeant was sick and tired of it.

'The way it is,' Charlie explained when authority came

a-calling, 'I haven't been able to get any sense out of
her and I didn't want to bother you with a comatose
woman and you so busy.'

Even he would admit that he had started out sounding like he was making excuses. Slowly it began to sink
in that he was in some trouble here. The Sergeant wore
the pained expression of disbelief that comes only from
an encounter with extreme stupidity. He was also red
in the face with the gobsmacking effrontery of margin-
alising the law and his high office.

'There're some countries where you'd be packed off
into a dungeon for kidnapping and the key thrown away,
though in my opinion that'd only be the tip of the bloody
iceberg. Did it never occur to you that you're keeping
this unfortunate individual against her will?'

'To be fair, Sergeant, she doesn't really have one at
the moment. It's kind of on leave.'

'Worse still. God Almighty, man, you could be up to
anything with that poor creature.'

'But I'm not,' Charlie reasoned, knowing that he was
in big shit if the Sergeant chose him to be. And things
seemed to be headed in that direction. No doubt about
it, he had been a complete fucking eejit at best and a
criminal at worst. What had he been thinking of, indeed?
He could be accused of just about every deviance known,
and unknown, to humanity and he had no witnesses to
tell otherwise. He needed the Sergeant on board and
quickly.

'What do you want to do?' he asked, lobbing the ball into the uniformed court.

'It's hard to know where to start, you've made such a fuck of it,' the Sergeant pointed out.

Charlie bit his tongue. God, but he hated having to be meek. However, there was a beggars and choosers line ricocheting along his brain canals and he thought better of dissing the Sergeant further with idle cheek.

'Did Gilhooley have a look?'

'Yes.'

The Sergeant narrowed his eyes. The doctor was in on it too.

'Very, very reluctantly,' Charlie added, by way of damage limitation.

At this rate of going he wouldn't have a friend or customer left in Kilbrody by nightfall.

'And I think he was bound by his Hippocratic oath, or he'd have gone straight to you.'

The Sergeant waved off this paltriness. 'It'll interest you to know that I've located her bag. At least some-one in this shithole of a situation is thinking straight and acting responsibly.'

Charlie thought it didn't suit the Sergeant to dwell on the moral high ground but he was in no position to point that out. He nodded at the plan to have the Guards call at regular intervals to maintain propriety. He also agreed to sponsor the rest of the under-thirteens summer season. The Sergeant had left before either of them noticed that he hadn't stumped up a rake of free pints. Both were unhappy with this for different reasons.

The woman's eyes scratched open. She blinked carefully, trying to minimise the irritation of lid on eyeball. Her mind was full of noise and pain. She turned her head groggily from side to side, unwilling to overburden herself and cause more discomfort. White curtains with a blue stripe blocked out most of the light, giving the room a mellow haze. It lulled her. Her mouth was dry. So dry. Her body ached heavily into the mattress. Down, down. She tried to fight it, to figure why the room was strange. Her eyes were too, too tired. She struggled to keep them open but could not match the strength of the weariness. Later, perhaps. Now it was time to give in to sleep. She drifted away again.

Cathy and Fiona lay tummy down by the bank of the short river flowing from Kilbrody to the sea. They threaded daisies on a chain, each having grown special index fingernails for the purpose. Slit halfway down the stem, then slot the next through. Repeat. Their fingertips were green and so was the smell of sap juice from the captured flowers.

'Frankie Marr says he likes you,' Fiona said.

'Urgh. He's *such* a pain.'

'I don't think so.'

'Yes you do. He's a nerd. You said so last week.'

'Well, maybe I changed my mind.'

'No way. Not about that eejit.'

Cathy rolled onto her back, and gazed at the dappled light playing through the trees. High above, leaves whispered to each other, sharing secrets humans could never understand. Beyond them white, balled clouds scudded across the blue sky on the way elsewhere. She closed her eyes and listened to the birds singing up a storm. Their happy chirps matched the day. She could be on the Mediterranean, a princess ruling her own, small country, beloved of all her subjects, especially—

'He says he doesn't mind that you're a ginger.'

Reality was overrated, no doubt about that. Cathy tried hard not to grimace. Fiona might be her friend but she was definitely lacking in the tact department. So much so, Cathy sometimes wondered if Fiona liked her at all, or was deliberately trying to hurt her. She took in her friend's mouse-brown bob and felt a keen envy.

'I mind that he's a freak, though,' was all she parted with.

'Are you having a party for your birthday?'

'Nah. Don't think I'll bother.'

'Knew you wouldn't.'

'How did you know?'

'Just did.'

'That's a miracle, so, 'cos I only just made up my mind this minute.'

Silence was all that met this. Maybe lying's not my forte, Cathy thought, in spite of her mother's opinion to the contrary. She was so bloody tired of all the pretence. All she wanted was to go to sleep and wake up in a world without the baggage of her life. Surely the next thirteen years couldn't be as bad as the first lot. Then again, each year seemed to throw up new shit, often with bells on.

'Let's go and get a Coke,' she said. 'I'm parched.'

They threw the flower chains into the river and didn't bother to watch them disappear.

She swam back in to the hazylazy room. It was darker now. Her eyelids had lost their abrasion and the tinny ringing had subsided, removing the sharpest edge of pain. She lay beneath the feathered duvet relishing its light embrace. Something was out of place though, nagging her. Each time she came close to identifying it, it fled. A streetlight shone dimly through the curtain. She closed her eyes to savour the night's silence. After a time a car passed, taking a leisurely pace along its route. Then the silence carried on its business. The notion came again, the idea that something was amiss. Warily, she opened her eyes again and reviewed the room. Her brain and body began to throb with apprehension. The bed cover was unfamiliar and surely those curtains were new? *New to where?* asked an inner voice. She didn't quite know. But what she saw clearly was that this was not her room. She was not at home. *Home?* the voice asked, persistent now. She sat bolt upright, her breath coming shallow and fast. Fear gurgled in her throat. *This was not her room.*

Charlie was ushering Old Mikey and the Whinge out of the door and into the small hours of the morning when the baby monitor issued a shriek. The small herd stopped in its tracks, then Charlie shoved them through the door and bolted it quickly. He heard hammering, and Old Mikey's voice insisting that he needed their help, as he raced for the stairs and the distraught woman in his bedroom.

Four

The words 'fight' and 'flight' stormed her brain. Although the traditional choice, she found neither a comfort. For starters, this place had the advantage over her, because she had no idea of its layout. She edged along a wall, hands spreadeagled to each side. A wooden board creaked underfoot, sounding like a crack of thunder to her ringing ears. Should she turn on the light? A redundant question, as she didn't know where to find the switch. Her legs felt weak and unused. How long had it been since she'd last walked? Had she been drugged? She was wearing over-sized pyjamas that were not hers. Perhaps a madman had taken her. Perhaps she was about to die. Her heart was thundering like a rocket launch and heaving so hard she felt sure it would burst through her ribs. Her breath rasped loudly in panic. She stopped to calm herself, taking a few large gulps, but these made her dizzier. Two paths were of paramount importance now, she realised: the first was to get out of here (wherever 'here' was) and the second was to find a loo. Quickly.

Footsteps on stairs, then a man's voice. 'Don't be afraid. You're safe here. Please don't be afraid.' Easy for him to bloody say, whoever in hell he was. Her eyes were accustomed to the semi-darkness now. She scanned the room for a weapon. Typical, she thought, as her eyes found a small lamp, the only light I can see and I'll have to use it to brain this weirdo. At least I won't have to look into his eyes as I bash his head in. She grabbed the stalk of the lamp and stood by the door, holding the makeshift protection over her head as she'd seen on television. All those wasted hours were proving handy at last.

Charlie heard the bump of a body colliding with furniture then pulling back as if the sound might be retrieved. A floorboard creaked softly: she was to his left inside the door, then. He had no way of knowing what the procedure was in such a situation. This class of thing wasn't covered by the tabloids or broadsheets at all, or perhaps he'd missed those articles. He had decided on a vocal approach, telling the woman that she had nothing to fear. He wasn't hopeful that she'd believe him, but at least she'd grow accustomed to his voice. Which was beginning to grate on him, reedy and insincere as it sounded. Squeaky too, if he had to choose an additional adjective. Now there was silence from the bedroom. She was probably waiting to pounce once he came within her range. That's certainly what he would try in the circumstances.

'I'm going to push open the door, but I won't come in,' he told her. 'I don't want to frighten or threaten you in any way. I'll step back into the middle of the hallway once I've done this and you can come to the door to look at me.'

Not bad for an improvisation, he congratulated himself.

She tried to build a picture of the man from his voice. It was squeaky. Was this normal, or was he as scared as she? Was he weak, a small man? If he was a little shit, she could take him. Adrenaline started to buzz in her veins. Yes, she could take this skinny little freak. She braced herself for action, shaking like an eight on the Richter scale.

Charlie reached for the handle, turned it slowly, and pushed open the door. He stepped back, as promised. Now what? Then he remembered a fundamental way of gaining trust, usually used by hostages to humanise themselves in the eyes of their captor. Seemed as good a time as any to try it out. He said, 'My name is Charlie,' and let it hang in the air. All those hours in front of the box hadn't been entirely in vain. He hoped.

She wasn't sure what should happen next, except for the part where she beat up the bad guy and went home. She edged towards the shaft of light spilling across the floorboards. Careful now, she told herself, it'll blind you and he'll have the advantage. She let her pupils widen and narrow at will, registering the strength of the brightness. She was hopping from foot to foot, limbering for the encounter and trying to distract from her urgent, painful need to pee. When she could wait no longer, she let out a holler, pitched at bloodthirsty, and leapt into the space before the open door.

In hindsight, it was an anticlimax; though the comfort of retrospection was a long way off, where the grass is always greener.

The man stayed still and, oddly, she felt a little foolish. He was not the sad, weird specimen she'd expected, but then nothing would ever match that undefined image of unnamed and unshaped fear. He wasn't at all unpleasant on the eye but who knew what meanness lurked under that pretty exterior? Ted Bundy had been attractive at first, it was said.

She stood there panting, breathing in the rancid smell of her own sweat, wondering where she was. All she was sure of was this bloke was called Charlie, unless he'd lied about that, which was no skin off her nose because she didn't intend to stick around long enough to care.

'Would you like a cup of tea?' he asked.

'Where's the loo?' she wanted to know.

There was a hiatus as the woman made to follow Charlie's directions to the bathroom. He turned to indicate where she should go then saw her jerk forward and back practically simultaneously. She landed with a painful thump on the wooden floorboards of the bedroom and lay there a moment.

'Fucking lamp is still plugged in,' she gasped.

'Are you all right?'

'I'll live,' she acknowledged.

She rose slowly, stretching her aches, and started for the door again. She raised the lamp for him to see. 'No funny stuff, mister,' she warned.

'You might want to unplug that if you intend to use it on me,' Charlie suggested.

The relief of the visit to the loo could not be measured. It was magic. As she washed her hands, she looked at the gaunt face in the mirror. I don't look so hot, she thought. And I don't feel too good either. She felt weighed down and didn't know why. It seemed she didn't know a whole lot about anything any more, if she'd ever known anything to begin with. Bile rose as it dawned on her that this reflection was the face of a stranger, in a foreign place, alone. In danger. Her body began to shake again with the horror of it, and suddenly she was leaning over the toilet spraying the bowl with vomit. Spent, she knelt and clutched its cool porcelain, trying to staunch the boiling heat of her terror. Hands under her armpits lifted her and helped her out. The stench of her sweat was overpowering.

'Back to bed for you, I think.'

This guy might be the devil himself for all she cared.

She needed that bed, and the tea he'd promised. She could smell the comfort of bread toasting and her saliva buds burst forth expectant moisture. She was starving. I'll beat him up later, she decided.

It was after she'd wolfed her fourth slice of toast smothered in butter that Charlie said she should slow down or risk being sick again. She nibbled daintily at her fifth, but was determined to finish it. Along with another pot of sweet tea. It was probably good of him to serve her in the bedroom but she had no time for the finer niceties of the situation. The lamp lay close at hand on the bed. She fondled it from time to time, as much for her captor as herself.

'Why are you keeping me here?' she asked, eventually.

'I'm not, really. You just turned up.'

'Do you usually collect people in this way?'

'No,' he admitted.

'Where am I?'

It was useless for Charlie to explain that he'd answered that question before. The last thing they needed now was a row about who said what to whom and when.

'Finn's pub, Kilbrody, County Clare.'

She gave the information a chance, then shook her head. 'Nope. Means nothing to me.'

'I suppose it wouldn't if you're not from around these parts.'

Her hands began to shake. She raised them to her chest and clutched them to the strange pyjamas. She gasped, trying to catch her breath. Tears spilled down her hot cheeks.

'I know this is going to sound really weird,' she whispered. 'But I've no idea why I'm here.'

'It's probably just the hangover,' Charlie reassured her. 'Your brain is still a bit scrambled.'

She began to rock to and fro, sobbing quietly. Charlie, precarious on the edge of his own bed, didn't feel master of his kingdom and was unsure whether he should comfort her with words or a hug. If he held her in his arms, would she mistake the action for aggression and beat the head off him with the lamp his Aunty Betty had left him in her will? He tried some cooing, but felt like a right prat, and she didn't seem to hear him anyhow. He stopped.

'No, don't stop, that was nice.'

He tried a bit more but it really wasn't his métier.

'Tell you what,' he said eventually, 'your bag ended up in Limerick and it's being returned this morning, so I'm sure we'll figure everything out. You should get some more sleep and it'll all be clearer later.'

Or as clear as mud, he could have added, but he didn't think that would go down as the best quip in the world. The tact of a barman hadn't failed him, on this occasion; a small thing, but a good sign. Of what, he was stumped to tell.

There was a volley on the front door of the pub that could only have been drummed out by a cop. Charlie put good money on its being the rookie McGowan, as the Sergeant was unlikely to be lured out of the cot for anything less than a grisly murder at this hour.

He was correct in his assumption and let the youngster in with the usual greetings suited to the twilight zone they were inhabiting.

'Mikey Byrne called me to say your mystery guest is awake.'

'Come on up and introduce yourself.'

But it didn't happen that way. Much to McGowan's disappointment, the woman from the bus was asleep again by the time they reached her side.

'Well, she's a grand sight all the same,' was the Guard's estimation.

'She is surely,' agreed Charlie. 'We'll talk to her in the morning.'

'Is there not a safety issue having that electric lamp on the bed?'

'It's not plugged in.'

'Oh, right so.'

Charlie was whacked and he shushed McGowan pointedly towards the door.

'Ah!' said the latter, halting in his tracks. He rubbed his hands together with gusto. Charlie held his breath. What now? 'Tea and toast,' said the Guard. 'Mighty altogether.'

Charlie sighed and set to. As he filled the kettle he saw that dawn was creeping along the skyline and another glorious day was insistent on a bright start.

Tom Long looked at the luminous streaks of orange horizontal to the darkness of the earth. The brightening sky let off shards of icy blue and flecks of grey-white. Another fine day, thank God. Not that he felt that fine himself. His hands shook as he used both to bring the mug to his mouth. He gagged on the tea, but steadied himself and willed it to stay put. He would have dearly loved a cure, but that would be to admit what could not be admitted. Wasn't he grand, anyhow? Wasn't he getting the work in and didn't a man deserve a few pints when his day was done? Too bad the day is done for by six every evening. He heard his wife stir and held his breath in case she decided to waken and join him. He didn't want her to see him till the sun had banished some of the demon still clinging to him. A good blast of air, that'll do the trick, he thought, throwing the dregs of his tea into the sink. He rinsed the mug and laid it upside down on the draining board. Then he crept into Cathy's room, as he did each morning. His princess was asleep, her soft breath blowing a flame-red tendril of hair from her face again and again. He could have watched her for hours. But he had a farm to tend to and a family to provide for.

He shrugged into his sleeveless jacket, dragged his

wellingtons on and left the house, whistling low for the dog. Then it came back to him: Dennis was dead. He felt his heart lower in his chest as he headed out through the fields, alone.

Five

The woman on the bus had her first shower in three days on Friday morning. She didn't trust herself to have a bath in case she lapsed into sleep again or felt so miserable she decided to drown herself. Both options were runners as far as she was concerned. She scrubbed hard but the shower didn't wash the world away as she would have liked. It did help freshen up her rotten aspect on life without augmenting it, and she almost felt human again.

A memory stirred in her exhausted brain, but instinctively she pushed it aside. It came with extras.

She cracked open a new toothbrush from its plastic and cardboard coffin, smeared it with Colgate and set to, relishing its minty action. Maybe she'd even get a ring of confidence like in the television ads when she was a tiny kid. Not today, it seemed, so she scrubbed her face until her skin shone pink instead. It was important to be pristine. 'Clean as a whistle.' Who used to say that?

When she returned to the bedroom, she found her clothes laundered and pressed on the bed. It was somehow embarrassing to see her underwear atop the blouse and trousers, although there was little doubt that Charlie had seen all there was to see and modesty was the last thing she should have worried about. This still seemed too intimate. He noticed her discomfort when she joined him in the kitchen for her second breakfast in five hours.

'The laundry was Mrs Daly's doing,' he said. 'She lives next door.'

'Thanks,' she returned, grateful for his sensitivity. Maybe she wouldn't need to bash his brains out after all. Just as well, since she'd left the lamp behind in the bedroom. 'You look wrecked,' she told him.

'McGowan, one of the Guards, called to see you when he heard you were awake. Only you weren't by then and he decided he wanted to talk hurling. I knew I wouldn't be rid of him till he'd related all his derring-do on the playing pitch. I was right.' He checked his watch. 'He didn't leave till six.'

'Sorry. That's all my fault.'

'Not to worry. You can buy a loaf of bread and some tea bags; that should take care of the damage.'

'I'm really thankful to you for being so good to me.'

Charlie flashed a smile. Nice teeth.

'Don't mention it. I was well looked after by strangers myself in my day.'

She lifted the teapot, idly deciding it would do as a club at a pinch, then gave an awkward half laugh. 'The kindness of strangers, eh?' She poured more tea. 'When does my bag arrive?'

'The bus gets in from Limerick at five past nine, and unless that bus driver has a death wish he'll have it with him to hand over to the Sergeant. Nobody crosses the Sergeant. I'd love to tell you his bark is worse than his bite but I don't want to give the wrong impression. He's not entirely overjoyed that you've turned up in his manor so be prepared for that.'

'I guess it'll be nice to have some details,' Ruth said, a cowardly cheat. Oh, the memories were close to the surface now but she lobbed them back. There was only so much unpleasantness a girl could take.

They gave way to ruminative chewing and the occasional slurp of tea, both trying to look as if this was the most normal of happenings. Charlie succeeded best.

'Don't worry,' he finally said. 'Some day I'll match you a few tales,' he promised lightly. 'Until then, why don't you take a walk around the town and get some fresh air. I'm sure it'd do you the power of good.'

And so she found herself strolling the streets of Kilbrody.

In his bedroom Charlie plugged Aunty Betty's lamp back into its socket. There wasn't much he could do about the teapot at large in the kitchen.

✿   ✿   ✿

Cathy Long was having a quiet breakfast with her mother and she intended to keep it that way. The adult had other ideas, naturally. Why were they all so fond of their own voices? Cathy wondered. And so bloody curious.

'What's the agenda for today?' the mammy asked.

'Dunno.'

'Sounds exciting.'

'Yeah.'

Cathy had answered automatically so it took her a moment to realise that her mother was smirking. She was perfectly prepared to let the side down normally with a sulk but decided to rally, convinced that it was true teenage rebellion, the last thing expected of her and bound to show her mother up in some mysterious and brilliant way.

'Actually, I think Fiona and me are going to walk to Lahinch to the beach again.'

'Just the two of you? Or might there be boys involved?'

Ah now, that was plain dirty: fishing for information as well as embarrassing a girl.

'I doubt it,' she retorted archly. 'We're not interested in any of the gobdaws around these parts.'

'Further afield, so?' the elder pressed.

Cathy sniffed imperiously, as if uninterested in dignifying this latest, most pathetic, ploy. 'You'd be hard pressed to find anything *but* fields "around these parts",' she rejoined, and left her mother for dead. Argument-wise, at least.

If Cathy hadn't known better she might have aired the opinion that her mother was trying not to laugh but, as this was beyond possibility and comprehension, she dismissed the idea, finished her cornflakes and headed for the bathroom.

'A shower wouldn't do you any harm,' her mother called after her.

Yeah, right.

It was obviously a small to medium market town, the woman found. She went to what she assumed to be the approach road and started back along the left side of the main street. She stumbled occasionally, as if walking was a new action not yet mastered. A former dairy kicked off the highlights, followed by a couple of dwellings that needed a coat of paint and to have their net curtains laundered, then a chipper called 'Mario's' which would open at six that evening, according to a grubby sign Blu-tacked to the glass door. Beside it, the menu offered plenty of grease and heart attacks. Next came 'Surf 'n' Turf', which seemed to be a bookies but had a few computer terminals going to waste inside also. It would open at 9.30 a.m., the smartly printed sign said, perhaps in time to capture the offerings of the Limerick to Dublin bus. Some more houses with jolly windows, then Finn's, where she was billeted, followed by a pharmacy, a drapers and a small café cum delicatessen which wafted forth delicious smells. She found she was hungry again and broke her grand tour to sample the local fare. The coffee, it emerged, was drinkable and the cream doughnuts a delight. She was going to have to roll herself out to the bus at this rate of eating.

She was aware of nudges and whispering but ignored them and no one approached to ask any questions, which suited her fine. Her mind was a jumble of misshapen images, snatches of conversation, incoherence. The café clock showed that the bus was late arriving, but somehow she didn't feel any surprise. It seemed the day had its own pace in Kilbrody and it was futile to try to chivvy it along. At last she had drained her mug, all but wrung it out, and had no more excuse but to return to base. She walked slowly back to Finn's where she found a large, florid Garda Sergeant in situ. Showtime could not be far off. They sat and waited, looking anywhere but at each other. The bitter smell of stale beer and used air was enough to make her eyes water.

Ten o'clock came and was followed by a quarter past. The Sergeant finished the *Irish Independent* and reluctantly started on the *Irish Times*.

'I find it a bit dense,' he told the small company.

'Feckin' bus,' Charlie muttered. 'It's a terrible service, never on time.'

'There's no rush at this stage,' she reassured him. Que sera sera. 'Que sera sera and all that.'

She had barely uttered the words when the bus rounded a corner into view. Her stomach lurched, but she made a huge effort to stay seated and calm. She watched the Sergeant cross to the vehicle and board it. When he returned he had the driver in tow and was carrying a tan-coloured leather satchel.

'It's a lovely bag, if nothing else,' she said.

Cathy sat, reading, on the toilet until she felt sure her mother had given up on her and gone off to tackle some housewifely chore or other. She flushed the loo and washed her hands, even did her face and teeth. She was crossing the hall to her room when her mum popped her head round a door and said, 'I suppose a swim later will do instead of a shower now.' When Cathy had recovered from the fright she managed to ask for money for her lunch.

'No lovely homemade sarnies?' her mother asked with mock hurt.

It was one of the great unwritten truths of the house that her mother was genetically unable to assemble a sandwich of any kind. Nothing else was beyond her in the culinary arena but sandwich-making had been neglected in her DNA. A stand-alone fact, and not to be questioned or debated. Cathy's dad never brought a packed lunch with him even if it was a mart day. He would travel home rather than risk a life-threatening concoction of bread and filling à la Mrs Long. Even Mrs Long wouldn't eat one of Mrs Long's sandwiches. And so she gave her only daughter money for chips and a Coke and instructions to collect her dad on the way home. Life moved on, all too slowly, but some things never changed.

'This is Jack Cunningham, the bus driver,' the Sergeant told them. 'He says you got on in Dublin at the terminus there, bought your ticket, slept till Kilbrody and the rest we know.'

If the woman remembered the driver she didn't show it.

'Hello . . . again, I suppose,' she said. 'Thanks for bringing my bag back.'

'No bother,' Jack replied. 'Sorry I didn't notice it in time to give it to you when you got off the bus on Tuesday,' he added. He was smooth, he told himself. Definitely. Now for the fun.

She took the satchel uncertainly and placed it on a low pub table.

'I presume you've taken a look inside?' Charlie asked.

The Sergeant cleared his throat. 'I'll deal with this, Finn,' he growled. He turned on the driver. 'Well?' he barked.

'Yeah, of course,' Cunningham replied. 'It all had to be logged, you know.'

'And?'

'You'll see for yourselves,' he said, licking nervous sweat from his upper lip.

The woman turned the bag upside down slowly and watched the accoutrements of her life tumble onto the wood. Make-up, purse, pens, a slim diary. She picked up a plastic bank card and turned it over a few times in her hand, reading and re-reading the details.

'Well, I'm Ruth Treacy,' she said. 'But I'm still not quite sure why I'm here.'

She picked up her mobile, which was beeping faintly, as if in pain. It was small and sleek and looked lost in her hand. 'This is in bad need of some juice.'

Charlie took the phone from her. 'Ozzy'll have something to plug it into.'

Two matching documents had slid to the side of the pile. Ruth sat on a stool and opened one, then the other. She read their stories then placed them back onto the table and put her head in her hands. After a while they heard her cry, softly.

'Her parents,' Jack Cunningham explained. 'Those are their death certificates.'

Their final postcards. Gone. Not forgotten. Wish you were here.

Six

Charlie would normally have called one run-a-day much like another in Kilbrody, and the townsfolk would have agreed with him, but there was no doubt that this was a week that was coming up a marvel in the difference stakes. Since Tuesday, life had definitely taken a rather interesting turn for the first time in an age. He had little idea where it was headed or, for that matter, where it had originated. Right now, no one gathered in the pub seemed sure of what to do next. They looked to the woman on the bus, who was becoming Ruth Treacy before their eyes. She sighed and lifted her head, evidently bent on survival. If she had been honest, just then, she would have admitted that her brain had taken on the aspect of cotton wool and she was finding the very act of feeling anything at all nearly impossible. From somewhere a course dredged itself to the fore.

'Did you not say you'd get a charger for my mobile?' she asked Charlie.

He shuffled to his feet, feeling that he should have some practical instructions of his own. The Sergeant, inspired by Ruth or shamed into action, intervened by reminding Jack Cunningham, 'You have a bus to drive to Dublin.' This was evidently far less exciting for the driver than delving into the Treacy woman's past, but there was no denying that he had to be elsewhere. He was dismissed, cheated by all of them. Had they forgotten that she was *his* woman from *his* bus? Ungrateful fecks. Still, what else could you expect from big, thick, country mulchies?

'I'll call in another time I'm passing, see how you're doing,' he told her.

She didn't have anything to say to that. As he left, he heard her announce that a cup of tea was in order, to which the Sergeant responded, 'It's early but I think I'll have a pint of stout meself.' It was all Jack could do to keep walking. He wanted to be there when Ruth Treacy had to deal with her life head on, when she couldn't stave it off any longer with tea and nonsense. On the bus across the road the passengers were in a foment. He could see the cross face of a Belgian student glare at him from the front seat. This would be one long, pain in the ass haul back to Dublin. But then, it always was.

Charlie breathed in the fumes of the extremely late 9.10 a.m. Kilbrody to Dublin and was reminded that a good lash of rain was badly needed to dampen the choking dust of this summer. He hurried back inside the pub.

'I didn't even need to tell Ozzy you were up and about, the bush telegraph is in overdrive since your walk through the town. I'll lock the doors and we'll take ourselves upstairs.'

They were under siege. Ruth suppressed a laugh, amazed that she could be the focus of such attention.

'She's awake,' Tom Long told his wife. 'I met Bert Fahy and he said she was in the café earlier.'

'What did she have?' his wife asked, grinning a little.

'Coffee and a doughnut,' her husband said, smiling too.

'Good choice.'

'Small world.'

'She's awake,' Ozzy said into the phone. 'Ruth Treacy. The Sergeant is in Finn's now. I'll see you there at half eleven when it opens.'

He clicked off and began to dial again.

'She's awake,' Deborah told the Whinge as she filled his wife's prescription at the pharmacy. Mrs O'Brien famously lived on her nerves and required the best medication her husband's money could provide.

'We can expect reporters and all sorts now,' the Whinge predicted. 'And Young Finn will make a mint. By God, but that fella would have a ladle if it was raining soup.'

'Does herself want more of the HRT or has she enough to be going on with?' Deborah asked, loud enough for the next county to hear. If the girl had a fault at all, it was her enthusiastic embrace of the matters that crossed her path and the volume she unconsciously allowed them. 'The extra hair thing is only a phase,' she reassured him. 'Sure hasn't my own mother stopped shaving because of it now.'

Ruth sat nursing her tea. She played with a spoon. She picked up the milk carton and shook it; not empty enough to throw away. She ate the last digestive from the saucer in the middle of the table, simply because it was there. Nothing more to fool around with, except the two certificates.

'I can't understand why I still don't seem to remember getting on that bus,' she said.

'Isn't it the thing that trauma often blocks stuff out?' Charlie suggested, thinking of her parents' deaths. 'Your mind doesn't want to deal with it yet. It's not ready.'

'I suppose.'

The Sergeant was increasingly uncomfortable with the psychiatrics and fidgeted in his seat. It didn't help matters that his rear end was too big for the chair and he hated it when it went numb, as was occuring rapidly during the above exchange.

'While ye work out the psychological aspects of this mess, I've to go and sort out a few practical details. Like, are you a missing person, Miss Treacy? Or maybe wanted for something?' He liked the momentous sound of that and decided to beef it up. 'Who knows what awful thing you might be blocking? A grievous crime, perhaps?' He unwittingly mispronounced the word as 'grievious' and left the kitchen to deal with the consequences of his words, real and otherwise.

'Looks like I'm in *big* trouble with the sheriff,' Ruth said.

Charlie was staring the teapot in the spout and remembering his earlier theories on assault. 'Maybe it's me who's in trouble, staying here with you, you murderer,' he quipped.

'Relax. I'm just going to have another cup before I brain you.'

'Grand.' He checked his watch. 'Actually, if it's all the same to you, I'll open up downstairs and we might arrange another time for the "grievious" bodily harm?'

'Fine.'

The mobile phone rang, an ordinary digital chime.

'At least you don't have a theme tune,' Charlie said.

Ruth looked at the flashing name. It read 'KATE.' She pressed the green button and said, 'Hello, Kate.'

Charlie didn't hear the words distinctly, but he could tell the thrust of the conversation was a tirade. Angry squawks, sometimes interrupted with information from Ruth: 'Kilbrody. County Clare . . . on a bus . . . sorry, I didn't realise you were worried . . . there's no need for that . . . no, really, Kate, don't.' She finally rang off with a sigh.

'A friend?' Charlie asked.

'More than that. My sister. She's planning a visit.'

Kate was hogging the bathroom and Ruth really, really needed to go. She danced around the landing outside, listening to Kate singing a song about rain. She hopped from foot to foot. She pressed her nails into her palms. She crossed her legs. Kate began to run the tap.

'Katie, I need the loo. HURRY, PLEASE.'

'You should have thought of that before you drank all the orange,' her sister shouted through the door.

'But I'm bursting. Oh please, Katie, please hurry.'

'Can't do that, Ruth. You'll have to go wee in the garden.'

But Ruth knew she didn't have the time to get there. Instead she went to their bedroom and hunkered behind her sister's bed. She didn't even get to pull her pants down before the hot pee started to flow from her, battering onto the beige and brown patterned linoleum.

'Mammy is going to kill you,' her sister assured her from the doorway.

'It's your fault for not letting me in the toilet,' Ruth said. 'You're older, you're supposed to know better.'

Ruth began to whinge in an annoying monotone.

'You really are the biggest pest in the whole universe,' Kate assured her. 'I'll help you clean up the mess. But you have to stop that racket.'

Ruth hiccoughed away the tears. She beamed at her sister. 'Am I the best pest?' she asked.

'This seems mad, but I feel like I need to get a little sleep,' Ruth told Charlie.

'Maybe it's your body's way of telling you it needs more time to figure all of this out.'

'Without my interference?'

'Uh-huh.'

'Think I'll give it a whirl, if you don't mind.'

'Not at all. I'll be busy. Kilbrody and the inquisitive wait for no man, or only for so long before they break down the door, so I'll be out of your hair.'

Charlie went to welcome the thirsty of the town to Finn's house of fun and Ruth went back to bed. But first she visited the bathroom: one can never be too careful.

Old Mikey floated his opener. 'It must've been a quare fright all the same, waking up in a strange man's bed.'

'Ah now, steady on,' Charlie said. 'I'm not that strange and there's manys the woman has been glad of waking up in my bed over the years.'

'I know I wouldn't like it,' the Whinge offered, adding his euro's worth.

'I don't want to destroy you,' Charlie said, 'but you're just not my type.'

'You'll get over it,' Old Mikey told the Whinge. 'The thing is not to let him see you're upset.'

Then he took himself to the gents so that he could let a guffaw rip. Lord, these were the days and no mistake.

Back in the packed bar he heard Charlie shout, 'One at a time now, *please.*'

Ruth woke with a thunderous start, vaulting upwards from the damp mattress. Glancing at the clock she saw that she'd only been out for twenty minutes. The dread had returned and was sparking cruelly in her head, flashing pain and apprehension. Sunlight streamed through the window, unwilling to leave her be. The duvet was cloying, now, comfort long deserted. She kicked it aside, but felt unable to get up out of the desperate pit she was in. A fine sheen of sweat clothed her skin, the undergarment of fear. Welcome back this was not. And where was 'back'? Steady breaths. Kilbrody, a pub, landlord a Charlie, maybe even a right one.

But you're not alone?

No, she was holding her dead parents in her hands. Clenching them, really, gripping tightly.

Too late for that now.

'There have got to have been better days,' she said, taking command.

She slung her legs over the side of the bed and sat with her head on her knees. It felt good, actually, as if some of the bad blood in her was prevented from coursing at will. She could hear the muffled sounds of a working pub below, dull chatter and the odd laugh, the ring of a cash register, commerce ongoing, life too. Without her. And without Ed and Rita Treacy, her parents. What difference had any of them made. Whoa. Big stuff and not a child in the house washed. Gloating in the recesses of her mind was the life she had fled. It could only be kept at bay in the short term, and she was in no hurry to think about it now. She laid Ed and Rita side by side on the pillow and headed for the shower, again attempting to kick-start this day.

Give it your best shot, kid. See you later.

Mockery had to be the lowest form of annoyance, she decided.

She said her name aloud a few times as the water beat and scalded her. Cleansed and crimson from scrubbing, she headed to tackle the hieroglyphics of her life that were held in the slim volume of diary she'd found in the tan-coloured satchel. She opened the black book to reveal the year-at-a-view inside cover. 'MY BIRTH-DAY!' was scrawled across 23 January. The trivia helped her move on. Kate was born on 4 May, a Taurus. There was a mention of a parent-teacher meeting, ends of terms, staff dos. Miss Ruth Treacy was an English teacher.

Come away, O human child!
To the waters and the wild
With a faery, hand in hand,

*For the world's more full of weeping than you
can understand.*

William Butler Yeats. Nice one.

'Tread softly because you tread on my dreams'; there's another of his greats, she thought.

Her eyes sped along the entries looking at the facts of her life. Her mother had died at the end of June, and her father four weeks later, just a fortnight ago. Yet still she felt no emotional tie with the events. The facts stood before her like a science project; existing, proof of life and death, without provoking reaction other than fear. And this fear was impossible to pin down. She was detached from the story of the death certificates, the diary, and almost grateful for that. She still had no real idea why she decided to come here.

'Fuck it,' she declared. 'If I don't want to remember the past, why not change it?'

Seven

Cathy lay on her towel, uncomfortably aware of Frankie Marr and some other boys playing football a few yards away. She could feel a pool of sweat and sunblock gather in the small of her back as she tried to be still and nonchalant. The beach grit was almost unbearable, scratching her skin and invading her tenuous calm. Fiona was shifting from one alluring pose to another, as she saw it. Cathy would have liked to swim in the sea but was afraid of looking fat as she walked the ten yards to the water. She needed a new pair of togs as well as the bra she'd requested for her birthday. And a paper bag to put over her head.

'I've been thinking,' Fiona told her.

'You amaze me,' Cathy heard herself say. If the statement dripped sarcasm, the other girl didn't notice and Cathy felt very grown up.

'You could ask for a mobile phone.'

'Why? Who would I call? Ghostbusters?'

'Very funny, I don't think. You could use it for telling your mother where you are. You could call me. Or Frankie, if he's your boyfriend then.'

'I don't want a boyfriend. Especially not Frankie Marr. He's a spot-riddled moron and I wouldn't go out with him if he was the last fella alive in the world.'

Fiona digested the information and remained nonplussed. 'What about a haircut then?'

'Maybe,' Cathy conceded. She had been thinking about one. But what could be done with a mop of frizz like she had? Shearing her like a sheep was about all she could come up with.

A spray of sand preceded the football's arrival. Both girls sat spluttering indignantly and waving their hands ineffectively in the air, a little late to ward off the sand-storm.

'Sorry, ladies,' said a voice hovering between boyhood and the drop zone.

Cathy didn't need to look to see that Frankie Marr was towering over them, but she shielded her eyes from the blazing sun and glanced up. It would've been too odd not to, and he might have seized on it and made fun. She would avoid mortification at all costs.

'You great eejit,' Fiona was saying to him, giggling like the schoolgirl she was. 'Look where you're going next time.'

'Sure wasn't I drawn to ye?' the pimpled Lothario declared. 'The two best-looking birds on the beach.'

Fiona was beside herself with joy and simpered accordingly.

'If ye're going for chips, me and the lads are off down the prom in about ten minutes. Ye could join us.'

As Cathy mouthed the words 'No thanks', Fiona said, 'Great. Give us a call when ye're ready. We're famished, aren't we, Cathy?'

'Later, alligator,' said Francis Marr, the Second.

'In a while, crocodile,' replied Fiona O'Reilly, the First.

'Hand me my barf bag,' Cathy Long muttered.

Her shoulders burned and every crack of her body seemed full of sand. She was convinced she'd swollen two sizes in the last hour and she could smell the rich and rancid scent of Frankie Marr all over her pocket of air. It was as if he'd removed the oxygen and left only himself. Clearly, he needed to wash more. She took a surreptitious sniff of her own underarm, logged it with the beach's deposit on her body and decided on a swim. As she set off for the sea, Fiona called, 'And you probably need new togs too.' Cathy walked a couple more steps and heard, 'But not a bikini.'

The cool water soothed her rage. After a few strokes out to sea and back, she settled in the shallows and let the gentle waves push her back towards the shore, inch by inch. First she tried it from a seated position, then lay on her stomach and 'surfed' in. The peace was thrilling, even amongst the screams and delight of the other beach-goers. The water pushed her landward, then returned to its own domain, taking a little of the shore with it, each tiny erosion proving its superiority over the landmass, like a genius over a dolt. It claimed more solid land each year, remorselessly chipping away, certain of victory at the last. Cathy licked her lips and enjoyed the salt taste of the great, wide ocean. Finally, as she was feeling clean and calm, she saw Fiona jumping up and down and signalling to the departing backs of the Marr gang. Reluctantly, Cathy got out and went back to towel off and follow them. The point of boys was lost on her and she hoped it would stay that way. For a brief moment she had a vision of her dad slumped before a pint in Finn's and it saddened and consolidated her opinion.

When Charlie went to check on Ruth she was reading a book of poetry entitled *Save Yourself*.

'Apt, eh?' she said with a twinkle.

'I dunno. If I remember correctly, there're lots of pieces in there about death that could make a person maudlin.'

'Just what I need.'

Ruth was weirdly elated and it worried her. She still had fearful shakes battling through her but felt liberated at the same time, as though she'd shed a burden. Charlie saw a woman on the edge of hysteria.

'I'm a writer,' she said, indicating her diary, open on the table.

Charlie smiled. 'One of the more acceptable of the black arts.'

Her mind churned with the lie but she had decided to re-create herself here in Kilbrody, to be someone and something else, and this was the start of it. 'Writer' won over 'English teacher' any day. Maybe she'd even write a book sometime. A section of her brain cackled at the notion, the rest of it held schtum.

'Would you like to come downstairs for a while?' he asked.

Her knees gave an inch. 'Is it time?'

'There's a lot of curiosity out there. If you appear now, it might leave you in charge.'

Her voice wobbled. 'Will they ask me questions?'

'Probably not. They all have their own theories about you and no one likes to be disappointed. So I'd say they'll keep it fairly general.'

'Right.'

'And they're unlikely to be rude just yet. That won't happen till they're used to you and can treat you as badly as they treat anyone else in the town.'

'I suppose I should start working off my debt too?'

'Actually, you've been very good for business so I'm not sure you owe me anything.'

'Still. It'd be no harm to know how to pull a pint, either.'

'Correct. Shall we?'

It was time to bite the bullet. 'Why not?' •

She hoped it would put off dealing with the tougher issues. She wanted to make the most of this false high. She tucked her parents into the diary and shoved them back in the bag.

Later.

Ruth patted the satchel. 'Alligator,' she muttered.

Passers-by gave the boisterous teenagers a wide berth. Cathy tried as hard as possible to blend with the concrete of the house next to the chipper. It had a low windowsill she insinuated herself onto, leaving her Coke alongside to preclude another sitter. She knew some of the boys from school, though only one was in her class, a dope called Pio. He spent his time braying at Frankie's antics, loudly proving himself a worthy acolyte. Fiona wasn't far behind with the fawning either, and would soon be eligible as a fully laughed-up member of the Marr Fan Club.

Cathy paid extra attention to her large single; salt, no vinegar. The chips were from a new batch and scalding hot. She popped one in her mouth, then rolled it around, lips open, breathing quickly in and out to cool the potato, before mashing it and swallowing. Delicious. Her fingers were slimy with the chip oil and every so often she gave them a lick, then rubbed them in the hard brown paper bag, leaving a dark greasy stain which crept across the surface. A slurp of sweet fizz then back to the savouries. She was enjoying this so much she'd forgotten the floor show.

She had other girl friends from school, but they lived far into the hinterland and weren't able to hook up every day. Hence the Fiona Fest. Fiona lived on the outskirts of Kilbrody too and her father ran a bookies in the town, with a few computer terminals they often fooled around on. Fiona was just telling Frankie about the porn they'd looked up when Cathy's attention returned with a bang to the conversation.

'Speak for yourself,' Cathy said. 'You're the one who wanted to see filth. I had nothing to do with that.'

'Ooh, get her,' Fiona taunted, trying to put on an American accent.

'So you're a dirty bird, are you?' Frankie said.

'No I am not,' Fiona disclaimed, but without much conviction.

To be 'dirty' was no blemish here. The company looked at Fiona with admiration. All but one lad at the back of the group, Cathy saw. His name was Peter and he had moved into the region only a few months back. His dad was a marine biologist or some such impossibility. He had dark, intelligent eyes and looked bored with his surroundings. Who could blame him? thought Cathy. I could almost scream myself with the awfulness of it. She met his eye. He grimaced surreptitiously and they both smiled.

The group continued their lunch, with Frankie laughing and jesting hardest and watching all around to make sure he was having the most fun. He was sprouting hairs on his chin and had fuzzy legs. It flummoxed Cathy to think that girls ever kissed boys, let alone that men and women did the other dirty thing. Inevitably (and Cathy was sorry not to have bet on it), Frankie called a farting competition, to the delight of his elite. They humped and huffed till Frankie was declared winner. He deemed it time to go look for magic mushrooms on the golf course.

'He hasn't a hope,' the new boy told her, quietly. 'The weather's been far too dry for fungi to thrive. Any fool knows that. The only mushroom he'll get is a deep fried one out of this chipper.'

'It'd be a shame to wreck his buzz by telling him that,' Cathy said, sweetly.

Peter smiled. 'Wicked.'

Charlie declared a Happy Hour while Ruth was learning to pull pints of stout. For the period of her training, the pint of plain would be a mere two euro. The orders were coming hot, fast and in multiples.

'Lads, anyone who can't hold the amount they're pouring into themselves will be barred,' Charlie warned. 'After they've cleaned up their mess.'

Ruth's euphoria was growing. She could do this. She could be a barmaid. What was it? Only serving punters and chatting. And they all seemed so charming, so kind. Charlie read her thoughts and shook his head. A wet Thursday in October and no money coming into the town, you'd know all about it then. Every man for himself. Every deal a cruncher. Every cow or crop lost a bullet through the heart of the farmer and all that crossed his path. Vengeance never far from the surface. And envy rife. Then he smiled as he looked around at the faces of his friends and adversaries. Wouldn't have it any other way.

Kilbrody Ruth was a natural at bar work. She had a ready smile and a pleasant action whenever the inconvenient threatened. She lobbed the awkward questions back at the askers as easily as she fielded them in her own mind. She was removed from her other troubled world, immune to its problems for this very brief time. Charlie let her be, again. Dublin Ruth would require different handling, whenever she decided to put in an appearance. She would be a polar opposite, he guessed. At the moment the woman had the manic happiness of a depressive before a low. The fall was always worst for those who shone brightest.

At no point did it occur to him to suggest she go home. Ruth hadn't mentioned it either. It was the Sergeant who felt they should be thinking along that line, and he said as much when he arrived in time for a liquid tea. As he supped a free pint of Ruth's finest at a back table he put it to them that she would be best off in Dublin, collecting together the rags and riches of her life. He said, 'There's a bus tomorrow morning that you should be on.'

'Am I being run out of town?' Ruth asked, incredulous.

'No. I'm just telling you what's best. How will staying here solve anything?'

The silence was stunned, or thumped into unconsciousness. Ruth found her mood shattered and tears slid along her cheeks. The Sergeant made a face that read, 'Women!' He said, 'Women!'

Charlie leapt in. 'If Ruth's sister is coming to Kilbrody, she should wait for her. They can go back together.'

The Sergeant shrugged. 'No skin off my nose.' Though clearly it was. He bridled to think he might have been bested.

'Thanks,' Ruth whispered.

Charlie, mindful that he had crossed the law, enforced the smoking ban that night and closed early, after only two hours' drinking-up time. It was half past one as he pushed the final, complaining remnants out through his front door. Across the road in a bright, busy Phelan's, the Sergeant sat drinking by an open window and watching Finn's. As Charlie saw his last punters off, they locked eyes and the Sergeant raised his glass in benevolent warning. The hairs on the back of Charlie's neck bristled.

The dream came for the first time that night.

Ruth was alone in a room. The air smelled of baking bread. She was happy. She glided as if on wheels through the open door and into a darkened corridor. The delicious smell was fading. Doors opened right and left. She looked into the first room and saw a box on a table. As she moved towards it, the box grew and morphed into an open coffin. In fright, she called for her mother, then realised that her mother was inside. She didn't dare look but rushed back across the corridor into the opposite room. Here her father lay, on a bed, ghostly and pale. He opened his eyes and said, 'Ruth. Get away.' 'Daddy,' she pleaded. 'Get away,' he called again. Gutted, she ran back along the blackened corridor until she reached the room at its end. The door closed behind her and she was in total darkness. She reached for a light switch but her hands felt only wood; close, closer, too close. She cried out. Her arms were pinned by her side. She was trapped inside a tight box. A coffin. And no one heard her screams.

She woke drenched and calling, 'Ruth. Get away.'

Eight

Cathy's mother had news. First up, the woman on the bus and her details, as far as they were known. It was entirely likely that some of the information given was suspect, but even gossip was acceptable at this juncture; legends have to start somewhere. Then, word of a youth project starting the following week.

'I took the liberty of signing you up. It's to clean the old church and graveyard and preserve some of our heritage.'

'Creepy,' Cathy declared. But the thought of getting away from Fiona was captivating. Even diluting that particular situation would do. There were principles to be adhered to also and, ever the wily girl, she asked, 'Will I get paid?'

'There'll be a small wage. Enough to keep you in drugs.'

Cathy's mum laughed out loud when she saw her daughter's reaction to this. 'You have a face on you like a slapped arse,' she told her.

There were times when you had to wonder about an adult's sanity, Cathy decided. As her mother's hilarity waned she delivered the coup de grâce: 'You start Monday.' Those last three words were the sweetest of Cathy's week. Salvation. In a graveyard. The Lord and His mysterious ways, no doubt.

Fiona was less impressed.

'No way would I be caught dead doing that place up.'

'Dead is right,' Cathy giggled.

Fiona was stung. 'It's only slave labour anyway,' she said. 'Probably be full of weirdos too.'

'Like me.'

'Whatever.'

The air remained frozen between them and Cathy was glad to use it as an excuse not to call, to stay at home.

Cathy loved to help in the gardens. As Fiona liked to remind her, she was 'nothing but a big farmer'. Directly behind the house was a walled area where the trapped sunshine ripened the delicate fruits and berries splayed across the brickwork. On the flat ground were the salads and herbs. Beyond the kitchen garden was a field of hardy vegetables with an informal orchard of pears, apples and hazelnut. The geese, hens and ducks ran free during the day and sheltered in their special coops at night. Now, Cathy joined her mother and worried for the birds; with Dennis gone, the fox might take to visiting.

❊   ❊   ❊

When Charlie found Ruth she was pacing the kitchen floor.

'You look like you didn't get much sleep,' he said.

'No. I had a bad dream,' she admitted. 'Now my head is full of questions and I'm trying to decipher the answers from here.' She indicated her diary.

'Any luck?'

'Not really.'

Charlie plunged the toaster handle, then set about pouring tea.

'I'm going to have to ring Kate. I've got to sort myself out.'

'Scary?'

'Yeah.'

They let that settle. Ruth's eyes fixed on the slice of toast before her. For want of something better to do, she picked up the knife and scraped butter across the surface, rasping magnolia over and back, over and back: a mesmeric rhythm. She was suspended, hypnotised, by the mundanity of it. Then her mind snapped at her, told her that she needed something beyond the immediate gift of this little sanctuary. With a sigh, she returned to matters in hand.

'You also have to take your room back,' she told him.

'I don't mind where I am, it was mine when I was a kid. I still sometimes feel like I'm sleeping in my parents' bed when I'm in that front bedroom even though it's not the same bed.'

They'd be shocked at some of the things that have happened in it too, he thought, but kept that to himself.

'Well, I mind taking your space. I've got to start making decisions and getting back to rights . . . if that's the way to put it.'

'OK, we'll swap. Now, what about the bar work? I fancy some afternoons off. And there are a few nights a week I have meetings. A girl called Deborah usually covers for me, but she's forever complaining that she has no social life so it might be best if we get you to do some of those too.'

'Done.'

'Good. You start today. One till six. Then we'll review your progress.'

'I need to buy some clothes. I've only got what I'm sitting in, so I'll need a few changes.'

'OK. Let's take to the mean street of Kilbrody and see what's on offer this season.'

'I'll probably need a power suit for my big new job.'

'I think the punters would vote for stilettos too.'

Charlie's toast popped up, done.

Tom Long leaned over the ditch, spilling his breakfast onto the dusty soil. It didn't amount to much: some yellow liquid pausing on contact to accuse him, then soaking into his land. The heaves repeated until there was little more than dribble to add to the dampness. He sat in the shade of the gorse lining the edge of the field.

His shirt was saturated and his body quaked and racked with spasms. He was poisoned. Above, rooks cawed and bickered as if fighting for his soul. He put his head between his legs and wept quietly for his health, his livelihood and his family. But he could see no way out. Pictured in his mind's eye was a drink. He craved it, ill as he was: a steadier, something to bind him and give him a boost. Just the one and then he'd be motoring again. He looked at his watch. He'd have to start a little early today, but start he must. He'd take stock then. No point in launching a new regime over a weekend. Monday was time enough to tackle what had to be done.

He got to his feet, gave one last dry heave and slowly, painfully, made his way back across the fields to the farmhouse.

Above him, on a hill and unseen, Ozzy O'Reilly was training his binoculars on the town and its inhabitants. Tom is shook, he thought. No surprise, with the amount he put into himself yesterday. Bert Fahy was showing Deborah from the chemist around his gaff. Odd that she was there so early. She must have popped in before work. And who was that courting with Frankie Marr? Some young wan looking for trouble. All in a day's looking, Ozzy told himself. And it might pay dividends yet.

The main street of Kilbrody was no Rodeo Drive and choices were quickly whittled down to Farrell's and Egan's. In the latter, the Finn's staff beat their path through the shillelaghs and peat sculptures and settled on a pair of jeans, embroidered with some Celtic swirls, and three distinctly promotional T-shirts, from the fashion department out back. Ruth kept in mind her aspiration to be whoever she chose and not who she had been to date. There was a threat of a baby and bath water scenario here, sure, but it was a risk she was willing to take, at least in the short term.

'Do I look sufficiently writer-ish in these?' she asked of the clothes.

'I've only met a few,' Charlie admitted.

'Even one is probably too many,' Ruth observed, pleased at the urbane sarkiness. It added a genuine detail to her deception, she felt.

'You look plausible to me.'

'Good enough. We'll take them, even if I do look like an advertisement for the Tourist Board.'

'They should be thrilled,' Charlie said, with a trademark glint.

'You, sir, are a ladies' man.'

'Certainly. What other way is there to be?'

She took herself into Farrell's Drapers to buy underwear and left with the last passion killers in the land: six pairs of huge, interlock knickers. The choice in the shop had been take it or go naked. Naked didn't seem unreasonable. These were certainly the equivalent of six chastity belts, padlocks and all; enough to quell any sexual feeling. She waved them at Charlie and posed coquettishly. They both laughed. It was wonderful to have a friend.

With an hour to go before her shift, and retail therapy exhausted, Ruth knew it was time to phone her sister. Her hand shook as she picked out the numbers. She wanted to talk to Kate and yet prayed for an answering machine. Her luck was out.

'Well, well, well,' Kate began. 'I don't hear from you for days and now we're in touch twice in a row. I'm not worthy.'

'Katie, please don't give me a hard time. I've got one already without you coming on board. I've been having a bit of trouble.'

'I would too, if I'd carried on the way you did over the last six months.'

Ruth felt her limbs turn to liquid. 'What do you mean?' she squeezed, through a closing throat.

'You know perfectly well what I mean,' Kate sniffed.

Ruth held her tongue, knowing that her sister had every right to be cross with her.

'I'm sure you'll be delighted to know that I can't make it to this Kilbrody place till next week, assuming you're still there, of course, and haven't upped and left it too.'

'No, I'll be here,' Ruth murmured. 'I've got a bit of a job. And I need the time to get myself together.'

'You don't hang about, do you? A job, no less. Still, I suppose if it keeps you out of Dublin it might keep you out of trouble, or from making an epic twit of yourself like you've been making a habit of lately.'

'How do you mean, an epic twit?' Ruth demanded, annoyance rising now.

'I'll just say the name Greg Deegan and leave it at that, shall I?'

Greg Deegan.

Ruth began to tremble. 'I'll see you when you arrive,' she stuttered. 'I'm at Finn's on the main street.'

'I can hardly wait,' her sister said and rang off.

Ruth went to her diary to remind herself of Greg Deegan. He was there, dotted through her life. What accompanied his name, she found, was apprehension and somehow shame. How long could she pretend he didn't exist once her sister arrived in town?

'You're on,' Charlie said, from the doorway. 'Good luck out there.'

Charlie also had a phone call to make. It was one he had been putting off making. The man's voice on the other end was friendly but somewhat disappointed.

'I wondered what had happened to you,' he said.

'I've been very busy,' Charlie told him, already feeling as though he'd offered a lame excuse.

'I heard. You missed our meeting on Wednesday evening.'

'If you know what's going on here, you'll know why.'

'Yes. I just don't want this to get in the way of our work.'

'It won't.'

'Will we see you tomorrow?'

'Yes.'

'How are you?'

'I'm well, really well.'

'I'm glad to hear it. But be careful of feeling too well, too happy?'

Charlie knew exactly what the man meant. He should be cautious. Even after all this time, nothing could be taken for granted.

'I'll be fine. See you tomorrow.'

Charlie took a moment to relax, breathing deep and beckoning calm. It felt good.

It was slicing the lemon that triggered the memory. An English couple had come in. He would try a half of Guinness, he said, and she, reluctant to change, ordered a gin and tonic. They sat by the window. As the stout settled, Ruth popped three cubes of ice into the slim jim glass and pressed it to the optic to decant the gin. A whole lemon lay on the wooden chopping board. She began to slice.

'Three c were a complete fucking nightmare today. Jesus, I need this.'

Greg knocked back his gin and tonic.

'Perfect,' he declared. 'Grasshopper, I have trained you well.'

'Would you like some dinner? It's just pasta.'

'No. I'll be having something at home later.'

A silence. This was never going to change, was it? Always 'home' in the way. Ruth felt useless, and used. Greg reached for her and though she tried to steel herself against his advances, she knew she would capitulate. Next time, she thought, next time I'll make a proper stand.

'Let's go to bed,' he whispered.

They did.

'Any sign of those drinks?' the voice asked.

Ruth looked at the lemon, smelled its acid freshness. She breathed in slowly and steadied her hand. 'Of course,' she said. 'Sorry for the delay. I just remembered something and it distracted me.'

And how.

She added two slices to the gin, snapped open a tonic and finished the glass of Guinness. No point in getting fired over an afternoon drink, she reasoned. Especially not one from the past.

Old Mikey slipped back in from the bookies.

'Any luck?' she asked.

'Ah, divil the bit. My lad is still running, on his three legs.'

'A pint?'

'The very thing,' he exclaimed, as if it was the newest and best idea in the world. 'Fling on the telly there till we see if my luck changes in the next one.'

'What did you back?'

'I have Mysterious Stranger at eight to one, in honour of yourself.'

Ruth laughed, presented Mikey's pint and rang in the money on the till. She felt her equilibrium return. Mysterious Stranger romped past the finish post and Mikey punched the air shouting, 'Ya good thing ya!' She was laughing again as the breath was stolen from her body by the arrival of a man she had never seen before. Her heart tangoed behind her ribs, then hit her toes. He wiped his forehead distractedly and a wedding ring glistened. *Here we go again.* Oh no, no way, not this time. She pretended to choke a little to cover her difficulty.

'Yes?' She kept it tight.

His dark, sad eyes seemed to burn through to her heart as he said, 'My name is Tom Long. You must be Ruth. I'll have a pint and a small Jameson, please.' As she reached, trembling, for a glass he added, 'Actually make that a double. It's been a hell of a day.'

Nine

Charlie was an only child in a town of large families. Neighbours often shook their heads in sorrow that he didn't have to share his every breath with a gaggle of other Finns. This merely puzzled Charlie. He enjoyed the sole attention of his parents as a child and, though assured to the contrary at every hand's turn, he never got to missing brothers and sisters. Other people had plenty he could borrow. The glass was certainly half full. His parents had married in their mid-thirties, which was considered old for their generation, and it took some time before Charlie arrived to complete their happiness. They wanted, and bought, the best for him, including an education with the Brothers of Charity at a boarding school in neighbouring Country Galway. As a result, Charlie saw and experienced Kilbrody only during school holidays and was regarded (with envy) as spoiled and exotic for most of those. Separated from family at school and lacking extended relations at home, he learned to fend for himself early on and grew into an independent, strong-minded individual. Again the town put it down to spoiling.

The great myth surrounding Finn's pub was that it had been bought with insurance money on a cousin who had drowned on the *Titanic*. Sadly, the truth was a lot more prosaic. Charlie's grandfather had worked as a farm labourer throughout the country and was frugal and ambitious enough to put together the money for a business. When he reached Kilbrody, and the end of his tether with travelling, he settled on the small pub in the main street and installed himself to live 'over the shop'. It was not the first time a wanderer had fetched up in the town, Charlie explained to Ruth.

'Some stay because they're tired of running. Some look around and decide they haven't run far enough. And some find the town just the right size to fit their private hell, be they native or stranger.'

The grandfather married a quiet, dark woman from a neighbouring village and they set about having a family: two boys and three girls. Between emigration and death only one remained to look after the family business and to see his parents into their dotage and beyond. This was Charlie's father, Francis Xavier Finn.

Charlie drifted from school to college in Galway, ostensibly to study civil engineering. He declared an interest in building a bridge for the nation to mark his, and its, greatness, but ended up escorting women to dances and the pictures and pretty much neglecting, in turn, his studies, the infrastructure of a new Ireland and his proposed contribution to it. Having scraped the most ordinary of degrees, a pass, he left for Europe to bum around and see other cultures, again with women the main focus of these cultural investigations. He devoted himself to pleasure with an easy grace that made him popular as a companion. He was an accomplished roué by the age of twenty-three, some sixty years too soon. Rudderless and without anchor, he travelled the length and breadth of Europe, laying waste to all who took his eye. He had a great time.

He occasionally returned to Kilbrody and was present, by accident, when his mother died of a heart attack. There were some who, unkindly, remarked that the very sight of her errant son finished the woman off. Charlie ignored this chattering, aware that his mother had wanted him to experience the world and actively encouraged his adventures. 'No point regretting it when you're dead,' she would admonish. Her own travels were minor. 'I'm a home bird, Charlie.'

He missed his father's passing by two days even though he received a call to warn him the event was imminent. He had business to finish in Dusseldorf, involving a married woman and a crate of fine wine. It was years before he felt the guilt of that one but it was acute when it came, like the agony following a hammer blow exponentially linked to the time taken for it to register: the longer the wait, the greater the pain. Even so, almost insistent on the tradition of Irish grief and mourning, he went on a bender to end all after the funeral. Four days later he came to in a ditch fifteen miles away, wearing only a pair of underpants and a vest. When he returned to Kilbrody he discovered he'd broken every window in Cross Street and pissed in the post office letterbox. He didn't care much for the residents of Cross Street but he'd always liked the postmistress and was sorry to have distressed her.

Charlie's mother, Esther, had loved gardening so it was a personal torture for her to live above a pub, stepping directly onto the concrete street from front or back door. But she was also a woman of imagination and though others scoffed at her ridiculous notion she decided to create a garden. She went up. Extra joists were added to the roof to take the weight of compost and dirt, and a drainage system designed to bear water to the roots and then take away the excess; Charlie would remark that she was the one who should have been an engineer. She laid deep walls of railway sleepers to the sides and planted them up with olfactory delights, her favourite being the rose. Amongst bushy honeysuckle rambled and climbed all the colours and scents of the *familia rosa*. A middle bed held assorted annuals, backed by standards, floribunda and tea roses, and cottage garden perennials on either side of a spine of green architecturally leaved stoics. It was a lush, erotic oasis, full of the miracles of procreation and death. 'Sure, isn't that what makes the world go round, Charlie?' she would say.

She taught her son to prune and deadhead and he rarely walked through the wonderland without unconsciously attending to some plant or other. Of a summer's evening, the Finns would luxuriate in their secret eyrie, glad to be alive, and aware of their special privilege. As a small child, gazing over the roofs of Kilbrody, Charlie would wait for an Irish Mary Poppins to breeze onto a neighbour's slates and walk across to admire their haven. As a middle-aged man, he still half hoped for her, especially on the damp days. She had an umbrella, after all.

He inherited the pub and, for want of something better to do, he took to running it. At first it seemed perfect for a man of his proclivities: the bar was well stocked and it was a way of meeting women. He bonded with the locals and renewed friendships. The early months were hectic as he grappled with the basics of his trade and he often wrote off the blackouts to stress and overwork. He also went off women, temporarily, after a dose of crabs, thanks to a passing Norwegian; a very modern Viking invasion, he thought, and unnecessary.

Although the pub did good business, Charlie couldn't account for all of the stock or cash; his drunken bouts were taking a toll. He made rules: no slate, even for the most loyal of customers. In fact, the more regular the regular, the greater the potential tab and the dodgier the debt. He stopped drinking behind the bar while on duty. Instead, he ploughed through vodka in his kitchen, thinking no one would notice. Then he would arrive, or return, to work, unable to function properly. It was Old Mikey who took him aside and attempted to talk sense to him. Charlie made more rules: no drinking till after teatime, but he redoubled his efforts thereafter and often couldn't get up the following day to open the pub. He switched to wine, hardly drinking at all, he reasoned, but went back to a lunchtime kick-off. Finally he was drinking beer all day, every day. He stopped eating. He quit women; the bald fact of it was he couldn't get it up. The only love of his life was alcohol. Even he didn't rate in the affair; it was all about the booze.

One November he came to on the roof in a shower of hail. He had no idea how long he had been there. All he knew was that he was in trouble. The freezing sleet lashed against his boiling skin, his limbs ached horribly and he was unable to move. He tried to call out, but only a low moan escaped. He slipped in and out of consciousness and torment for four hours, hidden from neighbourly view by the plants and ramparts of the garden. The louring sky tumbled past, marking time in an excruciating slow motion, and, when it was blocked out, Charlie was visited by the dreams and accusations of his scrambled mind. It was Old Mikey who finally convinced the Sergeant something was very wrong. They broke down the front door and came to his rescue. A spell prone in hospital dealt with some of the cold turkey as well as the pneumonia he had contracted. When he returned to Kilbrody he was two stone lighter, sober, and afraid for his future. But he was home.

He often tried to riddle that notion: home. As a concept it was slippery. Just as he thought he'd grasped it, it was gone again. Was it a refuge, a sanctuary? Or perhaps a shot at redemption? Intangible, inexplicable, yet welcome in its harsh warmth and fierce love. Perhaps it was simply belonging. Then again, to solve the riddle might mean the end of all and a moving on, earthly or otherwise.

Putting the pieces of his life together was tough by any standards. But in time he reached a reconciliation with himself and the town. He even fell in love.

Charlie broke off his thoughts. He always did at this point. There were places it was better not to go. Some things were dealt with more easily than others, and some were best avoided altogether. He went to get Ruth. He had something to show her.

He heard Deborah before he saw her, which was no surprise.

'GAWD,' she was exclaiming. 'I'd've been scared shit-less.'

'Eh, well, I was, actually,' Ruth said.

'I heard you drank a fierce amount of brandy so you must have gawked your ring up too.'

'Oh, I hadn't thought of that.'

'It's a very dangerous thing, you know. A person could be killed stone dead if they keep throwing up all the time.'

'I don't think I even like brandy,' Ruth offered sheepishly.

'The mammy has an aversion to the stuff. Just looking at it sets her off. Same with turnips. No one knows why. Just one look and everything's out. We've had some awful messes to clear up in our time.'

'It's as well you work in the chemists, so,' Old Mikey suggested.

'You can sing that,' Deborah told him.

Charlie appeared at the door by the stairs.

Ruth's eyes searched for an answer across the dusty gloom. 'Was I sick too?'

He shrugged. 'A bit. Not worth mentioning.' He gave the last phrase some welly but knew he was wasting his time and, as expected, it sailed right over Deborah's head. She spoke as she saw, usually oblivious of the consequences; this was her gift and Kilbrody's burden.

'Great stuff for your book,' Mikey said.

Ruth smiled evenly. I've become a consummate liar, she thought.

Cathy Long appeared in her usual rush of anxious hassle.

'The gorgeous Cathy Long,' Old Mikey acknowledged. She threw him a perfunctory greeting and went to her father's side.

Charlie saw Ruth's eyes steal to Tom and he recognised the look. He also saw that Tom was beyond them all by then. He knew that one too. They let the youngster haul him out with as much dignity as they both could muster.

'It's a bad way to be, all the same,' Mikey said, when they had left.

'It is,' Charlie agreed.

'Aree,' Deborah exclaimed. 'Isn't it great for business?'

There was no answering that.

Charlie was uncharacteristically nervous as he led Ruth up the stairs, further than was usual.

'The attic?' she asked.

'More or less,' he replied.

This might have been weird or even scary to her a day ago, but she trusted him now, wise or not. She was overwhelmed as this was repaid. She squealed lightly and danced about, clapping her hands.

'You know, I've only seen the front of the main street so far. And now I'm on top of the world.' She turned full circle in delight. 'How did this happen?'

'Dunno. Men came in the night and left it this way. The Sergeant is still looking for them.' He felt stupid to have made a joke. 'My mother. She made this. After that, all I had to do was love it.'

Ruth trailed her hand through the plants and held it

to her face. Lavender. Honeysuckle. 'So many roses,' she whispered. 'Beautiful.'

'This garden has saved me a few times,' Charlie told her. 'There's a theory that if you can't be happy in a garden, you can't be happy anywhere. I'm inclined to believe that.'

She crossed to the rail at the back of the roof and saw the river for the first time. The pub opened there onto a narrow street with a rampart by the water where a small, energetic cascade beat across the rocks and rushed towards the distant sea. Crossing the bridge above it was Cathy Long followed by her dad. Every hundred yards the teenager stopped and turned to berate the man and urge him homewards.

'He's lovely,' Ruth said. 'Does he have a problem with alcohol?'

'Oh yes,' Charlie said, trying to keep an agenda out of his voice, trying desperately not to feel and sound bitter that Tom Long had ruined his moment of revelation to Ruth. Her wonder was curtailed by another man. He knew it was unreasonable to feel jealous but he could not help himself.

'How can you continue to serve him when you know it's ruining him?'

Charlie told the truth, but it emerged as petulance. 'Only Tom Long can help Tom Long. He has to want to change. No one else can do it for him.' He turned and left the rooftop paradise.

Ruth couldn't shake the feeling that they had had their first quarrel.

'Why is it that two plus two is always four with you?' Greg asked.

'Because it just is,' she replied. *'Everyone knows that.'*

'Could it never be five, not even once?'

'I guess it could, but what would be the point of that?'

'You should loosen up sometimes, Ruth, you might like it.'

Her heart jittered. From where she stood, the ivory moon looked trapped in a tangled rose. A ghost wind shook red petals loose, like bloodied tears falling on the world.

She hurried downstairs, calling Charlie's name, but received no reply. She began to panic, wanting him close, wanting to see her friend, even if it meant continuing the row. She tried each of the living rooms but didn't find him. She descended to the busy pub. Deborah was loudly telling her audience of ancient male drinkers that they were all turning into women because of high levels of oestrogen in the water. Old Mikey wanted to know if that made him gay. He seemed worried by the idea. Ruth might have laughed, another time. Now she couldn't even muster a smile. Charlie was nowhere to be found.

Deborah caught her eye. 'He's gone out the door like a scalded cat,' she said.

'Oh,' Ruth managed.

All eyes were turned on her.

'I forgot to ask him to get me something,' she spluttered.

She left before she could catch their knowing expressions. She had better things to worry about than their boozy conjecture.

Had she ruined something special? *Again*.

Ten

She woke to the delightful smells of brewing coffee and frying bacon. Her heart lifted after a night of dreams, of demons and wraiths, and her father saying, 'Ruth, get away.' She leapt from the bed and rushed by the bathroom to freshen up and check that she looked carelessly tousled. Fragrant, and with heart thudding, she sidled into the kitchen. Charlie stood at the cooker, a similar study in casual. He glanced up after the briefest, calculated pause and smiled.

'Fresh orange juice,' he said, presenting her with a glass. 'And breakfast, as an apology for my behaviour last night.'

'You have nothing to apologise to me for,' Ruth told him, truthfully. 'I'm fairly sure it's me who should be making breakfast and trying to gain some brownie points.'

They held a gaze, smiled and chinked glasses.

Ruth surveyed the culinaries. 'Oh, sweet Lord, are you making a hollandaise?'

'That I am. And there's no need to call me lord, Charlie will do for the moment.'

She cuffed him lightly and began to poke around the pans: spinach, bacon, eggs, sauce and something else in the mix. She sniffed the air. 'Croissants?'

'But of course.'

Ruth began to laugh. 'Where did you learn all this?'

'I once spent a summer with a married woman in Tuscany. We were hiding from her jealous and estranged husband, so we stayed in a lot and she cooked and taught me how.'

Ruth smiled slyly. 'And that would have been in return for?'

'She left a more experienced woman than she arrived,' he acknowledged.

'And would married women be a feature of the Finn lifestyle?'

He seemed distracted as he pondered that. 'Sometimes I get them just before that momentous occasion.'

Ruth's antennae perked. What was there in his voice? Why did he seem in another place now? The poaching eggs boiled over. He returned. 'Shite! Shite 'n' onions.'

'Joyce,' Ruth offered.

He dropped his spatula. 'What?' he exclaimed. 'What did you say? What do you mean?'

Ruth was bemused but repeated, 'Joyce. That's a James Joyce quote, isn't it? Shite 'n' onions?'

'Oh, yes.' He bent to retrieve the spatula. 'Sorry, bit of a senior moment there.'

'A petit mal, as the French might say.'

Or a grand mal, in my case, Charlie thought. *Joyce*. A silence settled.

'Is that a big love thing?' Ruth asked.

'Have we just jumped a few steps on the getting-to-know-one-another scale with a question like that?' Charlie asked softly.

'Probably. But I think we might have anyhow, so why waste time?'

Charlie nodded and began to serve their meal. They ate in silence for a while, then he spoke again. 'I suppose I find the married ladies that bit safer.'

Ruth kept her voice neutral and steady. These were delicate moments as their friendship moved up a notch. 'But not so much that you'd marry yourself and have your very own safe lady?'

'I did come close once. Or at least I was close to the leap but I misread it. She chose someone else.' He toyed with his spinach.

'Joyce?'

He didn't answer.

'Does it still hurt?'

'Love always hurts.' He searched her eyes. 'And you?'

Ruth took a deep breath. 'Right now, I'm plain terrified. And I don't really know where love, or maybe lack of it, fits in.'

It felt good to say it, but in no way diminished the magnitude of her situation.

'Shouldn't we be eating in the garden?' Ruth asked.

Charlie smiled. 'You were paying it attention after all.'

'Let's try to get happy,' she suggested. 'Let's take that on.'

They began to gather their meal in a rhythm of people at ease with one another. Once their hands brushed comfortably and without bashfulness. Ruth relished the kindness, Charlie the company. They moved upward and tried to give their lonely spirits room to soar. It was a start and it was slow. But it would do for now.

Cathy Long was wishing her life away, again. Sunday was easily the deadliest and most boring of the week, and this one could not pass quickly enough. She yearned to start her new course and resented the slow, ambling day that was holding her from it. First, there was the obligatory Mass, at which everyone pinched her and said how huge she was getting, and what was she being fed to have her so big and healthy, and won't Daddy soon have to beat the boys from the door. It was excruciating. It made her feel fat. And ugly. And hot. If the weather didn't break soon, someone was going to get murdered or the whole town fried insane. At least the church was cool. Father Kilcullen's sonorous voice wafted over and above without disturbing her. She thought of her birthday and her new job and almost got happy. Careful, she warned herself, it can't last.

After the religion, she and her mother went to visit her grandfather and spent a terse time not mentioning her father's problem. Tom had gone to Finn's, sharpish, and by now would be on his way to another oblivion. And still there were twenty hours to go till Monday morning and her release from tedium. When God made time, he made way too much of it.

The locals were present in force.

'You'd think they never got out any other day of the week, wouldn't you?' Charlie whispered to Ruth as they manned the bar. 'Of course, you haven't lost your novelty value yet.'

'I'll grow on them. They'll have forgotten how I arrived by next Tuesday. I'll be a former one-week wonder.'

'Ah now, you'll always be a wonder,' Charlie said and gave one of his killer smiles.

Ruth had seen him unleash this before but didn't mind that he was including her in the 'women to be flirted with' category. His eyes had an amazing capacity to glow and lifted him from good-looking to handsome in a nanosecond. Still, though, he was not interfering with her breathing the way Tom Long was. It was a mystery; it's not as if the man had said more than ten words at once to her. What was happening was almost chemical, in essence. It was a raw desire, and one to be suppressed. This was wanting for something she didn't need, that's for sure; a married man and a troubled one.

She avoided serving him, not certain that she could prevent her hands from shaking if she did, or her voice from quivering, or her body from betraying her in a language everyone could read. She had all but got away with it when Charlie said, 'It's beginning to look rude that you're ignoring Tom. Grow up and deal with it.'

Ruth felt she'd been stung with a lash. His voice was harsh as he reprimanded her and she began to crumble. How could he be so kind to her one minute and so bitingly mean the next? Dutifully, she started a pint but, as if sensing he had gone too far, Charlie finished and served it. It could not save her from looking into Tom Long's soul as he collected his drink. He paused and broke her heart with a sad smile. That man is a danger, she told herself.

The new aspect of the Sunday drinking, for Ruth, was the presence of the wives and girlfriends. Charlie introduced a few: the librarian, Carol, who clearly had the hots for him; her friend Linda, who sported a wedding ring but no husband and who watched Charlie's every move from the corner of her beady eye. They perched like birdies on high stools at the end of the bar. Or vultures, maybe. They seemed unimpressed with the woman from the bus, and Ruth felt confrontation hanging in the air. Silly, perhaps. She was probably imagining it. After all, she didn't know these women and rushing to melodramatic conclusions wouldn't help, especially if there was a tension. She needed to calm down, ground herself and get real. And that would include some nasty, lonely, solo question-and-answer sessions later. She deferred naming her time for these, sure that they would occur with or without her blessing.

The women were smartly dressed and accessorised. Carol favoured a floral print, bias-cut skirt with a mauve wraparound top. Her curling hair was held loosely at the base of her neck in a cream scrunch, which matched her bag and bangles. Linda had opted for a more dramatic ensemble in black and white vertical stripes, dangerous heels and deep red mouth. Her black hair was scraped off her face by the Chanel sunglasses so carefully placed on her head. Bet that took a while to get right, Ruth thought, then admonished herself with a silent 'bitch'. She felt frumpy in her jeans and tourist T-shirt, and very aware that she was wearing a pair of the passion killers recently purchased on Kilbrody's High Street. There was no doubting that Linda was in an itsy bitsy thong, matching lace bra and the heady scent of Cristalle. Ruth had to be content with Nivea soap and deodorant.

Her heart lifted to see Old Mikey enter. He squeezed

himself onto his stool and looked around. 'So, they've arrived to suss you out, then,' he said, gesturing to the well-dressed pair. 'They'll be back for more tonight and that's when you can expect the inquisition.'

She served his stout.

'I'd even lay money on Mrs Whinge hauling herself off her sickbed to check on you.' He laughed gently. 'She's very protective of her husband. And him such a catch.' He winked and downed his pint in three swallows.

'Are you filling this woman's head with idle spite and nonsense?' Charlie asked congenially as he cleared the dead soldiers of the afternoon from the counter.

Old Mikey hooted, pleased with his villainy.

A large, good-looking man entered, trying to hide his size in a stoop. He quickly took in the room, clocked Carol the librarian and reddened slightly. Ah, thought Ruth, I'm getting good at this people-watching thing. He ordered a pint 'and whatever the two ladies are having'. Ruth filled the order and delivered the vodka tonics. Linda sniggered but Carol lifted her glass in salute and thanks. There was hope for her, even if her friend was a rotten specimen. Old Mikey introduced the arrival as Bert Fahy, 'a grand catch and a gentleman'.

'Pleased to meet you,' Ruth said, extending a hand.

He seemed to steel himself as part of a personal process he'd adopted. He's shy, thought Ruth. What a way to be for such a looker. He could have his choice of women.

Then his eyes locked onto hers and made her feel like the only person in the room. 'You're very welcome to Kilbrody, Ruth, and we're all delighted that you're up and about.' He turned to Mikey. 'Isn't it great to have another fine woman on board?'

'It is indeed.' Mikey smiled at him appreciatively, pleased with Bert's mammoth effort and progress.

Ruth felt attractive and worthy of the compliment just then. For the first time in a while, she suspected.

He had touched her hand, that day in the staffroom. She was so surprised she looked all around to see if the others had noticed. They had not.

'You are lovely, Ruth, you know,' he said.

Heart almost stopped at the unexpectedness of it. Why would he do such a thing?

'Thank you, Greg.' Then, lightly, 'Flattery will get you everywhere,' and a laugh.

Stupid, stupid, of course.

His turn to laugh and then he was away.

She was still preening a little from Bert and Old Mikey when she saw Charlie watching her with an inscrutable expression. Back in your box, she told herself.

'No harm in a compliment,' he told her.

You'd have thought not.

Sunday was when Tom Long came home early from the pub. This was due to the tradition of the family dinner, always accompanied by a bottle of wine. Today was an exception, he realised when he sat at the table: no wine. Cathy stared long and hard at her plate. The crisp, white cloth beneath it jarred with the close, green stripes of the dish, dazzling her vision.

'Will I open us a bottle of red?' Tom suggested.

'Oh, I forgot to get some,' his wife replied, knowing the lie rang loud in the room.

The plate and cloth were strobing off each other now.

'Ah, I'm sure there's something somewhere,' he said, rising in search of a cache.

His wife let him, certain that she had found all of his hidden stores. It had been an exhausting task that week, unearthing the secrets of the alcoholic and disposing of them surreptitiously. And what a selection she had found: whiskey, vodka, two kinds of sherry, even a manky bottle of rum. She had also cleared out her own few cans of beer and all the sauces that mentioned booze in their make-up.

'Will you have a bit of everything?' she asked her daughter.

'Suppose.'

'What, even the broccoli?'

'I'll give it a go.'

'Mirabile dictu.'

The background symphony continued, now speeding from legato to a more urgent rhythm, growing louder and more desperate.

'I think I got everything,' Cathy's mother said, breaking

with tradition and referring to the family problem directly with her daughter.

The staccato of banging cupboard doors moved along the corridor to the living rooms and on into the bedrooms.

'You missed a half-bottle of brandy behind the water butt in the orchard,' Cathy said. 'I looked after that.'

There was no hiding from this any more, nor any point in ignoring it.

'The only room that was clear was mine, wasn't it?' Cathy asked.

'Yes.'

A tiny act of love?

'It just seems time to tackle it all,' her mum said.

'Mirabile dictu,' from Cathy.

They both smiled, cheerlessly grateful for the small joke.

'I'll take some of the ratatouille too, Mam. It's growing on me.'

'Good girl. And thank you.'

'Thank you.'

After a busy afternoon, Ruth and Charlie staggered their breaks before heading into the evening session at Finn's. Charlie went first, leaving his newest staff member to deal with the quietest time of the day. The regulars had drifted off, promising to return for a 'proper session' later. Their capacity for the gargle was impressive, Ruth thought, and

not a little formidable. In stark contrast to a couple of
French tourists who had each nursed a glass of stout for
a record-breaking hour. She had just served them a second
(they'd lost the run of themselves) when the door opened
and Tom Long returned. She reached for a pint glass,
anticipating his choice, and managed, 'Chaser?'

He turned to her and said, 'A double.' She stepped
back. He had tears in his eyes.

'Are you all right?' she asked.

'No, but that's up to me.'

'Of course. I didn't mean to pry. Sorry.'

'No, no, please don't be. I wasn't referring to your
question. It's a bit more complicated than that.'

He knocked the whiskey back in one slug. 'I have a
lot to think about just now, a lot to deal with.'

'If there's anything I can do . . .' Ruth offered, haltingly.

'I wish it was as simple as asking for help.'

'Perhaps it is,' Charlie said, appearing from upstairs.
'At least it would be a start.'

Tom Long smiled, wryly, paid for the drinks and
retired to his usual spot with the pint. The air crackled
oddly between them. Charlie watched Tom, his face an
unreadable confusion of thoughts. Ruth sensed a distress
she had not noticed before in his dealings with this other
man.

'Will I break now?' she asked, as much to dispel his
mood as to go and eat.

'Huh? Oh yeah. And I'll have to go out for a few hours tonight so I'll get Deborah in to help you. I'll be back in plenty of time to lock up.'

Tom Long signalled another solo round.

Eleven

Ruth grilled a steak and married it with the salad Charlie had left prepared. Freshly made dressing, she noticed. Was that another legacy of a love affair? The idea led her dangerously close to an area of her own experience that she knew better than to tackle on an empty stomach. She scarfed back her meal. It didn't impart great perspectives on life and things universal, but she wasn't so low as to be hijacked due to sheer hunger.

The tan satchel sat by an armchair, vaguely accusing her. Its indolent hide had a deceptive blandness. It knew some of the truth, but what was that other than perspective, a slanted version belonging to whoever was deciding what was and wasn't relevant or true? Wasn't all life based on some sort of lie or exaggeration, from Santa Claus on? She didn't seem to remember any great gutting when she realised her parents were in charge of Christmas and not the mythic man with the beard and sleigh. As long as the placebo of the gifts continued, forgiveness was available to all involved. You got over it and went on, like losing your religion.

She wondered about her lie to the citizens of Kilbrody. She wasn't a writer, rather that other walking cliché: one who 'couldn't' and therefore taught. But surely it was harmless for her to pretend a while until she felt up to facing her old life? She found the lie liberating and a necessary distraction to keep the undesirable at bay. Needs must, she told herself. Some facts had to be faced, however. Ruth knuckled to. She acknowledged that she was single, thirty-eight years old and childless. In itself, none of these facts was necessarily a bad thing, so why did they worry her? Was it that she was getting on and alone? Perhaps. Something was halting her on that. Why? Was it to do with Greg Deegan? She summoned up an image of the man. Tumbling fair curls, deep brown eyes with long lashes, a way with a puzzled, boyish frown and a devastating eye bat. Total devastation, to a lonely singleton. She'd fallen too far after that first hand touch.

It was a hard day's work later. The dull communal staffroom, smelling of stewed tea, sour coffee, disappointing biscuits. Mountains of copybooks festered and multiplied in front of each of them. 'Lisa sucks cock' was the helpful information on the back of the last one Ruth corrected. Indeed. I'm sure her parents are very proud.

'I think a drink is in order, don't you?' he'd said.

She did, but didn't want to seem eager. Careful, Ruth, he's married. But surely that also made him safe.

They had been joined by a couple of the others: Sean, the science teacher, and Ray from phys. ed.

Nothing outwardly playful or untoward in the pub. Two drinks, some bitching about salaries, then the simple offer of a lift home.

'You're still with your parents?' He seemed shocked.

They were sitting outside her house in his warm car, the winter rain pelting down. It was the archetypal textbook scenario, if she'd cared to notice.

She had been abashed. 'Yes, I know it's silly, in this day and age.'

She was ashamed of her disloyalty, dripping so easily from her lips. She loved her parents. They were good to her. She had a whole section to herself at home, practically cut off from the rest of the house. They never interfered, except to look for her share of the bills.

'Big mistake, I think. You should get out of there and live your life, Ruth.'

Why had she listened or considered this to be reasonable? She had wanted him to like her? To admire her independence? Of course, independence was the last thing she got from him until he didn't want her any more.

Ruth was delighted to hear Charlie's voice call her for duty. Too much time alone was to be avoided. She didn't want to face her dirty laundry all at once. The best would be to avoid it for ever. Could she do that here in a new place, with a new life? The mad notion tided her over.

Linda had chosen a well-cut, red linen coat-dress for the evening. She teamed it with black heels, bag and matching vamp lipstick. Oh, and her husband, Frank, who spent most of his time on a mobile phone discussing hurling. Her cold eyes roamed the pub hungrily. Charlie's out, Ruth intoned smugly in her mind. I know something that you don't. I know something that you don't. She felt like laughing. With Linda marginalised by her spouse, Bert Fahy took his opportunity to talk to Carol, who was clad in a sober but classic green trouser suit. Clearly, these women did not shop in Kilbrody. Ruth was back in her linens but cut no dash in comparison.

'They make a nice couple,' she whispered to Deborah, nodding at Bert and Carol.

The latter was uncharacteristically quiet.

'Don't they?' Ruth prodded.

'Yeah. Well, he's only got eyes for her and she's got her eye on Charlie, so everyone's a loser.' Then she clammed up again.

The bar hushed as the Whinge entered with a scrawny woman who clutched her chest and wheezed a lot. Old Mikey chuckled.

'I told you you were in trouble,' he said to Ruth.

The woman's claw summoned her along the bar counter. 'Are you the Dublin wan?'

'I am.'

'Are you married?'

'No.'

'Hmm. Asked for?'

Ruth's heart filliped. 'Eh, no.' This appeared to be the truth, and another area for self-confrontation. At her age, why was she not asked for? Had she been? No, was the answer. *Greg Deegan.*

'Well, I just hope you know that there are a lot of respectable people in this parish who don't have any truck with foolin' about in other people's marriages.'

Ruth felt eyes boring into her back. Linda was sneering at her.

'Thank you so much for the tip-off, Mrs O'Brien. It's nice to have my card marked by one of the most respected of the respectable people,' Ruth said.

'And another thing,' Mrs Whinge said, waxing to her subject. 'I hear you're some class of a writer. Well, I can tell you that I won't take kindly to my image being used in any way. It's my . . .' She was stuck for the words and consulted her husband with a hand wave.

'Intellectual property,' he provided, grandly.

His wife agreed. 'That's it.'

'I understand completely,' Ruth said, unable to decide between laughter and tears. 'Can I get you and your husband a drink?'

'You're not supposed to have alcohol with the antibiotics you're on for that rash,' Deborah called, loudly. 'Remember the cut of you the last time?'

Ruth silently cheered and made a note to buy Deborah a drink later.

'He'll have a pint and I'll have a shandy,' Mrs Whinge announced. 'And bugger the antibiotics.'

'And the rash,' Ruth added, grinning. She turned to Linda and zapped her a mouthful of teeth too. Come on, the lot of you, if you think you're hard enough.

Ozzy O'Reilly entered with his better half, a glamorous, hourglass of a woman, a head and a half taller than her husband. Mikey was shivering with laughter. Come one, come all.

'I'm Angie O'Reilly,' the woman told her. 'You're welcome to Kilbrody.'

A different approach, then.

'How long will you be staying?'

And yet . . .

'I'm really not sure. My sister is coming to town next week and we'll discuss it all then.'

Ruth felt her blood chill and her brain whirr with anxiety. Back to work, she had nearly said, the new term. Icy tentacles reached for her heart.

'Our loss, I'm sure,' Angie O'Reilly purred, and headed down the bar to join Linda and her still chattering husband. 'Frank, give me that fucking phone this instant,' she snapped, grabbing the mobile from his hand.

'Frank's sister,' Mikey explained.

'I get the feeling mine might be a bit like that too,' Ruth said. 'Formidable.'

Old Mikey shrugged. 'That's what God invented families for.'

Tom Long had stopped communicating. He had even stopped ordering drink.

'I'm worried about him,' Ruth said.

Mikey checked his watch. 'Cathy mustn't be coming today. Deborah, give the hackney a call and get him to bring yer man home. He's done in.' No love lost there, Ruth noticed.

When the cab arrived it was clear that the bar staff were expected to see Tom Long to the door. Ruth was fixed to the tiles as Deborah signalled that she was busy and couldn't help. She agonised her way across the floor and gently told the man his lift was here. He looked into her eyes and said, 'I think I may need a hand, if that's all the same to you.' She reached out to him and he leaned on her for their short journey. She could feel the strength of his body coiled under his shirt, his heat and sheer manliness. Her head began to spin and she felt a faint ebb and flow of consciousness. Oh God, no, not now; body, do not let me down. As they reached the car and she steadied him to sit in it, he squeezed her arm and stopped her breath. Then, almost imperceptibly, he seemed to kiss her cheek as he disappeared into the car. Ruth boiled and gasped.

'He's a beauty all right,' said a toneless voice to her side. Charlie stood in the shadows, grim and watchful. And telling the truth. Tom Long was all that. 'I'll introduce you to his wife one of these days,' he said, disappearing before the sound of his words had faded.

Ruth sat on the sill of the front window to compose herself. She stood, eventually, walked back into the pub and told Charlie she was taking a break.

'You going up-up?' he enquired, almost blithely.

'Yes,' she admitted.

'Will I bring you something later? A drink?'

'No, thanks.'

'Would you like company at all?'

'It's up to yourself,' she said.

Something was going on here that she didn't quite get and, until she did, she intended to stay as neutral as possible. Hey, she wanted to scream, I've got some problems too, so keep yours to yourselves and let me get on with my own short, useless life.

The honeysuckle was playing a blinder. It enveloped her in a rich, intoxicating comfort. She wanted to disappear into it, to become part of its natural gift to the world, rather than blighting it with her misery and failure. She felt winded and jittery. The encounter with Tom Long had been so subtle as to be imagined. But her face stung, as if she'd been slapped, from the brush of his lips. There was nothing to do but put it behind her and avoid the chance of any similar situation. She had a knack for trouble and that was something that would have to change in her new regime.

Numbly she leaned over the roof and watched the punters leave by the front door. The now familiar gait of Old Mikey ambling along. He seemed to be singing to himself. The Whinge was supporting his missus, frail and langered. Ooh, that rash would have a flare-up tomorrow.

Ruth looked at the moon. Was Kate seeing it, in Dublin? And our parents. Where are they now? Can they see it too? Do they even want to any more?

Kate always said Ruth was wired to the moon. Sometimes that was a positive thing, apparently, sometimes not. Lunar, loony, lunatic lunacy. Tonight it cast a gelid stare upon her and offered little comfort beyond its existence. You'll be there a long time after I'm gone, she told it. And good riddance to me. She was steeped in inadequacy. What was the bloody point of her at all?

Cathy lay in bed unable to sleep: a mixture of dread at her father's return and apprehensive excitement about the morning and her new assignment. A car pulled up and she heard the sounds of one man helping another to the door. He was home. The house was unnaturally quiet, every room holding its breath. The key rattled in the lock, the door opened too widely and quickly, knocking into the wall, the clamorous bang reverberating throughout. Yet, still, the loud human silence persisted. Her father staggered to his bedroom, but all Cathy heard after that was his fumbling efforts to get out of his clothes and into bed. Her mother was not helping him, not speaking to him, no doubt pretending to be asleep. It was somehow worse than when they fought. Cathy shivered. They were headed into unknown territory now, a new phase of a campaign with unwritten rules. She buried her head under the bedcovers and began to hum.

Ruth walked slowly down the stairs, identifying the few remaining voices as she went. Deborah was holding forth on the merits of depilatory creams versus shaving.

'The itch is something terrible and nothing is worse than scratching "down there" all day. No, give me the Nair any time.'

Carol said, 'Thanks for sharing that with us.'

'Not at all. I just wish Mammy would listen to me. She's a holy show.'

Ruth was grinning at the notion of Deborah's ancient mother having trouble with bikini line regrowth when she heard Charlie say he would check on one of the lager barrels. She didn't want to face him alone yet so she crept back up a few steps. After he'd passed down into the cellar she counted to five and was about to continue her journey when Linda excused herself from the company, pleading the 'powder room'. Wanting to encounter her even less, Ruth hung back once more.

But the woman overshot the ladies and headed to the cellar too. What? Ruth crept along to the top of the stairs leading to the storeroom. She could hear the rustle of clothes and ragged breathing.

'Show me,' Charlie's voice croaked.

'You told me not to wear any.' A dangerous, honeyed tone.

'Good enough to eat.' Lascivious now.

'You'd better.' A low, predatory laugh.

Ruth was fixed to the spot, heart pounding, breath painful. She shuddered, horrified, and then she fled, unable to hear or imagine any more. She felt hollow. And although she knew she had no right, she also felt betrayed.

Twelve

It could not have happened! Although Cathy couldn't sleep with excitement, she had finally nodded off and was now being hauled late out of bed by her mother. Well, not exactly late, but half an hour after she'd planned. Now she had no time to try on all her outfits again and choose the right one. She'd had a go with them the previous evening but she never knew what way her hair was going to sprout from day to day or how her skin might look, so that usually meant repeating the process. With no such luxury available, she grabbed her oldest jeans (tears on both knees, hurrah) and a black T-shirt with 'hip' written across the front. She ran a hand through her mop and even she had to admit that it wasn't too bad; the curls were nice and relaxed due, no doubt, to the half bottle of conditioner she'd used and another of Frizz Ease.

Midway through a rushed bowl of cereal her father appeared and she halted her chewing. He was still in his pyjamas. Who had looked after the animals?

'I went out this morning,' her mother said, warning against comment with her glare.

It made sense. If anything would penetrate Tom Long's thick hide, it was surely his responsibility to his herd. That's us too, Cathy felt like saying, but hoped that the profound silence around them would speak it better than she ever could.

He looked wretched; not just terrible, wretched. Dark shadows along his cheeks and black circles around his eyes made his face look skeletal. The colour had drained from his skin and lips and his hair hung lank. His hands trembled fiercely as he forced tea into his mouth, holding it there forever before swallowing in a huge effort. His knuckles strained white through his skin as he battled to keep the liquid down and tried to wrestle charge of his life back from the pit he had brought it to.

Her mother checked her watch. 'Cathy, time to go. You'll need a hat and sunscreen, so go get them. And I'll give you a lift over if you like.'

This was her mother's escape. She would remove herself from confrontation over these next days, hoping to shake her husband into remedial action of his own. Tom Long was, after all, the only one who could decide to save Tom Long.

Ruth woke in the spare room. It was small, snug. She listened for the sounds of other life. None. Was she the first to stir, or had she missed that by a long shot? She squinted at the alarm clock. No, it was 8.45. She lay still, thinking, remembering the night before and Charlie and Linda's secret meeting. She began to squirm, yearning herself for the sexual attentions of another. Slowly, she reached down and began to stroke herself.

She found Charlie having coffee in the roof garden. He was looking fresh and relieved, she noted.

'You really scrub yourself hard in that shower,' he commented.

'Yeah, I guess I do.' She had, as usual. 'Cleanliness, godliness and so on, I suppose.'

What she did next felt liberating but she couldn't help suspect that she wouldn't have done it even a fortnight ago in Dublin. The power of the remove? 'Why are you shagging Linda?' she asked. 'She's a complete bitch.'

Charlie laughed and drained his cup. 'She is, and that's why. She couldn't give a shit about me, nor I about her. It's convenient. We use one another, and the system works.'

'As long as no one else finds out about it.'

'No one will.' He looked out from under those long lashes. 'Will they?'

'Not from me they won't,' she shot back. 'And don't do that to me.'

'Do what?'

'The eye thing. I'm not one of your creatures.' She was sounding prim now and hated it.

'All right, all right, keep your knickers on.'

'Unlike Linda.'

Charlie smiled but it was clouded. 'Get any tips from your voyeurism?'

Guiltily, Ruth thought of earlier that morning. She blushed angrily. 'It wasn't like that,' she muttered. 'It was an accident.'

'I must say I might have enjoyed it more if I'd known we had an audience. Perhaps you'd like an official invite next time.'

Her head snapped up indignantly, poised for retort, but she saw that he was teasing her. Time to locate a sense of humour, Ruth. She was searching for bon mots to assuage the situation when Charlie got up and disappeared. She boiled with temper at his apparent nonchalance. How did he do it? He knew all the right buttons to press to take her from indignant to regretful and over to bloody well angry.

He returned with a hose. 'Got to water the kingdom.' Now she felt like a clumsy, paranoid dolt.

Charlie got to work and Ruth reached for the fruit basket. She calmed to the music of running water and the velvet smoothness of a peach. She was leaning back in the warm sun and rubbing away stray juice from her chin as the rain began. Smiling, she sat enjoying this first light shower, then realised that it really couldn't be natural. She opened her eyes to see Charlie standing at a distance pointing the hose up and over her to ensure the lightest of water kisses. They regarded one another longer than was necessary, charged and combative then suddenly conciliatory: détente. This guy really does know how to play me, Ruth thought. She grinned. He makes me feel as if I've been here for ever. I'm kind of comfortable, she realised.

'The wet look suits you,' he said.

Ruth saw that she was all but naked from her drenching. Charlie disappeared into a tangle of rose and fuchsia, all smirking and pleased with himself.

She looked around her refuge and allowed the safety to thrust her forward. Today is Monday, she reminded herself; as good a day as any other to start over. She shivered in her damp clothes, a tremulous mixture of excitement and chilly apprehension. Where to start?

Ozzy was checking on the youngsters of the parish arriving for the Youth Project at the old churchyard. Fiona had refused point blank to join up. Now he could see her sitting on a wall with the ne'er-do-wells. He'd have to fix her up with a wee job in Surf 'n' Turf and get her off the streets. No way was she going to spend the rest of the summer hanging around with the likes of that gurrier Frankie Marr. The Marrs never had an arse in their pants and never would. The father, a painter and decorator; hunh! A job-a-day layabout who hadn't done an honest hand's turn in two decades. And the state of the house they lived in. If that was an advertisement for the family business, those people were in deep doodoo.

There was Cathy Long and her mother. The wife had had to do Tom's work that morning, he'd noticed. Couldn't be much left in him at the rate he was hitting the sauce. Mind you, he had a bit of a head on him himself with the feed of pints he'd put away last night. Angie didn't often come to the pub, she preferred to hang out with her own crowd, but when she did, it was a marathon session. He blamed that Ruth. Since she'd arrived they didn't dare miss a moment at Finn's for fear she might turn out to be a fugitive, or worse. Didn't look very likely now, though; she seemed normal enough. Well, things might hot up when her sister arrived. He let the binoculars roam to the roof garden above the pub. Charlie Finn seemed to be hosing the Treacy wan down. Ah, no, he was looking after his plants. Never water your roses at night, wasn't that the advice Charlie had given him? Young Finn probably had lots about the women too; he was the man for the ladies, for sure. But Ozzy couldn't very well go asking that sort of question and disgracing himself by seeming not to know it all. Besides, marriage had curbed his curiosity. He was happy to learn by observation.

He lowered the binoculars and rubbed his tired eyes. He'd been up since seven checking on the comings and goings at the various homesteads. He hadn't managed to identify the woman who left Bert's place at eight but he would, he would. Everything comes to he who waits, he told himself. And he could wait.

The old black bicycle was in good nick and had obviously been loved over the years. What had her mother called this sort? A Mary Hickey, wasn't it? She had no idea why, but it suited it. She dusted off the seat and walked it out of the storeroom and through the back door of the pub. A blast of hot air hit her, as if an oven door had opened. The tyres were plump, the chain a trained baritone, and the wheels made satisfied clickedy-clickedy-clicks with each complete turn.

'Charlie,' she called. 'Can I use the bike?'

He ran down the stairs, surprised. 'No one's wanted to since . . .' he paused.

'Is it a problem?'

'No, not at all. Eh, it was my mother's, originally. I'm sure she'd be delighted for it to get a run out.'

'I thought it'd be good for me to get some exercise and do a bit of thinking along the way.'

'Excellent idea. Nothing like Mother Nature for grounding a person.' He folded his arms and leaned against the door jamb. 'We have many local delights.' He gestured across the water. 'Just a few miles across is Ennistymon, our closest enemy. They have a bigger river cascade, a lovely hotel, better shops and they won the bingo jackpot twice in a row recently, which went down like a cup of hot sick everywhere else in the county. Further on is Kilfenora, treasured for its musicians and world-famous ceili band. Unfortunately for Kilbrody, our most talked-about moment in history was when a bunch of gutties decided to burn down the Galbraith demesne in the twenties, even though the family were as Irish as any other in the town and had been nothing but brilliant to their tenants for ever. What the brave arsonists weren't to know was that Dizzy Galbraith was sheltering some rebels on the run from the Black and Tans. They were trapped in the cellar and burned along with the house and its contents. An ignominious footnote in the annals of County Clare and not one we're ever allowed to forget.'

'Did Dizzy make it out?'

'I'm glad to report that she did. She moved into the gate lodge and lived to the grand old age of ninety-eight on a diet of whiskey and cigarettes. She never married and the line died with her, which was a pity. They were decent people, the Galbraiths.'

'Anywhere else I might like?'

'If you take the road across the bridge you'll get to Lahinch, or if you take the other fork you'll see a lot of countryside and eventually hit the sea at Doolin.'

'Mmn, the sea, I think. And quickly. I'll try Lahinch and go up the coast a bit.'

'Have you money for tea and buns?'

'Yes, Dad.'

'Take a bottle of water with you and don't forget your shift starts at three this afternoon.'

'Yes, boss.'

Is that how she sees me, he wondered, as he watched her shaky start along the street: a father figure, an employer? She gave a rusty tinkle of the bell. Jeez, I hope she gets steadier on that contraption, he thought, or she'll wind up as mincemeat to the country drivers, let alone the crazy touristas. 'Bon voyage,' he called. She raised her hand in salute and wobbled madly. Charlie winced and went back inside with fingers crossed.

Ten jittery young Kilbrodians lined up before the group leader. Their parents hovered close by to make sure all was well, before breaking into splinter groups for a gossip. Frankie Marr and his gang sat opposite, mocking. Fiona's face was a picture of derision. They're jealous, that's all, Cathy told herself over and over. Frankie lit up a cigarette and turned purple as he tried not to cough and spew. It was all she could do not to laugh out loud.

'Twat,' she heard from her side.

The town's newest resident, Peter, was standing beside her, also suppressing a laugh.

She chuckled appreciatively. 'You're not wrong.' She gave him a surreptitious side glance, which he met full on. Eek. She hid behind the peak of her baseball cap.

'I'm nervous,' he whispered. 'Are you?'

'Oh yeah, big time,' she managed, cheeks burning savagely with bashfulness.

'Still, can't be that hard.'

'Hope not.'

Behind them, Cathy's mother introduced herself to Peter's father, a swarthy type with a wild blond thatch and kind eyes. She heard her mother's laughter trill and saw her throw her head back at whatever Peter's father had shared. Cathy didn't like the look of it but couldn't put her finger on why. Her mother looked her way and gave a wave. She pretended not to notice and studied her shoes with great interest. Why am I like this? she chided herself. She's actually happy for a few moments. Let her be.

Frankie and co. had started to chuck small stones at the church wall. Idle dunts of stone hitting stone punctuated the morning air. Finally, a parent broke and ran the lot of them off. They seemed relieved to be able to vacate the area, looking like rebels as opposed to the idiots they had made of themselves. Now they could embroider their tales of revolt and weave a magical adventure of Youth versus System. Everyone was happy with the outcome.

The group leader gave them a pep talk and they were divided into units of three. Cathy was hooked up with Peter and a girl called Rachel, who was as lost for words as Cathy was. Good job they had lots of manual labour to do before they started recording the names and dates on the graves and in the church. Surely they'd have an easier rapport by then. This growing-up business was a lot harder than anyone knew.

Ruth was not as fit as she should have been and the bike was made before gears were profitable or fashionable. Two miles down the road and her legs were walloped, her breath tight. She decided on a rest, leaned the bike against a ditch and took herself into a stony field to sit in the sun and review her state of play. The heat seduced her and encouraged a closed-eyed adoration not entirely conducive to the figuring out of a life. Besides, all she could think about was Charlie and that Linda woman. He was worth better and something would have to be done to prise them apart. None of your business, she told herself. But the thought of that scornful witch having any foothold in the pub was beyond endurance. Was I this egotistical when I was with Greg? she wondered. The question jolted her physically. *Greg*. A different kettle of bitch, surely. She had no right to decide what was and was not fit for Charlie's life. She was a blow-in and would be gone soon enough. Home. Wherever that mystic place was. Did it exist at all? Did she have a home now that her parents were dead?

'Mam, I just think it's best for me to have a place of my own. I mean at my age, you know. I'm practically a figure of fun in the staffroom, living here still.'

Oh, the easy lie. Greg Deegan was the only one ever to find issue with it. But of course it was all for him anyhow. A place they could be together, their own little bolt-hole, while he dealt with an unhappy marriage. Sure, that seemed a cliché to others but they didn't know the ins and outs of it. They were wrong; it was different with him. He needed her and she would be there for him.

'What's brought this on?' her mother wanted to know.

'Nothing,' she lied again. 'I've been thinking about it for a while.'

'Your father's heart will be broken. He loves having you here.'

'You did too, Mam, didn't you?' she whispered. 'I'm sorry, so, so sorry.'

God, but regret was a poisonous thing, especially straddled by the grave. Two graves. A cold shame crept over her and she began to sob.

'Mourning and weeping in this valley of tears.'

Her mother had loved that prayer.

'I'm not religious, Ruth, but I do love the language.'

She let out a cry, feral and raw.

'Ruth, are you hurt?' Tom Long was hovering above her, his silhouette etched painfully against the startling light of the sun. He shifted from foot to foot awkwardly, unsure of how to help.

She wiped her eyes, angrily pushing the tears aside. 'I'm fine, really.'

Tom reached out his hand to her. She took it and stood. But on her ascent she stumbled and her cheeks wet his shirt. Neither dared breathe. They avoided eye contact. Then an imperceptible signal allowed them to step away from each other. Tom held the bicycle while Ruth brushed imaginary dirt from her clothes.

'Joyce used to ride this around the town,' he said, then felt like an idiot for having spoken at all.

On a hill in the town a pair of matching glass orbs flared as they surveyed the countryside.

Thirteen

Ruth sped along the country road wondering at her close encounter. That was as near as she wanted to get to more emotional disaster. She could see Kilbrody and, rather than lift her spirit, the sight of the town threw her heart around her chest so hard she thought she'd pass out. Would Charlie suspect she was now more adrift than when she'd left this morning? She needed to shower, to wash away her foolishness and then throw herself back into work.

She screeched to a halt outside the back of the pub, took three gulps of the river air, then dashed inside and up the stairs. Charlie heard the commotion, and it didn't sound to him like a calm woman. What had she dealt with on her trip that had turned her into a whirling dervish? She appeared, pink with washing, several minutes later.

'Ruth, you'll scrub yourself to nothing if you keep this up,' he told her.

'Suits me,' she said and started to stack glasses. To vanish, to be of no more trouble to anyone. Wound up like a mechanical toy, her tension gave off an air of danger. Charlie stepped to the other end of the bar in case breakables started flying.

Cathy stood to ease the strain in her back. They had spent a wearying three hours pulling up weeds and tidying borders. She knew, from her own family garden, that this exercise was cosmetic. Sterner measures were needed for the pernicious specimens rampant in the graveyard. She almost hoped they wouldn't succeed in their eradication. She liked the weeds, admired their colonising tactics, their single-mindedness and cheeky beauty, tempting and seducing all of the elements they needed to survive.

The group moved purposefully around the gravestones. Some were plain sheets of stone, inscriptions barely legible, some crosses, conventional or Celtic, and there were a few tombs with battered guardian angels and rusted railings. She had grown accustomed to the names now, recognising some, hoping to get to know others. The babies were especially sad. Jane Elizabeth Ford, 1890–91, precious daughter of John and Mary Ford. Sarah Anne O'Brien, 1912, aged four months, sadly missed by her family and loving parents Michael and Eva. Were they related to Ozzy and his family? The place reeked regret. Lost lives, some hardly lived. She sat on a kerbstone and bowed her head, ashamed at wishing her time to pass quickly. She was wasting it by wanting it gone. A hand passed water to her.

'Don't worry,' Peter said. 'I'm here.'

She took the offering.

'You know, if you weren't actually so nice, you'd be a bit creepy,' she told him.

'That's the best thing anyone's ever said to me,' he grinned.

The only customers in the pub that afternoon were Old Mikey, who sat at the bar, and Tom Long who took to his usual low table. Neither spoke to the other, and only really addressed Ruth to order drink. Even at that, Tom Long gestured more than he talked. She supposed this was a blessing, really. Old Mikey seemed preoccupied. The presence of Tom darkened his mood and left him introspective. He contrived to study the racing form, but clearly was getting nowhere with that. Tom Long was elsewhere, in his head. The air was charged to atomic levels. Ruth decided to clean all of the shelves, rigorously.

An hour and a quarter into their ordeal, Mikey left for the bookies. A strange pall hung over Finn's. Ruth took a breath as if to speak, but Tom shook his head and looked deep into his pint. She left to check on the stock in the storeroom and as she returned, Tom was in the corridor. She stopped dead, unable to speak or move.

'Ruth, get upstairs now,' Charlie's voice barked.

She yanked away, hitting the back of her head hard on the stone wall. Then she automatically did as she was told. He followed. She was stunned at his expression; he had obviously got the wrong end of the stick. She tried to gloss. 'Jesus, Charlie, what are you sneaking around for?' she squeaked.

His face was black with fury.

'What the FUCK do you think you're up to?' he shouted.

'I beg your pardon?' she spluttered.

'Well?' he spat.

'Well, *what*? I don't know what the problem is.'

'Then maybe you can explain what you and Tom Long were up to.'

'Oh, I see,' she returned, bitterly. 'It's all very well for you to shag married women but I'm to stay away from married men?' She faced him, twisted with anger. 'Maybe *I* like the *safety* of them?'

He backed up, stung. Ruth gasped. She had gone too far. She had betrayed his earlier confidence, ruined their delicate accommodation.

'You're right,' he hissed. 'It's none of my business. But what is, is that pub downstairs in which you were engaged to work this afternoon. Now get back down there.'

Ruth began to crumble. 'Oh God, Charlie, I'm so sorry. I shouldn't have said that. I'm so confused.'

'I'm really not interested in your excuses,' he said coldly.

'I haven't done anything.' She couldn't understand why he was being so unreasonable. 'You've got this all wrong,' she wailed.

Charlie stood rigid and took a chance. 'And what about earlier?'

She reddened. Who on earth had seen them in the field? 'Nothing happened earlier. Tom helped me with the bike, that's all.'

'Sure,' he said.

She sagged, all the fight gone. 'I could always leave.'

'Oh do, run, that'll make everything OK. Look at the success you had the last time you did that. Look where you ended up.'

She stood swaying with uncertainty, limbs liquid and useless.

'Get back to work,' he threw at her.

She scuttled away, cheeks flaming. How dare he speak to her like that. Where did he get off giving her such a lecture? He was the one who was actively cuckolding a neighbour and she was having the brunt of his problems dumped on her. Talk about an overreaction. The sooner she got out of this hole the better.

Grow up, Ruth.

Or had he reached into the heart of the problem? He wouldn't have been the first.

'Grow up, Ruth. He's a married man. There's no future for you there.'

'He loves me, Kate. He said so.'

'Talk is cheap, Ruth. How many times do I have to tell you that?'

'You can't brush me off with clichés. This is different.'

'What? And I'm the one accused of the cliché? Listen to yourself. He's making a fool of you. He's using you. And you're rolling over like a lovesick puppy and letting him. Grow up, Ruth.'

Tom Long sat in the field supping from the whiskey bottle. The local off-licence wasn't as fussy about serving him as Charlie Finn. He tried to reason his position now, both at home and abroad. One more week, that was all he asked. One more week and he would try the meetings and voodoo and whatever else it was that everyone wanted, but not until then. His wife understood. Deep down she knew he could kick the habit any time he wanted. And aside from this morning he hadn't ever missed work, or at least not that much work. He had overdone it yesterday. He would take it easy on the whiskey tonight and be bang to rights again tomorrow.

'There's no need to see me home,' Cathy said, as they walked along the dusty road.

'I'm not. It's on the way to my house too, you know.'

'Oh yeah, forgot.' How lame. She was going to have to brush up on some smarts or face serious opprobrium at the hands of Peter Finan (she now knew his full name and he had explained the meaning of opprobrium to her earlier, though she couldn't now remember why).

'Did you enjoy today?'

'Yeah, I did. I mean I'm totally knackered and starving and all, but yeah, it was good.'

'Me too. I'm glad I signed up. Will I call for you tomorrow on my way in?'

Cathy's brain did a quick tot. Unless her dad had another unusually late morning, the house would be clear of him from seven or so. Dare she take the chance? Hang it, she couldn't live like a prisoner all the live-long days. 'Yeah, why not. I'll see you whenever you get here.'

Right, that meant some serious wardrobe research this evening. Everything she was wearing needed fumigation after the sweat of the day, so they were straight into the laundry pile. Maybe her combats with a plain white T-shirt and her camouflage baseball cap? She skipped happily up the driveway for the first time in a long time. The day had been full of delights, not least Fiona being dragged away by her dad, Ozzy. Word was she would spend the rest of the summer trapped behind the cash register at Surf 'n' Turf. Hey, I can work with that, sister. I don't even need another go of the bra, I'll be getting my own next week. She laughed out loud, then pulled herself up. No welcome: they needed another dog.

❖   ❖   ❖

Charlie was curt. Well, Ruth thought, two can play this
game. He gave her a perfunctory tea break before
announcing he was off to a 'meeting' for the evening.
Yeah, sure. Shagging Linda, more like. What kind of
complete eejit did he take her for? She was fast growing tired of this little place with its silly feuds and petty
nastiness. It was time to think about getting back to
where she belonged. Only with that thought came the
ghost winds of heartache and uncertainty. For all the
small town bitching, at least she felt part of a greater
whole, and not an ignorable element in some vast equa-
tion that could well advance without her. She knuckled
down and got ready for the evening rush – hoped for
one, to take her mind off the storm settling over the
roof of Finn's.

Joyce Long was gobsmacked. Charlie Finn was at her
door.

'It's been a long time since we've seen you,' she said,
awkwardly. 'How have you been?'

'Well, and you?'

'Good, yes, apart from . . . you know.'

Charlie prayed that his voice would remain steady
and low. He kept his arms tightly by his sides to hide
the perspiration marks that were spreading on his shirt,
and to prevent his hands from shaking.

'Is he here?'

'I thought he was still at your place.'

A tight, 'No.'

'I'm sorry you appear to have had a wasted journey.'

'Wouldn't be the first.'

'No. But thank you anyway.'

'You're welcome.'

'See you in another hundred years, I guess.' An attempt at reconciliation, friendship.

'Hopefully.' Rebuffed.

Charlie pulled himself together. He was being unnecessarily sharp with Joyce. He hadn't come here to make her life any more difficult than it already was.

'I thought he might come to an AA meeting with me. See how it works. Maybe another time.'

She watched his back as he walked away towards his car. A familiar sight of muscled shoulder, slim waist (slightly thicker than in his youth, but who of their age could claim otherwise), long elegant legs. And yes, she had to admit, his ass still looked great in jeans.

She shook herself back to the present and the ever-present problem: Tom. Her heart grew sore. How much more of this can one woman take? She watched the tail lights of the car bump and flicker away in the dusk's haze. They begged a question: where the hell was he? Cathy was right, they needed another dog. Not so long ago she could have taken to the fields and byways with Dennis and the old faithful would have located him. Now she just did not know where to start.

'Cathy,' she called. 'We have a problem.'

Oh, the baldness of truth.

But help was available, as Cathy pointed out. They didn't need to head off blindly into the countryside. They were clutching their sides with laughter as Joyce placed the call to the mobile, and couched the nature of her request in neutral terms that were unlikely to offend their man.

'Ozzy,' she said. 'I'm wondering if you might have seen Tom around and about over the last half an hour. I can't seem to find him in the usual haunts.'

'I bet his binoculars steamed over when you asked him that,' Cathy chuckled. 'The big feckin' pervert.'

'Let's go and get your dad.'

Two miles away, Charlie pulled into a lay-by and got out of his car. Then he let out one long roar until his breath ran out.

Fourteen

Ruth was building up a great head of steam. The things she would say to Charlie Finn when he got back from his latest foray into the forbidden world of the Marrieds. So the wind left her sails when Linda and Carol walked in. Actually, she was replacing mixers with her back to the door, smelled Cristalle and didn't need to look up to know it was the vile siren in all her awful glory. Painted talons clacked on the counter and a crisp, impatient voice said, 'Two vodka tonics, at your convenience.'

'Only if you're wearing knickers,' Ruth wanted to say. Instead she heard an overly pleasant 'Be right with you' emerge.

Old Mikey arrived with the news that Patch Collerane had shuffled off his mortal coil. 'As decent an aul skin as ever walked the earth,' he said.

Ruth assumed, correctly, that he referred to a man and not a household pet. Patch was a widower from the Mount Temple area to the north of the town, it emerged.

Here, then, was one of the defining differences between her life in the big smoke and the country: nicknames. She didn't have one, nor had any member of her family. They were Ed and Rita and Ruth and Kate. Patch Collerane could have been a prize heifer for all she'd known.

Mikey's companion was introduced as J.J. Gilhooley Senior, former doctor to the town, his son the present incumbent. He was a gnarled old wrinkle with playful eyes and a dicky bow. His bulbous nose was purple and heavily veined, the imprimatur of an habitual spirits drinker. 'Poor Patch was forever trying to offload that bit of land by the river,' he said of their fallen comrade. 'The "for sale" sign is all but bald at this stage of the proceedings.'

'Is the land no good?' Ruth asked. 'Is it too swampy?'

They looked upon her with something akin to pity.

'All land is good,' Mikey said. 'Sure couldn't you run a duck farm on it and it marshy, or raise plants that love the wet and sell them on to garden centres and the like? Land is never wasted or bad.'

The gnarl nodded. Ruth felt like a dunce. This day was on the downward trail. Gilhooley made short work of two whiskies and announced his departure.

'Herself has the pig's head on the boil,' he told them. Then he held her eye. 'Mary is very fond of the tongue.'

The dirty old goat. Ruth smiled. 'I'd say you like a bit yourself,' she rejoined.

His face widened, ear to ear, with merriment. 'You'll do nicely for this place,' he said and made his goodbyes.

Mikey watched him go and reminisced. 'He helped me deliver a calf one time and the two of us stocious through the drink. He reached in to free the animal from the umbilical cord and all I could see of him was a pair of wellingtons.'

Bert Fahy and Deborah came through next, stalling briefly to check out the clientele. Carol gestured for them to join and they did, though it seemed to Ruth that Deborah was not overly thrilled with the arrangement. A handful of tourists played bad darts and drank too much beer and the local priest held court, at Tom Long's usual haunt, over the group leader of the Youth Project at the old graveyard. Old Mikey filled in the details there: a Father Kilcullen and a Margaret Cahill, teacher at the primary school in Lahinch but daughter of the parish of Kilbrody.

'She drives a huge old Ford and we all call it her Cahillac.' Mikey laughed. 'Smashing fodder for that book of yours, eh?'

Ruth had a guilty twinge at her subterfuge, but squashed it. The plan was to live another life for as long as she could, so why not enjoy it? And the lie was a harmless one, incidental to anyone who believed it. 'I must get hold of my notebook to jot things down,' she said.

Mikey toyed with a beer mat. 'There was a bit of a

scene between Tom and Charlie today,' he remarked casually.

'Really? I didn't see anything.' Her heart sank. Had she been the cause of more trouble?

'Ah, it's all a bad business, that.'

Ruth filled pints. 'I notice his daughter usually calls for him. Why not his wife?'

Old Mikey thought about it. 'The day she sets foot in here will be a day of great change,' he said. 'For all of us.'

She desperately wanted to quiz him but the tourists were having another large round and she was steered away. When she returned, Ozzy was in debate with Mikey about whether or not to buy the leg of a local greyhound, tipped for great things. Foiled by a man talking to a man about a dog, she thought, shaking her head. It didn't improve her mood. And something in the way Mikey held his head while listening to Ozzy reminded her of her father, and she was racked with a confusion she couldn't begin to contemplate there and then. The layers of the evening were stacking up against her. Then Charlie returned and she was aflame again with indignation, ready for battle.

He didn't rush to join her but sidled up to Linda and co. Linda looked at Ruth over his shoulder and let an indolent smile play at the edges of her darkly painted lips. Charlie barely turned to gesture for another round. Ruth burned, the fingers of an ice-cold fury lacing about her. She banged the drinks sloppily in front of him.

'What about you?' she demanded, in an ugly bray. Christ, she sounded like a nagging old whine.

He smiled at her indulgently. SMILED! How dare he. She began to sweat with the rage of it. 'Just a Coke, Ruth. I'll be stepping in to help you soon.'

'She certainly looks like she could do with help,' Linda chirruped venomously, as grey eyes drilled through her object of scorn.

I could murder some wine, Ruth thought. And I will, when we get rid of this lot. It was the first time in a week she had considered a drink. Now she could hardly wait. Maybe the booze would expiate this day, and she couldn't give a tuppenny damn if it brought her and Charlie closer as friends again. Let him rot in his own vices and devices. A glass slipped from her hand and smashed onto the wooden slats lining the floor behind the counter. She knelt to gather the shards and cut herself in her haste to clear them away. Charlie was quickly at her side, kneeling also. He took her trembling hands in his and steadied her.

'Ruth,' he whispered. 'It's going to be all right. Trust me.'

'Get away,' she hissed. 'I don't need you. I don't need anyone.'

'Look, it's nearly closing time. Why don't you knock off early and I'll lock up.'

She straightened, veering away from him, reached into her trouser pocket and put a tenner into the till.

She took a bottle of house white from the fridge and stormed off.

'What's up with her?' Mikey asked, concerned.

'She's angry.'

'Is it anything we've done?'

'Maybe, but mostly I think she's angry at herself.'

'Ah,' he nodded, understanding. 'The poor creature. Sure isn't that the worst way to be?'

Tom Long was weary to his bones. He had one last drink from the whiskey bottle and looked at it, stunned. Empty. How could that be? He had only intended a few nips to steady himself. He must have spilled some of it. Yes, that's surely what happened. Best hide it in that hedge in case people got the wrong impression and thought that he'd had the lot. Which, of course, he could not have. He tried to stand, but his legs were traitors. He rolled over and clambered onto all fours and rested. Then he began to haul himself upright. He fell face down into the soft, understanding grass. Ah, the comfort of the land, his land. What else did any man need but a bit of comfort and a nice drop of something at the end of a long day? The weariness washed over him again, and then repeatedly in waves. And then he realised that the waves were dizzying him and it wasn't so nice to be face down in the field any more. The grass was brittle and scratching, sucked dry of moisture by the endless hot weeks. His insides erupted and he was spewing onto the grass and himself through his mouth and nose and unable to pull himself out of it. He rolled with the heaves, unable to stop or resist them, and when at last he was spent, he groaned once and let sleep take him away. As he left consciousness, a question popped into his fevered brain. *Why did you kiss Ruth Treacy's cheek as you got into the car?* Just because she was there and she was new and uncomplicated and because it was easier than kissing his wife. He had no shame left. He had never been so low.

Ruth was halfway down the bottle when Charlie appeared.

'I suppose you're looking for an apology,' she snapped.

'Another one?' he chided.

She turned her face away from him. He looked at her straight nose, full mouth, perky chin.

'I do not appreciate lectures about my behaviour,' she told him archly.

'I've noticed.'

'Don't be glib with me. It's cheap.'

'If you say so.'

'Are you deliberately trying to hack me off?'

He supposed he was. Tell me, Ruth, he urged, tell me what happened to you. 'Why are you so angry?' he asked.

'I think you know that, or have you forgotten your sermon earlier?'

'I may have been a bit heavy handed,' he conceded. 'I just didn't want you making a fool of yourself, especially over Tom Long.'

Her eyes narrowed. After a while she pushed the bottle towards him. 'Have a drink,' she said.

'No, I don't want wine.'

'Get yourself something else, then, it's not as if the gaff isn't well stocked.'

'I'll leave it for the moment.'

'Your funeral,' she said. That caught her short. 'Funeral,' she repeated, amazed at the word. She was drifting away from him.

'Is this really to do with my "sermon", as you like to call it?'

She switched back sharply. 'Of course it is. I'm stunned that you can come over all moralistic with me, about something you know nothing about, I should add, while you're balling another man's wife.'

The gratuitous vulgarity was meant to provoke, instead it made him sad. Had he pushed her to a low common denominator? Or was she simply on the road to being drunk?

'Why are you so angry? What happened to you, Ruth?'

'Have we skipped some more steps here?' she asked from under a creased brow.

Were they getting back on their track? 'I guess we have.'

She sank in on herself, defeated. 'I let them down, Charlie. I wasn't there when they needed me. Sometimes, lately, I think I may have killed them.'

'Your parents?'

158

She nodded.

'That's foolish talk.'

'Is it? I upped and left. I moved out. For no good reason, as I later found out.' She gulped back emotion. 'It was after that they got sick.' Now her breath was rapid.

'And?'

'And now I'm mad at them . . . because they left before I could make it up to them.' She began to rock. 'I never got to apologise.' Her face twisted and she was furious again. 'I can't forgive them for dying. How dare they die? I'll never forgive them for dying.'

'Maybe they didn't need an apology.'

'Well, they fucking deserved one.' She imploded, sobbing into her chest. 'I hurt them. Two good people.' She fought to control herself. 'I'm mad at me for not making it up to them.' She shook all over. 'I loved them, and I'll never forgive myself.' She shook more, and sobbed more, and ran out of steam. 'How could they leave me? Them, of all people?' She mewled her unhappiness, breathing unevenly.

Ruth looked at Charlie, trying to gauge if she had alienated him with her outburst. She didn't want him to leave, she was afraid of being alone again.

'Have a drink, please, I'll feel weird if you don't. Please.'

'I can't, Ruth.'

'You mean you won't,' she snipped, disappointed, rejected.

'No, Ruth. I can't. I'm an alcoholic.'

She looked up, watching for the joke, or at least a jibe. There was none that she could see.

'But . . . all this . . . the . . .'

'Pub. Yes. The ultimate irony?' He shrugged. 'Or something about keeping friends and enemies very, very close.'

'I'm sorry, I didn't know.' Her hands fluttered. 'How could I be so stupid?' She gestured again, aimlessly. 'Am I ever going to stop telling you sorry?'

'Who knows? I've grown accustomed to it now. I'd miss it if it was gone tomorrow.'

'Will it be? Will I be?' She was beseeching him now, eyes wide with the possibility of eviction. 'Do I have to be . . . gone, after all . . . this?'

'Not on my account.'

She sank into her chair. 'I don't deserve you.'

'Maybe it's me who doesn't deserve you.'

'And then maybe we both deserve one another?'

They took a moment to smile.

'Say it again,' she whispered.

'I am an alcoholic.'

In the darkness he might have said 'I love you'. Though of course he had not.

Fifteen

Kate hammered relentlessly. 'Open the door, Ruth, I know you're in there.'

She stood, not daring to breathe, perspiring with anxiety, waiting for her sister to give up. She could wait till Doomsday and that wouldn't happen. She knew it, but hoped against all hope that she was wrong. She was not.

'Come on, stop wasting time.'

Ruth capitulated, opened the door and prepared for the onslaught.

'You can tell Deegan to come out, I know he's here. Either that or he's taken to parking his car a long way from home.'

Ruth did her best goldfish impression.

'Oh, stop that and close your mouth or we'll have dribbling next.' Kate waited a few minutes. 'I should have known,' she said rolling her eyes. 'He's too chicken to appear. Well, let him hear.'

'Kate, can this not wait?' Ruth interrupted.

'No, it can't. Mammy is sick. It's cancer and she hasn't long.'

Ruth's world began to spin off axis. 'That can't be right. She would have told me. Or Daddy would.'

'And when, pray, would they see you to tell you? It's hardly the stuff of a casual phone call. And you haven't exactly been a regular visitor over the past few months, have you?'

'I come over on Sundays,' she declared, pathetically.

'No, you don't. You say you will and they get a dinner ready and get all excited, God love their innocence. But you haven't shown for a month now.' She laughed bitterly. 'A month of Sundays.'

Ruth jerked awake. Her legs were leaden and stiff, her ribs exhausted and muscle-bound and her lips felt crushed. She had obviously been run over by a tank and her mouth invaded by a colony of sponges. She tried to move further but was pinned down by an arm lying across her. She turned to see Charlie above the bedcovers, she below. He looked peaceful, almost angelic, his hair tousled across a vaguely furrowed brow, facial stubble outlining a strong jaw, and his mouth was almost plump from sleep. The fine hairs on his arm were bleached blond by the sun and set off by a healthy tan. Altogether a nicely packaged package. The woman who got him for keeps would be a lucky one. And I'm glad it can't be that bitch, Linda.

She squirmed out, still reeling from the shameful

memories she couldn't now staunch. Her head boomed, hungover; after a week of sobriety a bottle of the Finn Ordinaire wrought havoc with her synapses. The wonder was her whole brain didn't short circuit with the amount of misery and self-loathing it had to endure. She shook her head, immediately regretting the action. Time to shower good and hard.

'If you get all nice and clean, I'll show you an even better time, Ruth Treacy. We can't be doing with a dirty girl, can we? Unless it's getting down and dirty, the way I like it.'

She had been so meek, so accommodating, so grateful for the attention. I deserve to be washed away. She grabbed a bar of soap and turned the water up high.

'A gentleman caller, no less.'

'Mam, he's not. He's just a friend. He's part of my group at the project.'

'Nice-looking and all, if I remember the right lad from yesterday. I was talking to his father, wasn't I?'

'Uh, yeah, I think so.' She remembered her mother's uncensored laugh, the abandoned tilt of her head and the way it had made her feel uncomfortable.

'His mum's dead, did you know that?'

Cathy quit her Coco Pops, shocked. 'No. Really?' How could she not have known such a thing? How could something so huge have happened and left him so, well, normal? She could see his smiling green eyes, picture his easygoing manner. 'But we're working in a grave-yard,' she said, agog at the new perspective.

'He must be well adjusted to the situation by now, I suppose. It's been a good few years. Five, I think.'

How had her mother learned all this when all Cathy saw was a brief laugh between her and Peter's dad? She felt uneasy again.

'I had coffee with his father yesterday and we had a great chat. Lovely man.'

Speaking of which, Cathy might have said, NOT. She bowed her head, unwilling to ask but compelled to. 'How's Daddy today?'

'He's sleeping it off. I don't expect he'll bother anyone till this afternoon.'

Her mother's shoulders stooped under the pressure.

'I'm sure it's nearly time for a change, Mam. Even he knows that now.'

'Look at you,' her mother said, shaking her head. 'Old before your time. You shouldn't have to go through this. When we get him well, I know he'll make all this up to you, pet. He loves you.'

'He loves us both, Mammy.' She turned before her mother could see the tears in her eyes. 'Just not enough,' she whispered to herself.

It was so obvious, Ruth wanted to kick herself. Where, particularly in a small country town, had she ever come across a state-of-the-art coffee maker in a bar, or a vast selection of fruit, herb and conventional teas? Put it this way, when had she last ordered a pot of lapsang souchong on holiday from a publican in the West of Ireland? When had she last sat down to freshly squeezed orange juice in an out of the way spot? Charlie regularly partook of all of these on duty and off. It didn't mean much by itself, but married with his latest revelation, the veils fell from her eyes and she felt like a klutz. She had been so wrapped up in herself she had noticed nothing important. Isn't that always the way? she asked herself.

It was her turn to do breakfast. She made for the local supermarket to buy provisions, wondering how to make amends.

'So you'll come for your supper?'

Cathy was stuck to the tarmac outside the house. Had her mother lost her marbles, asking someone over when it was virtually certain her dad would be back in action by then? Before she could intervene, it was sorted with 'I'd be delighted to' from Peter and 'This evening it is' from her mum. Cathy had a sudden urge to slap them both, scream loudly and run away.

It got worse.

'We can discuss Cathy's birthday. It's the week after next, you know.'

She headed onto the road like Bambi learning to walk.

'Is supper OK with you?' Peter asked, catching up with her. 'You don't seem too keen on the idea.'

She was weary of the cover-ups and decided to come clean. 'It's not you. It's my father. He . . .'

'Drinks.'

'How did you know?' Was the whole town discussing them? Actually, she'd have been surprised if they weren't a regular topic and laughing stock.

'Your mum told my dad yesterday, and he told me.'

They walked on. Cathy felt awkward that her mother had shared so much with a stranger.

'That must be really tough,' Peter was saying.

She decided to give in. If her mother thought it appropriate to discuss the problem, why shouldn't she? 'Yeah, it is. And it's getting worse lately. Don't know why.'

'I guess you know about my mother too.'

'Yeah. Sorry . . . and all.'

'We miss her, but all our memories are good, so that helps.'

'Are you finding the graveyard spooky because of it?'

'Oh no. We scattered her at sea. Her ashes, like.' He thought about that briefly. 'Wow, imagine that, throwing arms and legs in? Far out.'

Cathy was wearing the careful expression of someone dealing with a lunatic so Peter got back on course.

'She was practically a mermaid, so it seemed the only thing to do. Now it's just Dad and me. But we have plenty of pictures and videos and her urn is on the mantelpiece.' He laughed easily. 'Dunno why we still have that. It's pretty, maybe that's why. We used to bring her with us everywhere in it for a while, then it was time to give her back to the sea.'

'Cool.'

'Yeah.'

There was no easy way to start this conversation, so over breakfast Ruth settled for opening her mouth and letting some words out. She wasn't too worried if they were relevant, making noise would be a kick-off and she'd manage from there. 'Charlie, I need to talk to you about yesterday.'

'Oh?'

Ruth halted, not knowing how to continue. She had to trust her brain's instincts, hoping that some of them were paying attention or functional. 'About me and Tom Long.'

He tensed. 'Yes?'

'I don't know why, but you've latched on to something that doesn't exist and blown it out of all proportion.'

Charlie felt a bit guilty but said nothing.

'There is nothing between me and Tom Long. I did meet him when I was out on the bike and later, in the hallway, we just got a bit wedged into a . . . small space. It really was nothing. I'm mortified that you've misread the situation.'

'I'm not sure I deserve to be told this, Ruth. In spite

of my preaching, in the end it is your business, not mine.' He grinned. 'I'm not usually this avuncular,' he admitted. 'You bring out a good side in me, even if it's a little too good to be entirely palatable. It'll ruin my reputation as a bad-ass mother if it gets out.'

'I wanted you to know.' Ruth felt massively crawly, but she persisted. Some things were worth saying, however naff they sounded. 'It's important to me what you think of me and that was getting grubby there for a while. Anyway, now you know.'

'Thanks. Genuinely.'

'You're welcome.' She reddened. 'I don't know what would have become of me without you.'

He waved a deprecating hand. 'Some other Charlie, some other place.'

'Jesus, I don't believe it,' Ruth exclaimed.

Charlie waited on tenterhooks for the latest bombshell.

'There are clouds in the sky. Shadowy rain ones.'

'At last, an end to all this niceness.'

'Yes,' Ruth agreed, her voice as laced with bitter relief as his. 'It's been far too lovely here for too long.'

'We do need to get back to proper damp Irish misery or we'll lose our sense of humour completely.' He held both hands out in extenuation. 'I mean that, no irony.'

'Charlie?' Ruth toyed with a croissant. 'When you were in your bad time, was it as . . . embarrassing as me going through my mess now?'

'Oh, much worse. There were times when I honestly didn't think I wanted to make it out, or deserved to. I still have days when I wonder. But each one is a separate entity now, or that's how I deal with it, them, whatever. Sometimes you have to cut yourself some slack. We're all only human and we make mistakes; some of them are huge and some, the worst maybe, are unforgivably small. It's hard, Ruth, no one ever said otherwise.'

It wasn't all that comforting to hear, but it was good to know that someone understood and might even be able to help.

Tom Long found the house empty and his lunch waiting on the kitchen table. A note was propped on the sugar bowl.

'We love you but we cannot share you with that curse. It's time to decide. We hope you choose us.'

He couldn't quite believe the words. He desperately wanted to ignore them. He distracted himself with the food, even though it held little interest for him. He put half a slice of quiche and some coleslaw in his mouth and fought the urge to hurl. He bolted for the door. He needed to think. He needed a drink, in spite of all.

His wife sat on a wall behind the orchard and watched his flight. Have you decided, Tom, or do we have any last weapons left in our arsenal? She would play the waiting game a little longer. It might even be time to give God a go.

Greg appeared as soon as Kate left.

'Sorry to hear about your mother.'

Ruth wiped away her tears. Expecting some comfort, she was surprised to see him reach for his jacket and bag.

'Where are you going?' she asked, stupidly. It was patently obvious where he was off to.

'Home, of course.'

'So early?' Still dumbly, wantonly misreading the situation's declivity.

'Look, Ruth, I think you're getting a bit clingy and this whole thing is feeling claustrophobic. I need time to think and to sort myself out. Maybe we should give ourselves some space. And now you have this big family thing to deal with and I'd only be in the way.'

'This is the very time I need you. You can't walk out on me.'

But that was essentially what he did, though she was the last to notice. They snatched time, when it suited him, and only then. He kept her neatly at arm's length, giving her just enough to hold on to. After an exasperated haranguing from Kate she opened her eyes to the obvious. And by then he was paying special attention to the new Domestic Science teacher, a pretty little scrap, new to the Big Smoke and green as cabbage. The rest of the staff shuffled and simpered around the twin liaisons, leaving Ruth humiliated and embarrassed.

She began to lose weight.

She began to bite her nails.

She bought complicated shoes.

Sixteen

Charlie chatted happily on the phone, lively background noise as Ruth drank tea and rifled idly through her diary.

'She wants to talk to you,' he said, finally.

'What? Who?'

'Kate.'

Her mouth opened and closed without sound. She didn't know what to do with her feet. This was unexpected. She took the phone and looked at it for a moment as if it was her first encounter with the modern miracle of communication. Gingerly, she held it to her ear. 'Kate,' she tried, careful still.

'Ruth. I was just checking in with Charlie and I hear all's well.'

'Em, yeah. We're mucking along.' She enunciated slowly. This could be a test.

'I'll be arriving tomorrow so I'm taking orders. What do you need brought from here?'

Ruth still wasn't thinking straight. She was hardly

listening to what she was being asked. Why were Kate and Charlie in touch, and how was it they seemed so pally? That was the big question. She let auto-pilot take over, momentarily. 'I could do with some clothes. Whatever is comfy for pub work. Plenty of underwear. And maybe shoes?'

'Would that include any of the mad things you've been buying recently?'

'I'll leave the decision to you.' She could feel her sister smile all those miles away. Was it weird that she knew that?

'Right-o so. See you tomorrow. And I must say I'm dying to meet this Charlie Finn. If he's anything like his voice, he must be one fox of a man.'

Ruth hung up feeling dislocated from reality. She looked bemusedly at the fox. He was more like a cat with a bowl full of cream. A tom cat. My sister is happily married, she thought, so don't you dare.

'How long have you been in touch with Kate?'

'Since the day your bag arrived. You told her where you were, she got the number from directory enquiries and made contact. She was concerned about you, naturally enough. She rings once a day, at least.'

'And you never thought to mention it?'

'Didn't see the need. You'd have got all paranoid and thought we were keeping tabs on you.'

'Which you were, as it happens.'

'Yes. Wasn't I right not to tell you? It's put off your

persecution complex till now, so I'm happy.'

Ruth was a maelstrom of emotions. How much had Kate shared with Charlie? Had she told him what she really did for a living? Did he know what an utter fraud she was? She wasn't brave enough to ask these questions now and she dreaded having to face them ever. It was time to stick her head in the sand. 'You are outrageous,' she said. 'Both of you.'

'But you love us.'

'Yeah, yeah, love, shmove.' Ruth could not believe she appeared so controlled when, at any moment, she might run, yelling her head off. It was time to take stock, and that stock said Kate and Charlie were on her side and had no intention of hurting her.

'What's she like?'

'Beautiful, fun. My dad used to say she was sharp as a gooseberry.' She grinned. 'Though not usually as green and hairy.'

'You're alike, so.'

'Oh no. Kate has all the chutzpah and I'm a bit of a wallflower.'

'I meant the hairy greenery.'

'If I had the energy I'd cheerfully beat the living daylights out of you. But then I'd be out of a job.' She waved a hand. 'Ah, I'll leave it for now.'

She was beginning to relax, have fun, bizarre as this was. Everything could come tumbling down soon, but so what?

'She's married, she tells me.' He let the evil twinkle in his eye dazzle its way over to her.

'Don't even think it, Finn. I know where you live.'

He wandered off humming 'Happy Days Are Here Again'.

Ruth felt tendrils of excitement uncoil in her belly at the prospect of seeing her sister. They had a lot to talk about, a lot to sort out. She's my best friend!

I'm terrified.

Charlie watched Tom Long. He was perilously close to falling apart. He would then have two choices, neither of them easy, in spite of the fact that one would take him upward and the other would kill him. At his present level of drinking he had to be doing himself profound damage, physically as well as mentally, though he was taking it easy today; must've got a fright yesterday. It was like watching a rerun of his own life. From a better place, he reminded himself. From a tough place, too, where it wasn't any easier to pass by the bottle, it just made more sense. And always the chance of a slip along the way. He threw the switch on the coffee grinder and savoured the pulverising grounds. He was steady, he was strong, he had to be.

'Mammy into hospital,' the entry read.

'It's the best place for her.'

Ruth quaked. Mammy and Daddy were the rocks. It

was unbearable to see one so helpless, strapped onto a gurney and wheeled to an ambulance. Her foundation was eroding, slipping slowly into confusion and worry. The shrunken figure was so frail. This was her mammy, the lioness who could see off any threat to her family. Until her family decided to fend for themselves, that is, and then were visited with all that they deserved.

'Put on a brave face for your mother,' her father whispered. 'She needs to worry about herself now, not us.'

Ruth smiled her broadest cheese and helped her dad into the ambulance. She hopped in to say, 'I'll follow ye over to the hospital, Mam. See you there.' She kissed the parchment cheek.

'That'll be great,' her mother croaked. 'Good girl.'

Crying on the phone to Kate.

'You have to pull yourself together, for Mammy's sake. For Daddy too, Ruth. He's in bits. When it's all over, we'll have lots of time to cry.'

Kate sobbing then, distant, down the thin line, yet unbearably close in time. She knew the truth.

'Oh God, there's no way she'll make it, is there? I don't want her to leave.'

Two broken hearts, unable to hang up, unwilling to give in.

'Why do you never bar him?' Old Mikey asked.

'He'd just go somewhere else and I think it's best if we're the ones keeping an eye on him.'

177

'He's a lot worse, isn't he?'

'It's a disease.' Charlie shrugged, unhappy to make the call. 'It's progressive. You remember what I was like.' He leaned wearily on the bar, feeling helpless in the face of Tom Long's imminent doom. 'I interfered yesterday, in spite of myself. I went over there to bring him to a meeting, but he was missing.'

'Something's got to give soon.'

'Oh yes.'

'Be it here or at home.'

They circumvented that with silence. Eventually one of them had to speak.

'Right. We'll wait and see a little longer, so.'

That was the plan, poor as it was.

Although the dying was happening at the hospital, the house knew of it too. An emptiness filled the rooms, in preparation for her mother's absence.

'I never realised the place was so big,' her father would say.

The family became as grey as the invalid.

'Are you eating?' her mother fretted. 'You look as bad as me, and that's not right.'

Ruth wanted to roar, 'None of this is right.'

'Don't make me get out of my sickbed and do something about it.'

Her dad smiled indulgently. 'She will, girls. You know it.'

Her mother jollying them along, too, with her threat.

Their little unit huddled round the bed, sharing the precious, numbered moments. On the corridors they saw other grey people leaving or arriving at their parallel vigils and, though they acknowledged them, they could not waste their solidarity by engaging or sharing their misery. It seemed to them that theirs would be the more important loss. They had to remain selfish to get through. They sat by the bedside waiting for the sky to fall in and their world to be torn asunder.

They didn't know then that they would lose another too, and soon.

Ruth saw the corner of the photograph sticking out from behind a flap at the back of the diary. She let out a small yelp. Here was her dad in the garden, swinging the young Treacy sisters in a circle. She could hear her mother from behind the camera.

'Eddie, you'll make them sick if you keep that up.'

Their heedless delight. 'Faster, Daddy, faster!'

Forever faster or higher or more. Their dad, their hero. Was he always that, or had his family made Eddie Treacy into a fully fledged, paid-up member of the Heroes Club of the Universe? It probably didn't matter, as long as he achieved hero status, and he had. And whereas she would never need another dad, she would spend a life searching for a hero of her own, to pass on to her daughter. Surely when she found the first she would be granted the latter? Heroes were in short supply, she soon realised. And she had not always looked in the right places.

'I never see you any more.'

'I don't know why you seem so surprised. I thought you might have noticed how busy I am, what with the small matter of my mother about to die, which requires quite a lot of hospital visits. Funnily enough.'

'Sarcasm doesn't suit you, Ruth. I only want you to have some constants in your life. I thought I was one.' He gave an especially manipulative deflation of his put-upon shoulders. She was about to point it out when he delivered his sucker punch. *'It's not as if I have so much time to choose from to be with you. I wish I did, but what with my . . . circumstances . . .'*

He was making an effort for her and she was being mean.

'OK, I'll make sure to get home to see you this after-noon.'

'You won't regret it. I'll take your mind off things.'

She was late back to the hospital. Kate held up a hand to stave off the excuse.

'Don't, I do not want to hear a pathetic fob-off. I've sent Daddy home for his tea and we'll be back in an hour and a half. Call us if there's any change.'

Her sister's back was rigid as she left. Ruth was alone with the sleeping patient, and all alone. She held her mother's fading hand.

'I can't seem to do anything right.'
She felt the tiniest squeeze and with it a little comfort.

It was quiet and Old Mikey drank Rock Shandy. There were two reasons. One was Patch Collerane's removal to the church that evening. Patch had been a dedicated teetotal in life and Mikey felt he should honour that in death, briefly. The other reason was sitting behind him in the bar.

'Cathy is on that youth course, so I'm not sure she'll be in for himself,' Mikey told Charlie.

Tom was slumped and motionless in his regular spot. Even the act of lifting a glass to his mouth was arduous. He was disappearing with each quarter hour.

'We should send him home,' Charlie decided. 'The longer he stays, the worse he'll get.'

'I'll do the phoning.'

'It would be best coming from you.'

History was repeating itself and Charlie could hardly bear to acknowledge it. He didn't want to weaken, not after all this time. He switched the kettle on and chose a green tea flavoured with orange.

The periods of lucidity grew further apart. Sometimes they were sharp but brief, sometimes longer and more scrambled. And then there were the times when the unconscious Rita Treacy brought them all back to their past.

'That jaysusin' trumpet,' she called out late one Thursday.

They hooted in the beige, overwarm ward.

Eddie had got the instrument one Christmas (from Santa Claus) and had driven the household doolally with his foul attempts at music.

'It's jazz,' he would declare.

'Were we mad?' his wife would exclaim.

In general, though, she was slipping further away with the hours. More than once they were called and told to expect the worst but, between medicine and sheer will, she rallied. In time, they moved from hospital to hospice, the inevitable now openly admitted. She was diminishing before their eyes.

Then came the moment when she could go no further. They gathered to help her through.

'One more breath,' her father urged. 'One more, Rita. Good woman, that's it.'

Each time they thought she was finished, she would take one more gulp of air, make one last Trojan effort at living. Each time, they encouraged and cajoled her. And so her mother struggled from life into death in a strange reflection of giving birth. It was oddly joyous and Ruth felt privileged to be there to help. Afterwards, exhausted, they hugged each other tightly, as relieved for themselves as they were for an end to Rita's suffering. The ordeal was over. And while neither Ruth nor Kate suspected it, another was about to begin.

✻ ✻ ✻

Tom Long went quietly. He was putting himself in other hands for the day. His burning mind didn't know what else to do. He would rely on other people till he could think straight. He was weary enough to sleep for a week. He might try that and wake to a new life, with fresh possibilities and no sickness. He was nearly gladdened by the notion.

Charlie steeled himself and took the phone from Mikey to give some advice. 'He's stopping early today so he'll have trouble sleeping through the night and he'll want a drink when he wakes up. You should probably talk to the doctor about getting something to help him along.'

He hung up wondering what they were doing here, and was it more harm than good in the long run to interfere where they might not be wanted? He could have slaughtered a vodka. He surveyed his stash and reached for a Blackcurrant and Apple Delight. He could still hear the catch in her voice as she had tried to stave off her tears. A very large vodka. He poured the boiling water on the tea bag and breathed in the fruity aroma. It was bound to taste shite.

Greg Deegan did not attend the funeral. His name appeared on the card from the staff at the school and was implicated in the catch-all note with a wreath of flowers 'from all at Rosemount College'. Later, Ruth rationalised that she hadn't wanted him to be there. She

*needed to compartmentalise her life to get by, and he
was one section she didn't want turning up in another.
She thought of him as a solace she didn't have to share,
and an escape whenever she could be with him. He
encouraged her to get away from the family rituals. He
discouraged her from moving home to her parents'
house.*

*'The important thing is not to panic into making a
decision like that. Remember, you have to think about
us too. Don't slide back into the past, Ruth, think of the
future. We're that future.'*

Now, later, and with miles between them, she could
still taste the sweetness leaching from him.

Cathy struggled with a particularly thuggish bindweed,
and was reminded all over again how tenacious these
natives were. It was even odder for her then to rip out
the latest generation of an old dynasty and be confronted
with a part of her own past. Here, under the vines of
the plant, was the grave of long-dead ancestors. She
read the names, determined to remember and ask after
them later at home. From her position in the graveyard
she could see the newer church and its reciprocal depos-
itory, where she knew she had two grandmothers and a
grandfather, waiting for other members of the family to
join them.

A car passed by on the road outside the graveyard
wall. Her father sat in the back seat, his head fallen onto

his chest. He opened his bloodshot eyes, saw his daughter and raised a tired hand in greeting. He was like a ghost already; pale, gaunt, a shadow of himself. Cathy shivered and looked away. Did they have long left with him at all?

'How do crazy people go through the forest?' a voice behind her asked.

'I don't know, Peter. How do crazy people go through the forest?'

'They take the psycho path.'

Cathy made a strangled noise and continued with her tasks.

Seventeen

The locals were in sombre mood and most of them dressed in black. It was the evening of Patch Collerane's removal to the church and each was considering how short life truly is. 'Another one gone,' they muttered and crossed themselves. 'We'll give him a good send-off,' they promised. Charlie pulled the blinds down over the front windows just short of seven o'clock and they prepared for the hearse to pass. As it did, the customers filtered out and joined the growing number of towns-people walking behind it. The bell tolled mournfully at the church, sorrowfully beckoning another of the fold for the final take-off.

'I've done a lot of this sort of thing in the last while,' Ruth remarked to Charlie. 'Too much.'

He put his arm round her and squeezed. 'Hang in there,' he said, before joining the cortège. 'You're in charge,' was his final instruction.

It was all so familiar; she had to remind herself that

she hadn't been in the town a wet week and was not expected to participate in all its rituals. Besides, she had a job to do. And the week hasn't been at all wet, she added to herself.

Perhaps they should have spotted something in their father's haste to clear the house. He had never expressed much of an opinion on the place and his wife would tease him that he wouldn't be able to name the colour of the landing wall without a big hint. Now he was fired up and he made it his opportunity to jettison a lot of his own paraphernalia. It seemed to make sense and Ruth and Kate supposed it was his way of dealing with the loss of his beloved partner.

They packed up Rita's dresses and shoes and his old suits into roll on roll of black plastic sacks and delivered them to the local charity shops. Eddie threw out a dozen shirts, all 'red rotten', he insisted. They pored over the family albums, reading their mother's modulated descriptions and elegant cursive script, the by-product of a careful education when good penmanship was prized. They divided trinkets and paste jewels.

Ruth found the handbags the most difficult to deal with, and the most moving. Here was the lasting essence of her mother: pressed translucent powder, lipsticks, bottles of perfume. Ruth remembered 'Tweed' and 'Charlie' from her childhood, moving on to more prosperous times with Chanel No.5. 'Isn't she the image of

Marilyn Monroe?' her father would declare. 'That's all she wore in bed, you know.' Her mother would blush and admonish him with, 'Eddie, not in front of the girls,' then giggle like a schoolgirl. Occasionally a mint languished at the bottom, still in its wrapping, waiting to be enjoyed. Stray hair clung to a fine-toothed comb. Sometimes a headscarf was packed into the side of a bag, just in case of that rogue shower of rain: 'Sure the weathermen never get it right.' There were little notes reminding of a niece's birthday, a hair appointment, the dry-cleaning. Pens leaked, still, into the faded linings. How strange, now, to look at the dusty bags, each item so redolent of the departed. How odd that part of her remained though she was gone.

Their mother's decorating style might best be described as busy, but somehow all of the elements blended. Rita had an eye for mad harmonies. There was always a plethora of patterns and styles in a room and often far too much furniture. One Christmas, they treated her to a new three-piece suite which she promptly installed alongside the resident furniture rather than replacing it. 'Why would I throw it out when there's nothing wrong with it?'

They came across presents of earrings, hardly ever worn because they were 'too good'. Everywhere her imprint was stamped on the house and its contents. Short of giving their lives up to the curating of a museum, it seemed prudent, logical, to move on. Their father *encouraged the cull, saying the ornaments and decor meant little to him.*

'It'll be so bare, Daddy.'

'Didn't she always say I noticed nothing?'

What he was really about was leaving his house in order, quite literally.

Two weeks after the funeral, Ruth paid an unexpected visit and found him semi-conscious in an armchair, mid-morning, surrounded by bottles of pills and clearly in difficulty. It was her first sign of the terrible cancer that had been racking his body long before her mother had been taken ill. As he left in an ambulance he croaked, 'I had to stay well for Rita. I had to see her off safely. And anyway, she'd have killed me if she'd known I was keeping this from her.' The doctors were astounded that he had avoided hospitalisation for so long. 'The man must have the stamina of an ox.' Their hero had come up trumps for others again.

Ruth couldn't sleep. She paced her room, moved to the garden and back to the kitchen where she joined the appliances humming through the night. You had to admire such automatic loyalty. Memories assaulted her and she went to the roof again. Under the emotions splayed forth was a belly-tingling expectation: Kate would soon be on her way. She was queasy to think of it. Before her, night merged with day and she was exhausted to realise that she had flittered away another six hours of her life. She slumped into bed as the sky brightened, clearly signalling another fine day. The clouds were banished, all hope of rain disappearing with them for the time being. A delivery truck rattled by. The birds belted out their chorus. Ruth stuck her face firmly into the pillow, determined to rest. All she got was the dream of her mother in a coffin, her father telling her to get away, her own choking terror. And always running along those endless corridors. *Running from what? Running to where?*

Tom Long was groggy but functional, which was a bad combination. It meant he felt better and capable of tending his farm. With this came the false idea that he was somehow cured. Granted, he ached all over, his head throbbed, his kidneys hurt and his stomach was churning, but he was steadier than he had been in days, and rested. He was not a stupid man but he desperately wanted to believe that he could continue on this present track. A life without drink was unthinkable. What he needed to do was to manage it better. The doctor had doled out various tablets and concoctions to help him through the night and, though these came with dire warnings on long-term use, he was happy to stave off any big or unnecessarily momentous decision by using them. His wife stirred beside him. He guessed she hadn't really been asleep, just biding time till he woke. At least she hadn't abandoned him for the spare room.

'Tom, you're probably feeling better and thinking more rationally, but remember you still have to tackle this situation properly, once and for all. We cannot continue like this. In fact we won't. It's down to you now.'

'I hear you,' he said. He had.

He needed to maximise this good time and make the right choice. He knew it. He felt it. He hated it.

Charlie was bothered. He lay in bed picking over the last week. He tried telling himself that the introspection was the result of a lack of rain and Patch's death. These had skewed his perspectives. Still, he couldn't shake the inquisition. It seemed to him that, barring the nonsense with Linda (which was sexual and didn't count), he led a very measured life now. OK, Ruth was a mess and anyone would seem a rock by comparison, but every time they had a bust-up he was so reasonable he wanted to puke. He knew the value of reining in destructive urges, certainly, in spite of the fact that his mentor placed the Linda adventure in that category, but surely there was a limit? Just because he was sober didn't mean he had no viewpoints or opinions, particularly unreasonable or feisty ones. Ah, where was the vehemence, the definitive statement, the grand gesture? The rage was gone, now, mostly, and that was no harm, but he wasn't dead, for Chrissakes. Was he never going to let off steam again, now that he was off the sauce? Where was the passionate creature of only a few years ago –

well, a decade or so, but surely still in there somewhere? The questions bombarded his mind.

Was he a boring git now?

Was he less attractive?

It had to be said that Ruth showed no signs of wanting him as anything other than a friend, which was fine as neither of them wanted more than that.

And yet . . . it rankled, somehow.

Everything had changed when Ruth Treacy got off that bus and came into his pub.

Suddenly he was no longer complacent.

That spelt trouble.

Cathy was on edge. Her father had left for work: good. The house was on tenterhooks: no change there. She was afraid of what might happen next: bad. She tried to grab one of the friendlier ducks for a cuddle but the bird was having none of it. She missed Dennis. Maybe she could do without a bra for her birthday and ask for a dog instead?

The place was unnaturally cold without her parents. Ruth wandered from room to room listening to the sad echo of her footsteps. She knew her father would not return and her heart broke into a thousand shards to admit it. She paused by the few, framed photographs he had allowed to stay, a handful celebrating the milestone events. A black and white of Eddie and Rita on their wedding day, the girls making their first Holy Communion and Confirmation (Ruth's mouth full of orthodontic brace in the latter), Kate getting married, Ruth graduating.

She compared their features. She had her mother's skin tones but her dad's strong nose and stubborn mouth. Kate's face was finely sculpted and she was dark like the Treacys. She'd also inherited their height and slim build. Ruth had managed to walk off with the curves of her mother's side.

'I wish I'd got the chest,' Kate would moan.

'I'll swap any day,' Ruth assured her.

Pitch and putt trophies lined the sideboard. Both parents had been keen competitors. She remembered the Saturday morning ritual of dusting the bric-a-brac and prizes, armed with her father's retired vests and boxer shorts. At Rita's funeral, members of the local society formed a guard of honour with their clubs. They would do the same for Eddie. Sorrow ripped through her like a hurricane laying waste to all in its path. Death was savage in perfection and they were being given ample opportunity to savour it.

'Your mum is great,' Peter told her.

Cathy shrugged. 'I guess.'

She didn't feel entirely comfortable talking about her mother with a boy who had lost his. He, on the other hand, seemed quite at ease.

'What's your dad like?'

'OK, when he's not . . . you know . . .'

'Must be hard.'

Cathy shrugged again.

'End of conversation?' Peter asked.

'I guess. Don't know what else to tell you, really.'

'OK. I have another one for you.'

Cathy groaned. She'd refereed a bad gags competition at teatime the previous day.

'What's the difference between roast beef and pea soup?'

'Dunno.'

'Anyone can roast beef.'

They broke into a run, as Cathy tried to beat him up.

'Would you like a cup of tea?' Charlie asked from the bedroom doorway. Ruth swam wearily to consciousness through a sleepy sea of exhaustion. A waft of cologne reached her. She sat up, yawned, then focused on the man before her.

'Why are you all dressed up?'

'I'm not,' Charlie insisted, a little too vociferously.

He was wearing a modish, large-collared white shirt with deep cuffs and a pattern of tiny flowers and leaves. His jeans were faded but designer and nicely taut over his buttocks and thighs. Does he work out? Ruth wondered. Italian loafers completed the ensemble. Were they from his time in Tuscany? Her heart gave a strange flip. His hair was freshly washed and falling casually over his left eye. She felt like a badly managed compost heap.

'I changed after the burial this morning,' Charlie offered, shiftily, Ruth decided, but she was still half asleep and unable to engage him on it. If he'd already been to the funeral, she had slept very late. She groaned.

'I think I may need to go the coffee route, a massive caffeine kick-start. And a good sluice-down.'

She climbed from the bed, glad she'd worn an oversized T-shirt he'd donated to her clothing fund. She was aware of her claggy breath and sticky body as she shuffled passed him. She wondered if her legs were a tad too hairy. Safely in the corridor, she began to hum 'You're So Vain' and suffered a towel flick as punishment. She gave a yelp and ran for the bathroom. Her face was happy in the mirror. As the shower pelted her she remembered that her sister was arriving that day. He hadn't dressed for her; he was preparing for Kate. She reached for the loofah and began her daily scrub.

'How can I help you when I never see you?'

'My father is dying, Greg, I have to be with him as much as possible.'

A predictable sulk. She was so tired of it. Wanted to scream, 'Don't be such a bastard.' She willed him to offer even a little comfort. I love my dad. You can't ask me to abandon him now. Though it was as if that was exactly what he was asking. What kind of warped affection was this? It wasn't listed as love anywhere she looked.

'Spend a few hours with me this afternoon, Ruth. You can't ignore the living. I'll be here when he's gone.'

Oh, really?

She would lose herself in him and to him, and for brief moments it seemed to justify itself, this lust, this obsession.

'What a fucking idiot.'

'I beg your pardon.'

'Sorry, just remembered something unpalatable.'

'Wanna share?'

'You'd be disgusted.'

Charlie's face perked up.

'No, not in that way, I'm afraid.'

He sighed. 'Pity. Nothing like a bit of filth to start a day well.'

Ruth narrowed her eyes. 'You are an incorrigible dog, Finn.'

He gave a bark, low and throaty, then laughed at his own goofiness. 'You've made an idiot of me, Ruth Treacy.' He bowed. 'I thank you.'

'Freak,' she offered, delighted to be of help.

Tom Long rested against a metal gate. His armpits reeked stale alcohol and sweat. His forehead glistened from internal combustion as much as the rising temperature of the day. His stomach burned and his limbs were cement. His breathing was ragged and sore. A thumping headache raged in his brain, pounding a bright, flashing light across his vision with each beat. He felt nauseous and parched. The only words functioning in him were urging him to a drink, just one, to still the shakes, to even the imbalance, to stop the jigs. His head was going to burst, there could be no doubt about that. Pain sliced through his diseased mind and eventually he was compelled to lean into the ditch and spew forth some of the badness coursing through his frame. He needed to get to Finn's but was weak as a kitten and couldn't make the journey. He sat by the hedge and let sleep overcome him.

Tom's wife sat in the empty church trying to talk to God. To reason with him, perhaps, and to make some bargains. Then she realised that this was a mistake. There would be no bartering, wasn't that supposed to be the other lad's gig: the devil, brightest of all the angels, the fallen one? She'd been badly let down in the past and wasn't sure she believed in a higher power at all, but it was a comfort to be in this cool place, and sanctuary was welcome no matter where it appeared. The scent of incense from the thurible waved over Patch Collerane's coffin still hung in the air.

She remembered the beautiful man she married, her bright angel, now fallen. He was still there, just, but this disease was stealing him away from her and from their daughter. She had to do something to help, and even if that involved foolishly talking to the air she would try it. In keeping with tradition, she knelt, blessed herself and clasped her hands together in supplication. Give me strength, she implored, and the wisdom to know what to do next. Help me keep my family close and safe. God, if you're out there and listening, please don't forsake us. Please don't let Tom die.

Eighteen

Ruth wasn't sure why she struck out for the church. Last two times she'd attended had been to see her parents safely off into the Catholic promise of a life ever after. She was only partially convinced that they weren't just going six foot under, but they deserved every chance of Eden, so who was she to argue the point? The rituals had done little to ease the pain of loss, or produce great hopes for the future.

She had been educated in convent schools and, strictly speaking, taught in one, though there were few enough nuns in the place, due to falling numbers of postulants and natural wastage through the Lord's recalling of his handmaidens. Lapsed was the word for her now. Still, hadn't she read somewhere that when they wet you they get you, and she had been baptised into that faith. They had her.

She hoped the trip would ease her, and she was jittery. Not knowing exactly when her sister would hit town was taking a toll. With any luck, the church would be empty. She'd grown weary of their local parish priest slyly mentioning how long it was since he'd seen herself and Kate at a service. He might have been disappointed to know his obvious barb didn't dent them and neither had undergone a re-conversion, or lost moments worrying for their immortal souls. Even though there was no hope of running into him here, she wasn't keen on meeting his counterpart. In general, she didn't have much to say to the religious and kept it that way by not saying much. QED.

It was a neat, medium-sized building in the old style. Grey granite with pointed arches, a wide main aisle to the main altar, flanked by two smaller ones. Some windows were of stained glass which cast splintered colour onto the dark wooden pews. A small organ sat to the rear. Statues of Mary and Jesus stared balefully from their plinths. It smelled of incense, polish and candle wax. She gave an automatic, shallow genuflection and slipped into a seat midway along. There was one other woman in the place, head bent in prayer. Ruth closed her eyes and let the silence take her.

Her father faded quickly before them in the narrow hospital bed. He had little interest in staying on without Rita. They had been together for forty-five years, married for forty of those.

'I'm like Darby without Joan.'

'Tarzan without Jane,' they teased.

'Will ye be all right?' he asked his daughters anxiously.

'Daddy, don't worry about us, you think of yourself now. Sure look at us two lumps, why would you be worried? We'll be grand.'

Sometimes Ruth even believed this as she peddled the reassurance. The placebo was always short-lived, though welcome for all its brevity. But something was keeping him and they couldn't figure it out.

Ruth visited before work one morning and found him more lucid and agitated than he had been in a while. He couldn't find the words he needed. He was of a generation that didn't discuss their feelings aloud. There was no vocabulary for it and no decency either, it seemed, only embarrassment. When it came time to advise or to probe, matters were kept to the ordinary, practically the business end of being a family. So, circuitously, he talked of Rita, how proud she was of her girls. And how . . .

'It's me, isn't it?' Ruth said. 'It's me you're worried about.'

She was the one detaining him.

'Ach, it's none of my business,' he sighed. He was so, so tired. He slipped away for some moments but shook himself awake again and returned to his theme immediately. 'Is he good to you?' he asked.

Ruth was gobsmacked. She didn't think her parents knew about Greg.

'Daddy,' she implored.

He cut her off, aware that his time was limited and

therefore priceless. 'You see, I don't think he is. And there's his situation too. He's not . . . available? And he's stifling you, that's what I think.' Then he looked into her very core and said, 'Get away, Ruth. Get away from him.'

She jolted on the wooden bench as her dream caught up with her. She was elated to remember that her father had not rejected her but gutted that he had worried, even a day, about her messy, unforgivable affair. Her poor mother had known too and was unable to broach it. What torture had those good people gone through because of her stupidity? She heard her choking sobs resound in the church. That was one thing you could not deny these places, the acoustics were great. Embarrassed, she stanched the tears and buried her head in her hands, but the sound continued. She was not the only one crying. Slowly the other woman turned to her. They both fought to regain composure. They paused. In that silent moment between strangers, they galvanised their resolve to fight for what they needed. They nodded and went their separate ways.

She was amazed when Greg announced his intention to attend her father's funeral.

'There'll be other teachers there, I won't stick out much.'

You did by not coming to my mother's, Ruth wanted to say. But she was grateful for the crumb of comfort and unable to have even the slightest of rows. It might signal a change of status for them. She was becoming a larger part of his life.

'You must be on something to think that,' Kate told her, bluntly. 'He's seen them all off but me now. He's come to crow.'

She paid no heed. Time would help her and Greg disprove her sister, she was sure. Amidst the grieving, she had hope. She could forge a life from this.

Old neighbours filed by, faces worried with their own mortality. They gripped both her hands and murmured, 'Sorry for your trouble', 'She'll be missed', then 'He'll be missed'. Her palms were sticky with sympathy. At last, 'Time is a great healer' was offered: that precious, necessary cliché. She grasped it. 'Thank you.' It held her together like glue.

Greg stood at the back of the church with her work colleagues, hugged her when they did, said how sorry he was, then cried off the burial and joined the others in the pub. When the diminished funeral party returned, for the traditional pint and sandwich, he spent five minutes telling her how strong she was, saw her to the ladies and was getting into a car driven by his wife when she rejoined the group.

'Greg said he'd call you later, see how you are,' said the new Domestic Science woman. 'He's such a good friend.'

'Yeah, he's just great.' The stuffing was so knocked out

of her by then she couldn't even muster some sarcasm.
Kate gave her the look of a lady confronting a very large
turd in her soup bowl.

Ruth stopped outside the church to let her eyes adjust
to the sun's glare. She saw a movement to her left by
the wall.

'Oh, hi, Ozzy,' she said. 'Beautiful day, isn't it?'

He seemed to be fidgeting with something out of her
sight and disinclined to make conversation. Behind him
a freshly turned mound indicated the last resting place
of one Patrick Collerane R.I.P. Ozzy must be paying his
respects to the dead, she decided.

'Are you on the doss?' she teased.

'Eh, yeah. Just a break, you know?'

She was sure she heard a small laugh from the other
woman. Well, the acts of laughing and crying were
closely related, kissin' cousins you might say. She could
also have sworn she heard the mutter 'Baldy conscience'
as well. Ozzy was thinning on top, rude as it was to
mention it, but what did the conscience bit refer to?
She was flummoxed and began to wonder if she would
ever know the real workings of the town. She might not
have the time. With Kate arriving, her own departure
drew closer. Was she ready to leave her haven, and what
did she have to return to?

Ozzy made his way out of the church grounds at
speed. Ruth would have called it hurried. Can't deal

with me out of context, she thought. She steered a course for Finn's. As she walked down the incline towards town, she could see the youth group hard at work and hear vague chatter in the air. Tom Long's daughter was laughing at something said by one of the boys. Ruth was sure she had seen Cathy somewhere other than the pub. She racked her brain but could only come up with the weird thought that she had seen the girl on the evening she'd arrived, in just the briefest of images, but a strange one too, because in the memory Cathy seemed to be waving at the bus and then barking. That couldn't be right. The product of her confused and intoxicated mind at the time, no doubt.

'Charlie tells me we can expect your sister today,' Old Mikey said from his spot. 'He's in high good form altogether over it.'

'Mmn.' Ruth couldn't believe how happy they all were at the prospect of meeting Kate. 'Hope ye won't be disappointed,' she said. 'She's only human.' Then, to prove her point, she added, 'She's a hairdresser.'

'I haven't heard him whistle in ages.'

Sure enough, Charlie was chirping out a ditty. It seemed an oddly old-fashioned thing to do.

'That shirt's not very practical for bar work,' Ruth pointed out.

He beamed. 'I know, but I look deadly in it.'

Was he deliberately baiting her? She gave a lofty sigh.

But he was right, he did look a million dollars. She gazed at her own ensemble and knew that it left a fair bit to be desired. She didn't make it any better by spilling two cups' worth of spent coffee grounds down the front of her 'Welcome to County Clare' T-shirt. That's when the bar hushed and she turned to see her sister in the doorway, immaculately dressed and shod, wearing the looks of a movie star and a cherubic smile.

Charlie was upon her in an instant.

'You look just like you sound on the phone,' Kate told him.

'I hope that's a good thing,' he smarmed.

'Oh yes.' A purr.

Ruth brushed off the coffee and tried to rub out the stain with a damp cloth. No luck.

'Don't I get a hug?' she heard Kate say.

Jesus, were they already in each other's arms? Then she realised that the request was for her and she sprang forward into her sister's embrace, tears rolling down her face.

'You great big ninny,' Kate said, brushing her hair with affection. 'Let's get you out of that heinously ugly T-shirt.'

'I'm going through a hippy-student-ish phase,' Ruth explained.

'I suppose it's not the worst,' her sister admitted.

She let herself be introduced to all before taking to the stairs, which necessitated a protracted round of goodbye-for-nows and promises that she'd return 'toot sweet'. Not a gnat's breath in the place and everyone fawning all over her. Stylish.

Upstairs, Ruth didn't recognise any of the clothes Kate laid out on the bed for her.

'Good,' her sister declared. 'I've always thought you dressed too conservatively. Hallelujah for a change. I took the liberty of bringing a few suggestions.'

Ruth wriggled into a halter-necked top with black and white geometric patterns and a pair of black hipster trousers. She paused before the shoes.

'It's obvious which are the recent purchases,' she grinned. She chose red patent leather pumps. 'They're not half as bad as I remembered.'

'Oh, they are, I just brought the least vomit-making.'

'Ta-dah!' Ruth struck a pose.

'Much better. You look well, Ru, and your hair is growing. I didn't like it short.'

You should get your hair done. It would suit you shorter.'

She didn't want to. She liked the length, thought it softened her features. Pleasing her lover took top spot. She cut her hair.

Her father, waning in his hospital bed, was surprised. 'Sure it'll grow back,' he comforted.

Greg adored it. 'Just what the teacher ordered,' he crowed.

Ruth hated the change, loved his approval. She made

a note to herself not to forget to draw a line on all the changes he seemed to want to make to her. Still, when it came down to it, she switched her make-up and began to wear a new perfume that he chose but didn't pay for.

'I should get back down to relieve Charlie. Strictly speaking, it's my shift.'

'He's one of the good guys, isn't he?'

'He's been one to me. I've been very lucky.'

'It could have been a disaster otherwise.' Kate hesitated, then said, 'But we'll talk later, eh?'

'Yeah.' She dreaded it.

'No rush, Ruth,' said Kate, reading her sister's terrified expression.

'I'm glad you're here.'

'So am I. Now send that handsome hunk of beef up here till I find out more about him.'

It was unsettling to Ruth that Kate knew anything at all already. And did it mean Charlie knew all about herself? Was her foolish cover as a writer blown out of the water? The knee-jerk reaction of wanting to be someone else brought with it the potential for major embarrassment. She had spent so long this year telling lies and shape-shifting she wasn't sure she could tell the truth, or recognise it, any more. However, there were, unbelievably, more basic worries now that her sister was here.

'You won't be forgetting that you're married?'

'No, dearest sister. I'm sure I'll be able to keep activities within the bounds of propriety.'

'Which is more than I did with Greg,' Ruth said.

'I didn't mean it like that, sis.'

'No, I know, but I did. If I could turn back time, as Cher is wont to sing.'

'And you really wish she wouldn't.'

'For sure.'

Below, in the bar, Charlie's mouth fell adrift as Ruth sashayed across the floor.

'It's a new me,' she said, neglecting to mention that there were a number of old and new Ruths. 'Kate says I have mumsy taste in clothes. She's appointed herself stylist.'

'Good work.'

She was behind the bar now and they were standing close. He put his arm round her waist. 'You look wonderful,' he said. Then he kissed the top of her head.

She murmured, 'Thanks,' and was happy with her lot. It was better than a poke in the eye with a pointy stick.

'Oh, much better than that,' he said.

Ruth had no idea whether he had read her mind or she'd spoken aloud.

Nineteen

Tom Long woke shivering in the field in spite of the glorious sunshine. His vision was clouded by headache and nausea. His body screamed for drink. His back ached, the poison of alcohol straining his kidneys and liver. His lips were cracked and his mouth foetid. He was shrivelled with dehydration. The pub and salvation from this torment was ten minutes away. He would consult the doctor later about more treatment to help him, but now all he could see, taste, feel was a drink. He would have a few to steady him, along with a few glasses of water to even things, and then work out a way of weaning onto a more sober life. If Charlie Finn could do it, so could he. He struggled to his feet, staggered towards town. A rare flash of honesty assaulted him. I'm in a bad way, he thought. And I'm frightened. Everything would make more sense after a cure.

✿　✿　✿

Kate sat at the bar with a Diet Coke and an attentive Charlie. Ruth watched them, heads together, sharing giggles and information. It unnerved her a little, delighted as she was to see two of the important people in her life bond so well. As long as it wasn't too successful a bonding, of course. She was desperate to eavesdrop on their conversation to monitor how much of it was about her. They had given no sideward glances her way, which might mean they weren't discussing her at all, and that unsettled her too. She was a cat on a griddle, which was as cruel a thing as it sounded.

Old Mikey checked his watch. 'Oh ho, it won't be long now before the hordes arrive to check her out.'

The Sergeant was the first. Kate greeted him like a long-lost buddy. 'It's very good of you to take time out for me,' she said. Although it was deemed impossible, the Sergeant simpered and practically fell at her feet. She was smooth, no doubt there. And she's on my side, thought Ruth. She felt safe. What she did wonder about was how long Kate had been in touch with the law. She was well in with the hoi polloi of Kilbrody, and no one had ever mentioned word of it to her. The Sergeant took his hat off, ran a hand through greased-down hair and ordered a pint. He appeared to be blushing. Charlie looked over at her, barely concealing his mirth. She widened her eyes and raised her brows to him in agreement. This was certainly a sight. The Sergeant who believed in bullying over cajoling. His modus operandi was to fell a man and (maybe) ask questions later. He rarely felt the need to charm his subjects, and relied on a primeval roar for those more delicate situations. Now, he was a lap dog. It was too much and Charlie had to quench his hoots under a coughing fit.

'Is there anything more foolish than a silly old man?' Mikey asked, also marvelling at the situation. 'She's some wonder, that sister of yours. Beauty and the beast, wha?'

On cue, Carol and Linda swanned in. They made a beeline for the action. Linda waved her spikes at Ruth and ordered 'the usual'.

'Please,' Charlie instructed her.

'Of course, *please*,' Linda scowled. 'And whatever you're having yourself, dearie,' she dismissed at Ruth.

Ruth decided on two pints, for Old Mikey and the Whinge who had appeared by magic forces. Mikey rubbed his hands in appreciation. 'Things are hotting up nicely now,' he said.

Linda was all over Kate like a cheap dress but getting nowhere. More than once her sister raised her eyes to heaven and made barfing gestures behind the woman's back. My sister's got discernment and taste, Ruth cheered. Charlie smirked. The Sergeant stood a round.

'A historical milestone in the annals of the town,' declared the Whinge, though just to Mikey and Ruth, aware what side his bread was buttered.

The Sergeant was loudly telling Kate that the town was glad to have a scribe in its midst once again.

'Over the years they've been in and out to us,' he intoned. 'And many's the good tale they got and made famous. Good luck to them, I suppose. Sure, we all could do that if we had the time.'

'Or the talent,' Kate smiled. She was moving with the conversation, cordially, though it was clear to Ruth that she didn't know to whom the Sergeant was referring.

'You must have to be careful yourself, not to end up in the books,' the big man offered.

Again this went over Kate's head. 'We should all be careful of writers *and* journalists,' she said, congenially.

'You'll have read them all, of course.'

Now a slightly quizzical expression settled on Kate's face.

'Have you a favourite?'

'In what way?'

'Your sister's books, have you a favourite?'

Kate let out a peal of laughter and, quick as her fideltiy to her sister allowed, said, 'Oh, they're like children, you couldn't praise one over the other.' She shot a splendidly communicative 'I'll talk to you later' at Ruth and deftly led the talk to the rising crime in the area, shocked to hear that there had been two cases of 'disturbing the peace' in the last month alone.

'Sure the hot weather has people driven demented.'

The Sergeant held the view that society was sparing the corporal punishment and spoiling the citizen, and couldn't get his head around sending deviants to 'shrinks and charlatans, when all that's needed is a good root up the hole for the most of the blackguards, begging your pardon'.

It was wisely granted with a nod. More porter flowed, the price of cattle scorned and the lack of single women bemoaned, 'with all the grand lads in the parish that're goin' mad for the want of a decent grab of another human being. Is it any wonder we're losin' them to Limerick and beyond?' The last spike of wisdom was donated to the company by the Whinge.

The afternoon was moving quickly along in a jaunting reel of conviviality when Ruth saw Charlie frown. She followed his eye to Tom Long standing frail, pale and unsure on the threshold. Slowly, he stepped in and moved along the bar. Charlie went to speak to him, clearly trying to talk sense to the man. Then he stopped and jerked back as if hit by a truck. A woman stood in the doorway, the woman from the church. She reached a hand out to the men, both wanted to take it, but Tom Long was the intended. Charlie's face was a study in anguish. The rest of the pub was oblivious to the drama and chuntered on with the business of enjoyment. The woman turned to Old Mikey.

'Hello, Daddy,' she said.

'Hello, my lovely. Have you come to take Tom home?'

'Yes,' she replied.

Tom Long put a hand over his eyes to hide his emotion.

217

Mikey had never called him by his name in the pub before, rarely acknowledged his existence. He thought him a bad husband to his princess.

'Good woman, Joyce. That's the right thing to do now.'

The penny dropped with a clang in Ruth's mind. She snapped her attention to Charlie. He looked shattered. He raised a hand to one of the pints standing in line on the counter.

'Don't, Charlie,' Joyce said. 'Please don't.'

He was defeated, as always, by the gentleness of her voice. His stooping back disappeared through the nattering crowd.

'Kate, could you step in here for a moment?' Ruth asked. 'I have to change a barrel.'

Charlie leaned against the coarse brick wall of the cellar. He couldn't believe the effect of her after all he'd been through. Worst of all, he realised it had ended a long time ago. He had let his emotions crystallise over the years into one beautiful impossibility. Now he must face that fact and move on. It didn't make life any easier. He despaired at the futility of all that wasted time. He was now staring at a void where he had once pictured Joyce. He began to pound the wall with his fists.

'Charlie?'

'Not now, Ruth.'

'Yes, now,' she said firmly. 'You need to take the night off and go to a meeting or see your sponsor.'

He knew she was right and nodded, shallowly.

'You also need to come here.' Ruth held her arms open.

Charlie went to her, grateful for the presence of another living being who cared. Her warmth seeped into him.

'It's going to be all right,' she said.

They heard a snort. 'And there was I thinking a blow job might be the answer.' Linda, lovely as ever, stood silhouetted in the doorway.

Charlie had known the Byrne family and their daughter, Joyce, from boyhood. Joyce was acknowledged as the bright spark, her elder brother Michael Junior universally held as a spoiled waster with no interest in anything but backing horses. However, this was to stand to him when he turned to breeding and racing, and became successful beyond the reaches of the Kilbrody imagination. Joyce, meanwhile, studied history and philosophy at college and returned with a good degree to nurse her mother as she died, and her father as he fell apart afterwards.

In the early days they saw each other during the holidays, when Charlie returned from boarding school, mostly at bingo evenings or the odd good funeral. Occasionally, a progressive teacher would run a youth disco, get told off from the pulpit the following Sunday and be discouraged from trying ever again.

Joyce was a pretty girl and an easy favourite with the

boys. She liked Charlie for his lack of parochialism (courtesy of his general remove from Kilbrody) and the fact that he always had enough to buy a girl a Coke or rise to a burger if the occasion called for it. Even in her awkward early teens she could admit to herself that he was also good looking and, mercifully, acne free. That one last attribute alone carved him as an individual from the flock for a good two years and made him extremely desirable to the young ladies of the town, and at least one of the boys, who later debunked to Cork to run a gay bar and restaurant called Manhole. A further boon was his attraction to the joys of washing, so lacking in many of his peers.

Charlie thought Joyce a cut above the rest from the beginning. She was smart and plucky, and had a sense of humour when it didn't seem fashionable in that neck of the woods. She was as keen on his early experiments with sex as was allowed by her upbringing, and they both learned a thing or two when they took themselves into the various fields on the edge of town for late-night kisses. It was generally assumed that they would hook up on his holidays and what they did in the meantime was their own business. Neither lost too much sleep over the other.

Their college years saw various mis-timings on returns to the homestead, and then Charlie disappeared off the map during his excursions around Europe. They gradually relegated the union and, never having had a formal arrangement, let the whole matter of growing up slide into memory. It became something that happened on the road to the age of (some) reason, achieving adulthood and the life that then presented. As Joyce cared for her mother, she began to see a young farmer from out the road: Tom Long.

Charlie's eventual return to Kilbrody (though he did not know it would be at the time) was shrouded in gossip and scandal. Not only had he missed his father's death and delayed the funeral, he then took to the drink in a big way and became the talking point of several townlands. As her father had always been fond of him, Joyce found herself on occasional missions of retrieval. More than once she wiped a bloody brow and often was kissed frantically by a plastered Charlie Finn. If he remembered these incidents he failed to show it and she didn't bother to mention them in case they embarrassed him. What unsettled her, though, was that she never minded that he kissed her and once, at least, was well on the way to making full and passionate love when she called a late halt. It took all her will power to stop and remind herself that she was now part of a relationship with Tom Long. She was left gasping and confused. Finn was a menace. But she cared about what would become of him.

Tom Long had studied agriculture in Dublin and took over the family farm when his time came. His parents shocked the entire community by upping sticks and moving to a small apartment in Florida where they revelled in their retirement and regretted not a jot. Tom was steeped in the land and livestock and chose to pursue the organic ideal, as far as economics would allow. The farming community of the region was old fashioned and considered him soft in the head for his approach. He was that elusive perfect ratio of tender compassion and all-encompassing fervour. He courted his love ardently, wooing her with a soul laid bare and practically tattooed on his forehead. He was head over heels for Joyce Byrne.

Joyce and Old Mikey saw Charlie through his demon days as he fought infection and then withdrawal. His dependency on alcohol was devastating and physically horrific, and the fight to banish it from his life almost carried him away. It led to an unspoken intimacy between all three. And by the time Charlie was ready to take up the reins of Finn's again, Joyce found herself thinking of him constantly.

Charlie was beginning a new life and he wanted Joyce to be a part of it. How to tell her this, and prove that he was worthy, was beyond him. She had seen him at his worst and he feared she might be repulsed. Gradually, he wove her into his new day-to-day. He often asked her to accompany him to trade dinners. He invited her to meals at home and beyond. Occasionally, he dared to take her to the pictures and once to a concert in Ennis. He was always careful not to impinge on her time with Tom, who was the official suitor. But the thought that he might not be her chosen in the long run was not an option. He would not let go. He would do whatever it took and be as patient as he needed. He would make her love him.

Joyce was anguished to discover that she had a choice. She spent long hours poring over her dilemma. Tom was openly making love to her, but Charlie seemed reluctant to. Nevertheless, it was clear that he wanted to, but was afraid of her bolting if he made an inappropriate move. She wanted them both, but knew that was not possible. She didn't know what to do. One evening in the roof garden she detected a different charge in the air. Charlie had been particularly distant and she had felt what she could only describe as peculiar all night. Her breath was catching, her hands shook and her body was disobedient. She fudged picking things up, bumped into chairs and scuffed against plant borders. Eventually she took herself to the railings and watched the river flow by. She heard him approach, felt him near.

'Joyce?' he whispered.

Her head began to spin. 'Yes?' She turned, haltingly, and found him so close she could kiss him by merely puckering her lips. They stood dangerously close, breathing in the other, then he reached for her and she knew she would be his entirely.

They made love there on the roof again and again, then moved to his bed. Neither wanted sleep to come to end this dream, this excitement, this exultation. Later, she lay breathing him in and watched his face in slumber. The lines of his struggle had disappeared with a new happiness and he smiled as he slept. She thought of Tom and her heart ached. She now had to choose.

When Charlie woke some hours later, she was gone. But her decision was made. She married Tom Long two months later. A note on Charlie's pillow said, 'Forgive me, I had to know. You will always have a part of me that belongs to no one else. I hope we can be friends again some day. Love, Joyce.'

Charlie went to the bar and poured himself a pint.

Linda stormed away in a waft of Cristalle. How she made such a wonderful fragrance so unpalatable was a religious mystery, Ru.h decided. She and Charlie were left as they had been found and awkwardness set in. They parted, left guilty by Linda's intrusion.

'I can't believe I can still be hijacked by the past,' Charlie said, quietly.

'We all are, constantly. It's one of the supposed joys of being human. Character definition would be lost without it, I'm told.' Ruth paused. 'It's a real pisser, eh?'

'We're a right sorry pair because of it anyhow.'

'Yep. And there's still a bar to run. Let's get back in there.'

Charlie's shoulders sagged. 'Jesus, life just goes on and on.'

'It does stop,' Ruth pointed out, remembering her parents. 'So let's make the most of it.'

'*Illegitimus nolle carborundum?*' He saw her puzzlement. 'Don't let the bastards grind you down.'

'That's the one.'

They headed up.

Twenty

Deborah was bribed with time and a half to take over
for the evening. Charlie drove the Treacy sisters to
Ennis, where they went in search of a bistro and he
attended an AA meeting. His knuckles were white for
the journey and he said little. Kate was oblivious, filled
as she was with observations on the good folk of
Kilbrody. Linda got thumbs down, unsurprisingly, Carol
a 'jury's out' and the Sergeant was declared a harmless
enough old bear of a thing. Charlie managed a snort for
that.

'He's just old style,' Kate argued.

'He's a medieval throwback,' Charlie agreed.

'Throwback?' Ruth scoffed. 'Hurl back, more like.'

'Sis,' Kate squealed, 'you made a joke.'

'She has a lip on her all the time,' Charlie pointed out.

'Really?' Kate seemed genuinely surprised.

'Do I not always?'

'At home, yes, but not so much . . . anywhere else.'

'Welcome to the All New County Clare Ruth,' Charlie said.

Kate thought about that for a few seconds, then asked, 'Does everyone drink all day long?'

'Ah no, not all day,' Charlie was waxing. 'If they're farmers, they'll have had a very early start so that usually means an early visit to the pub, maybe late afternoon for a few hours. The townies come in after office work. They all mix the drinking with raking over the past and creating feuds for the future. Gossip, poker and darts get a look in too. All bets are off at the weekend when it can be a bit of a free-for-all. It's a full dance card.'

'Not to be sniffed at,' Kate said. 'I don't know where they get their energy. A glass of wine with my dinner and I'm slaughtered. The Treacys were never very good at drinking.'

'I made a fair stab at it recently,' Ruth observed.

'Yes, we'll have to get to the bottom of all that,' her sister told her. She saw the horror and added, 'Only when you're ready.' She smiled, wickedly. 'Was it research for a book, I wonder?'

Ruth ignored her by appearing fascinated with the electricity lines strung above the hedges. Her interest waned after five hundred yards.

'I will say one thing for sobriety,' Charlie piped up. 'At least I don't wake up with that awful false panic of a hangover. That chemical fear. Now all I have is the real thing.' He clammed up again shortly after that.

The lights of Ennis glittered far away, orange diamonds shimmering on the black velvet of the night. Thousands of people there were living through similar problems to their own, but each with a personal journey to make. There are no short cuts, Ruth thought. Even if there were, we'd probably avoid them in our vanity and mistrust. Worse luck.

Joyce looked at the kindest, best man in the world, devastated that he had come to this. Tom was sedated and comatose in their bed, bathed in an aura of unhappiness and pain. He jerked and fidgeted in the agony of withdrawal and small moans escaped his dried lips. Joyce wiped his sweating forehead with a cold flannel and spooned water into his mouth. She tried to soothe him with whispers of love, and encouragements that everything was now going to be OK.

'We'll see how he is tomorrow,' the doctor had said. 'But I think it's time to let the experts deal with him. I hear the Parklands Centre is good.'

He left her to get her mind around what had to become a fact in their lives. She marvelled that Gilhooley had spoken a modicum of sense, let alone the vast truth of what was needed. Maybe he was not as much of a quack as they all feared. And what colour did that cast on some of his dodgier diagnoses? That's all the town needed: to discover that they had a medical seer on their hands. She wasn't about to be the one to break the news. People had been burned at the stake for less.

She heard a figure creeping along the corridor. Cathy stuck her head into the room. 'How is he?' Her face was etched with worry.

'He's comfortable, pet, but I think we'll have to get him into a clinic for a while, just to get over the worst of the detox.' Her voice broke as she expressed the major concern. 'That's if he can make the decision that he wants to . . . I hope he does.'

She felt odd to have so adult a conversation with a girl who was only just touching thirteen. However, they would never get through this without honesty, and she was determined that they were going to get through.

'I don't know why we're whispering, he's out cold.'

'Still, we don't want to disturb him any more than we have to,' her daughter said.

My God, where did she get the sense from? Who was this level-headed, patient girl? How had they been lucky enough to make her?

The sisters linked arms as they roamed the streets of Ennis.

'What we need is the Latin Quarter,' Kate declared.

Ruth found herself holding her head back in the warm breeze and enjoying the very act of breathing, close to her best friend, back where she belonged. She wished Charlie could be on her other side.

'We want somewhere cheap as chips and cheerful as a bus load of nuns on a good, long pilgrimage.'

They came across Le Place and decided it had to be the one. Within a fraction of 'Hello' the patron was offering a free glass of fizz. Ruth basked in the trail of her sister's conquests. Kate need only smile for a major player to swoon.

Kate sipped her drink, and gently wrinkled her nose. 'Tart, but full of good intentions.' She giggled. 'Like me.'

'How do you do it?'

'Being honest? I look available, and not too much of a moose.'

'Naive as I am, I thought it was your sex appeal.'

'The day I know what that is, exactly, is the day I lose it, according to Lar.'

Lar was Kate's musician husband; an unlikely gangle of raggy hair, hooked nose, straggly limbs and intense green eyes. He had a razored wit and ready laugh and played piano as naturally as most people drew breath. Together they were quite a sight: Kate, all elegance and polish, Lar a clumsy fallabout. His charisma was devastating and groupies abounded wherever he played. He only had eyes for his beautiful wife and they were as happy as any pair was allowed in a capricious world. Ruth called him her favourite brother-in-law and docked points from anyone idiot enough to point out that he was also her only brother-in-law.

'He wanted to come along but he's doing a residency

at that dive we know and love as The Pit. Money in the bank, Weetabix on the table.'

He had played the organ at the funerals, even composing a short requiem for both, firming the original piece into a more masculine opus for Eddie when his unfortunate turn came. Ruth had a vision of Lar hammering on the clapped-out upright in the front room, managing to make even its tinny sound acceptable, the family surrounding him with adoration writ large on their faces. 'Moonlight Becomes You' was one of Rita's favourites, and Ruth could still hear her mother's peal as Lar changed the lyrics to 'mooning becomes you, it leaves you all bare'.

They tucked into garlic mushrooms, steak, frites and a cheeky burgundy, and left the chat to neutral subjects, like the shenanigans at Kate's hair and beauty salon.

'The new nail technician, Jasmine, is running rampant through the male staff.'

'That's a grand total of two men,' Ruth remarked.

'Yes, but we did think that Dougie was gay. Actually he may still be, if he was in the first place. Experimenting is allowed, I believe.'

'I'm tipsy and filled to bursting,' Ruth groaned, opening the button on her trousers.

'You could do with putting a bit of weight back on. You were getting very thin.'

You know I like your shape, but there's a bit too much of it here and there. It's either the gym or a diet for you, my dear.'

It was both, as it happened. Then the illnesses, the deaths, the sorrow. She didn't notice hunger, only misery, and engaged in a disregard for matters corporal. Besides sex, that is, whenever available to her. Then she relished the abandonment of sheer rutting, the harsh thrusts, both liberation and punishment all at once. She found the loose waistband satisfactory, liked the shape of her ribs which were so defined now. She looked at the new Ruth in the mirror, a makeover with changed shape, hair, cosmetics, smell. She didn't recognise her, but there seemed to be a familial resemblance to someone she had once known.

She let her eyes wander. She saw an apartment filled with the gifts she had given Greg Deegan. He could not take them home. Home to his wife and children.

The waiter brought two flaming sambucas, gift of the smitten proprietor. Kate did her trick of wetting a finger, dipping it in and waving the ignited digit proudly in the air. Ruth saw her father playing his magic tricks, with cards and ash and matchsticks, and her tears rose to join the night.

Charlie was more relaxed on the drive home. Kate sat in the front passenger seat beside him and conducted a mini interrogation.

'Do you not mind being around drinkers?'

'I used to get very envious in the beginning,' he explained. 'But the fact is I run a pub, that's my living, so I got over the envy thing in double quick time. I still have my moments. That's why they say it's one day at a time. Or sometimes it's only an hour.'

What a confusing concept it was to 'make a living', Ruth thought. It was the practical end of earning enough to survive and also the pinnacle of ambitions: to attain the means that would enrich life, produce happiness or even simple content. She had made her living a war zone of pitfalls. She was indifferently employed, churning out the expected number of partially educated youngsters, no more, no less, passing them on to others to sort out, meanwhile settling on another woman's husband. Her own living was a mess and, not content with that, she was a cuckoo in someone else's nest, someone else's living; queering up lord knows how many lives on her shambolic journey.

They drove another mile in darkness strange to city people, that blackness negated by the neon sarcoma of orange light they were so accustomed to. Dark, bushy shapes raced by, the white line of the road, the luminous eyes of startled sheep frozen on the verges and walls by the car lights.

'I haven't always been successful in staying off the sauce, either,' Charlie said, still with his own theme.

He remembered the fog of drunkenness after Joyce had left. It was fuelled with the news that she was engaged to Tom Long. He went on the batter and found himself constantly in danger of turning up on her doorstep to beg her to reconsider. In fact, he did just that on more than a few occasions, each more craven than the last. Tears, wailing, begging, then anger. He smashed three pots of geraniums from her windowsill with a sweep of an arm once and lay bleeding in the clay and plants and dirt, sickened by what he had become. All the time he knew he was just digging himself further into the hole he was in and that the only realistic way of getting her back was to sober up and live a better life. But, in his heart of hearts, he realised she had made an unalterable decision, so he kept on drinking. His second hospital stay was the one he knew would be his last, one way or another. His compromised system was on the brink of total collapse. If he died he would never see Joyce again. Perhaps best to live, and love her from a distance? Or maybe there was someone else out there for him?

Kate sat on the end of Ruth's bed, removing her nail varnish. 'I don't want to look too like that witch Linda,' she said.

'How long will you stay?' Ruth asked.

'A few days, I suppose, or until you feck me out. How long will you stay?'

'Like yourself, until I'm fecked out. Nah, term starts in a few weeks' time, and I'll have to go back for that. Face the music.'

'We'll have to decide a few things, like what to do with the house and so on.'

'How did I get so out of hand?' Ruth blurted.

'You thought you were in love, or that someone was in love with you. It's all any of us wants.'

'I chose badly.'

'I think he did the choosing, and you were susceptible at the time. He's a very manipulative man, that Greg Deegan. You were unlucky.'

'Why am I not getting a bollocking from you?'

'I'm too mellow, and I haven't the energy right now. But you know how it is with family, I'll get around to it.' Kate leaned in to kiss her forehead. 'Night night, sleep tight, don't let the bed bugs bite.'

Ruth snuggled into the bedclothes.

'I am fascinated by one thing,' Kate admitted. 'This writer business.'

'Ah, yes, that. Well, I suppose the simple answer is that I wanted a change. It seemed an easy job to pick, woolly and mysterious enough to pass muster without too many questions. All the proof you need is a tattered notebook and a furrowed brow. And there was no one to contradict me. I got the chance to be someone else for a while.'

'Did it work?'

'Sort of. It was a distraction anyhow. I haven't gouged out a novel, but I didn't have to discuss the workings of the education system either.'

'All very well, but you'd better get scribbling, miss, or there'll be questions asked.'

It didn't seem like the worst idea of the day; must be the delirium of the wine and a need for sleep. Ruth yawned and asked, 'Why was it so surprising that I made a joke earlier?'

'You don't usually open up like that, unless you're with family or someone you trust.'

'Well, there's your answer. I was with both, earlier.'

Charlie lay in his bed listening to the soft tinkling of women in his house. He liked it. He thought of the sham of the last thirteen years, when he had wasted all opportunities of settling down because of an impossible love, a situation so idealised in his mind by his stubbornness that he couldn't see how hopeless it was. A dark thought lurked at the back of his mind. Had he deliberately kept Tom Long on a short leash, hoping that he would spot a time to jump in and run off with his wife? And if that was indeed the case, how stupid and self-delusional was he for thinking such a thing? Not to mention how mean. He was not proud of himself and turned on his side in a state of self-disgust. He needed to make amends to the Longs and to himself. Tomorrow is another day, he told himself, though in fairness you're no Scarlett O'Hara.

Ruth lay gazing at the ceiling, tracing hairline cracks and imagining them to be shapes, a dog here, a cup there. Her head began to pulse slightly and she hoped she'd get to sleep before a hangover got hold. The house was still, barring the odd creak of sheer old age. She finished the water Kate had left by her bed and knew that she would need another. Quietly, she slipped out of her room and into the kitchen. She left the glass on the draining board and picked up the telephone. She dialled her parents' number and listened as the distant phone rang in an empty house for people who could no longer answer.

Twenty-One

Breakfast at the Long house was eerily still and quiet. Joyce had seen to the farm work with help from her father, who now sat tucking into a fry and pretending that everything was as normal as day following night, which it had dutifully done, in age-old tradition. Cathy allowed herself to be spoiled by two pop tarts and her mouth was stuck in on itself with sugar. She made dry smacking noises as she tried to free it up. The radio said the weather was due to break but didn't mention when exactly, then indistinct tunes followed one another in a blanket of sound. Joyce loaded a tray of scrambled eggs and toast for Tom and disappeared with it.

'How is the project going?' Old Mikey enquired.

'Grand. It's good fun. I saw a few Longs in there. Are they anything to us, do you think?'

'Oh, I'd say so,' her grandfather said. 'It'd be hard to throw a stone and not hit someone with a Long connection in this part of the world. Your dad will be able to fill you in better on that. Did you come across the Byrnes yet?'

'No. I'll keep an eye out.'

'Do. We're there too.'

'Grandad, do you think people can change?'

Suddenly and unexpectedly, they were on dicey territory.

'Ah yes, I think so. In spite of what you hear about a leopard and its spots. When it's important, we can all make a big effort.' He decided to go for broke. 'Sometimes a problem doesn't go away, but we can get it under control. And if someone was to have the best of support, sure who could topple them?' He stood and rubbed his belly. 'That was a mighty feed and I'm getting old, so I think I might head home and have a wee snooze. Tell your mother I'll be in touch later. And I'll see you when I see you, hah?'

'Sure.'

Cathy pushed a sliver of pastry and goo around her plate and wondered why life was so hard. There seemed to be nothing for it but to get on with it. Dennis would have loved the last of her breakfast, she knew, and she could imagine the heavy thump of his tail as he lay in wait for the treat. She dumped the remainder of the tart and loaded the dishwasher.

Her parents' voices barely reached into the corridor leading to their bedroom. She took a major breath and pushed open the door. Her father was propped up in bed trying to deal with the food in front of him. He was pale but for the emerald gills. He gave a wan smile and said, 'You should see the other guy.'

'I'm off to the project,' Cathy said.

Her parents exchanged a glance.

'I might not be around for the next few days,' her father told her. 'Could be a week, maybe two. I hope you don't mind.'

Just get well, she wanted to say but went for 'Right' instead.

'But I'll see you for your birthday, of course,' he rushed to say.

'Right,' again. 'I'll miss you' wanted to rush out but 'I'll see you when I see you' emerged. She waited for an age then went forward and kissed him on the cheek.

He gripped her hard to him and whispered, 'I love you,' in a ragged voice.

'Good,' she said. ''Cos I love you too.'

She was exhausted as she walked down the drive. She looked to the right and saw Peter loping along. She waved and let the day brighten.

Ruth slept late and woke with a furry tongue and an overwhelming feeling of doom. She had dreamt that she was awake but couldn't open her eyes, even though she knew there was someone in the room and she had to see to be able to protect herself. Then it came to her that the other person was Greg and she didn't want to be at his behest without full command of her senses. She was trembling in fear of an unseen but known presence. Why was he so threatening to her? She tried with all her sleepy strength to waken but could not. The heaviness was too much and as she gave up she thought, well, he's fond of me, so what could possibly go wrong?

She was pinned to the bed, shaking, as she slowly swam to consciousness, yearning to sleep off the dream for another two hours, at least. Charlie and Kate were breakfasting cheerily in the kitchen below and that comfort allowed her to turn on her side and drift off again. This time the sleep was uneventful. When she finally made it as far as the kettle, groggy and stupid with too much rest, a note propped against it announced, 'On roof.' She loaded a tray by rote and went to the garden. Charlie and Kate were prone in sunloungers.

'The Kraken is amongst us,' her sister intoned.

'Shuddup.'

'Hope you brought biccies.'

'You may not live long enough to find out.'

'Ah, the sweet harmony of a family together again,' Charlie noted.

'You're not above a smack either,' Ruth growled.

'Sore head?' Charlie enquired.

'No, Mr Smug. Bad dream, is all.'

'Diddums.' Kate got a bread roll on the noggin for that.

'I thought life couldn't improve, but now a bitch fight on my own roof. I'm in heaven.'

'Sisters, too,' Kate pointed out.

'At no extra charge. Thank you, Lord.'

'I'm off for a shower,' Ruth conceded, unable to join their level of joviality.

Charlie was about to comment but left the thought in the ether.

The long driveway into Parklands was pleasant, fringed with flowering shrubs bursting with cheer. The Rose of Sharon was a major contender.

'I love the yellow, but it's an awful bully in a garden,' Joyce said, for conversational noise as much as information. 'Still, I suppose that is its job.'

'Pretty,' Tom agreed. 'Or should that be pretty dreadful?'

She appreciated his attempt at normality and forged what she hoped would pass as a smile. She suspected her face had merely distorted.

They found a parking space without difficulty.

'No great rush on today,' Tom said, looking at the handful of cars.

They dallied in their seats, looking around.

'We better get a move on,' he said, after a century.

'Are you sure you're all right with this?' Joyce asked, immediately feeling like a right thick. She didn't want to give him a way out, or they were lost.

'You know I am. I'm terrified too, but I have to do this. I know that. The alternatives are unthinkable.'

In his traitorous heart a pain emerged as a paean for his great days in love with alcohol. He would never truly lose that. Only conquer the craving. That was the hope. He knew he was a strong man, apart from one important aspect of his life. The very one he now had to tackle and vanquish. Terror stirred in his veins. When the inevitable could be put off no longer, he got his bag from the back seat and let his wife link him to reception. They were bent in regret and trepidation.

Ruth was beginning to see Charlie's house through new eyes. It seemed the first time she had noticed that the kitchen and living areas were an open space, the entire length and breadth of the first floor, and filled with books. It must have seemed odd to him that she'd never commented on it, and her a writer. The furniture was modern and sleek, yet comfortable, in creams with splashes of colour. Kate was scanning one of the multiple shelves.

'I thought blokes were supposed to be phobic about having things in order,' she said. 'I can't detect a plan here.'

Charlie looked sheepish. 'It's my new addiction, buying books. Eventually I'll get around to reading all of them. But I've never obsessed on alphabetical order, which is odd for someone as compulsive as I am. I guess I don't have a system, I have a problem.'

'You certainly like Jane Austen, and she's all in one place.'

'Oh, yes, Ms Austen is special.'

Ruth remembered a section of *Pride and Prejudice*, the culmination of Lydia and Wickham's liaison: 'His affection for her soon sunk into indifference; hers lasted a little longer.' Greg Deegan and Ruth Treacy, so many years later. Was anything in life new, or was everything a repeat of the same mistakes? History might echo the errors but if it tried to teach a lesson, who paid attention and learned what could so easily be avoided? What was the line from *Macbeth*, a play she was forever hammering into her pupils? 'And all our yesterdays have lighted fools / The way to dusty death.' It was all folly, ultimately, that tale told by an idiot, 'signifying nothing'.

'Time to get you out for a tripette, young sister. There's far too much going on in that head of yours, and not enough getting out. I fancy the seaside, for I do like to be beside, and so on. You have five minutes.'

Joyce sat crying onto the steering wheel of her car. She had driven a mile from Parklands so that no one could see her, especially Tom. She had been so up, so positive, as they checked him in (easier to call it that than 'admitted him') and he had matched her mood. He was shaking with the effort, she was very still and deliberate; how, she didn't know, when inside she was churning and shattered.

She tried to remember how the problem had escalated. Tom had never been a drinker before their marriage. They were under no more pressure than any other farming couple in the area. Outside factors were at a minimum. It was a disease he suffered from, that's what the counsellor had said as she left the clinic. It happened to the best of people and the worst, an equal opportunities destroyer. No one was to blame. Right now, she wouldn't have minded a scapegoat. Right now, she wanted to beat the living daylights out of someone or something. Right now, she wanted her husband back and her life restored to the normal tumult of a family growing old together. And weirdly, right now, she'd have loved a gin and tonic. She wiped away her tears and turned the car for home, where she ate half a packet of digestive biscuits and went to bed to sleep for as many hours as her battered body wanted. As she drifted off she was accosted by the thought that no matter which man she had chosen, she would have had to deal with an alcoholic. Equal opportunities again.

Back at Parklands her husband slept too, but with less incident; he was drugged to his eyeballs and, in this way, content.

They sat in the sand, licking ice creams.

'You're wondering how I ended up here,' Ruth said. 'Bet you are too.'

Ruth allowed herself a laugh. 'Yup.'

'OK. Let's go back to Mammy and Daddy dying.'

'I miss them.'

'No shit, Sherlock. Me too.'

A teenage girl lay on a towel close by, ears swathed in headphones, her Walkman hissing forth sibilance and rhythm. Occasionally she let out a yelp in time with the music. Her eyes were closed and she shook her head from side to side. Kids ran around after balls and frisbees, and competitive dads tried to outdo one another at beach football.

'Should they not be at work?' Ruth wondered aloud.

'The sort of laissez faire attitude that has the Celtic Tiger flailing. Sure look at me, for God's sake, skiving off. The country is in a state of chassis, as someone once had it.'

'Sean O'Casey.'

'Righto, teach. To be fair, it is holiday season, so they're entitled to be off having a good time.'

'We had some great holidays with Mam and Dad.'

'Certainly did. I'd be hard pushed to pick a favourite.'

Ruth had demolished the ice cream and was now biting off the end of the wafer cone and sucking out the delicious remainder through the bottom and crunching the rest, so dangerously close to becoming soggy. Timing was everything and she hadn't lost it yet. Way to go!

'Charlie says you're angry.'

'Could you blame me?' No point in beating around whatever bush was adjacent.

'What exactly are you angry about?'

'I feel like I had no time to apologise for my . . . behaviour. And I know that it's a lot to do with me and my disappointment in myself and the way I . . . behaved. I don't know what to do to make retribution, and I can't with Mammy and Daddy 'cos . . . well . . .'

'And you don't know how to make it up to yourself?'

'Probably not, no. I've let us all down.' Her head sagged.

'You almost sound sorry for yourself.'

'If you're trying to needle me, it's working.'

'Fact: I had the bereavements too. And though I am in bits, I didn't disappear off the face of our known earth. Either I'm an unfeeling bitch or that's not all that's upsetting you.'

'Kate, I just can't, don't, want to remember what tipped me over the edge.'

'I'm gonna take a wild guess here and suggest Greg Deegan.'

The smell of dripped ice cream on her face was souring quickly and she wanted to leave. The sun was too bright, too hot. The situation was too tense. Her throat constricted and her breath refused to follow regulation. The tish of the Walkman became waspish and chased around her.

'I have to get back,' she wheedled.

'We're not letting this go indefinitely,' Kate said. 'So don't think I'm going to forget about it or let you off the hook. Until you confront this, you're not much use to anyone, least of all yourself.'

'Great to have a vote of confidence,' Ruth muttered, too low for her sister to hear.

'You're welcome.'

Ruth kicked her way along the beach back to the car, lifting the sand, choking herself. The usual self-destructive nonsense, she thought. That historical aspect, chasing her still. It depressed her to think that only the past existed, full of sorrow and joy, the pendulum swinging to favour one or the other according to the individual's season. The past would get them all, and cherry-picking highlights only served to delay the unpalatable. Might as well wallow in the muck, pig out.

She shouldn't have been surprised at the note. The cowardliness of it suited him. Even without reading it she knew what she'd find. He felt they were better off not seeing one another for a while; she had issues to 'work out' and he, graciously, acknowledged that perhaps he did too. Best leave it for the summer; in brackets read 'for ever', she knew. She sat in her alien apartment, parentless and ashamed. It's a glorified bedsit and he's left me in it to stew and stagnate. I've let him isolate me from everything precious in my life and now I've been dumped. A howl built up inside her. I don't belong here, it started to yell. She didn't want to hear it.

She sat for hours at the tiny Formica table, so expertly

chosen by some anonymous architect to suggest sixties chic, and amplify a sense of space where there was hardly any. She stared at the note, hastily scribbled on a spare piece of copybook, dumbly waiting for the words to change. Finally she roused herself to action. I have to see him, she decided. If I can see him, I can talk sense into him. This cannot be allowed to end like this. She listened to that thought and set forth.

In retrospect, she wished she'd let it trickle away.

Twenty-Two

When they reached town again Kate wanted to see the sights. Ruth confessed to having holed up in Finn's for the most part and so was nearly as strange to Kilbrody as her sister. They wandered by the supermarket and the gate leading to the lone hotel, the Travellers' Rest, an uninviting, one-star affair that always truthfully announced vacancies on its battered sign. Several benches were dotted along the banks of the river and they sat on one by the bridge, shallow cascades flowing beneath. Silver flints of water danced over the stones, gurgling busily as they rushed by. The air smelt fresh after the dull heat of the seaside sun.

'How are you feeling now?' Kate asked.

'I get the impression that you mean in general as much as at this very minute.' She was buying time, but it couldn't go on indefinitely. 'I don't know what's come over me lately. I'm just so aimless. I don't know what it is I want, or hope for. Everything seems somehow futile.

That's the general overview. But day to day, I'm enjoying being here, on a basic level. I like the work. I like Charlie. I like some of the locals. It's not the worst.'

'Have you come from the worst? Is that what you're running from?'

'Maybe.'

'What possessed you to bolt?'

'Greg was involved, all right. I remember arranging to meet him and having too much to drink. We had some sort of row and then I turned up here. Beyond that is a bit of a mystery, but not one I seem to want to unravel in a hurry.' She closed her eyes and listened to the river's music. 'Do you think Mammy and Daddy died worried about me? Did I make them unhappy in their last days?'

'All they ever wanted was for you and me to be happy. So it wasn't any new worry, if that's what you mean. They wanted us there to help them in the end and we were. We should be glad about that.'

'I still feel shitty about it all.'

'That's understandable. I do myself.'

'Really?' She was genuinely astonished. 'What have you got to feel bad about?'

'Oh, the usual bollocks we whip ourselves with. Did I tell them I loved them enough? We never did go in for that much in our family. I look at Lar's lot and they're forever hugging and kissing one another. It makes me feel a bit frigid.'

'I know exactly what you mean.'

'They were very proud of you being a teacher.'

'And they were thrilled that you have your own business.'

'I suppose death puts too much pressure of perspective on those left behind. Makes you wonder what it's all about, what's your part in the cosmic scheme of things, and whether you're worth the skin you stand up in or the air you're breathing. The Big Stuff. It doesn't help that none of us is getting any younger.'

'Mmm, my regular hairdresser tells me I have grey hairs out back.'

'I only mentioned that because you dragged it out of me. And they are really, really sparse, unlike my own thriving colony. It's as well I employ a brilliant colourist.' Kate sighed dramatically, then realised that Ruth wasn't paying much attention. 'Ru?'

'Sorry to seem melodramatic but I don't feel I have anything to show for my life so far. I think that's the root of my problems.'

'Everyone feels that way at some time or another.'

'Even Mammy and Daddy?'

'Probably. Although they had us.'

They looked at one another and exchanged a weary smile.

'What a legacy,' Ruth said.

Tom Long had the feeling he wasn't at home but it was impossible to wade past the wall of sleep hemming him in to check on his whereabouts. The colour yellow clung to his limited vision and he heard Joyce say it was a bully. It looked beautiful to him. He clucked his mouth, trying to ask for water but the effort was beyond him. His head filled with the sounds of faraway voices, wheels turning, metal clanking. His body was pleasantly wallowing in paralysis. No need to fight this. No point. He began to let go. Yellow's fine, he wanted to say, it's happy, it's hopeful.

They went to McGrath's Medical Hall to get after-sun for Kate. McGrath's was a typical country pharmacy, selling everything from penicillin to worm drench, to gold jewellery guaranteed to turn your neck, ears and wrist green. Deborah was on duty. A mountainy hulk was standing at the counter, bewildered, holding a four-pack of Duracell.

'No, love,' he boomed. 'I said Durex. It don't need batteries at all, at all.'

Deborah set about correcting her mistake.

Linda glided in, cleverly disguised in the darkest pair of shades since Jackie Onassis was on the American throne. She affected not to know anyone, so it was with added pleasure Ruth heard Deborah disgrace her. Linda proffered a tube of Preparation H for payment and packaging.

'Did you know,' Deborah asked as loudly as usual, 'that some people use this on their eyes?'

'It *is* for my eyes,' Linda sissed.

Ruth found herself hiding behind a carousel of sunglasses and stuffing a fist into her mouth.

'Is she for real?' Kate whispered.

Ruth nodded. 'Isn't she the greatest?'

'You'd want to be careful with that or you could blind yourself. The applicator is very pointy, so it is. You'd have your eye out before you could say—'

Kate sallied forth. 'Linda, how are you?' She raised her eyebrows in perfect pseudo shock at the purchase. 'Oh, I am sorry, what a nasty thing to have. Ruth, come say hello and sympathise with poor Linda.'

Joyce stood at the entrance to her kitchen garden. There were early plums ripe against the wall, hanging dangerously close to a fall and ruination. She grabbed a wicker basket for her harvest and began to think what she might do with the surplus. Tom liked her recipe for plums poached in cider, but that would obviously have to change. It was time to experiment with unfortified apple juices. It was time to change a lot of things in the Long household to reflect the altered dynamic, and the plums were one of the easiest areas to adapt. These are opportunites for change, she told herself, not impositions. Change must be embraced, she intoned, like a party mantra. How very jingoistic and what a bag of horseshit, but if it helped to get by, she'd mouth the platitudes. She bit into the fruit and

255

wondered why it needed alcohol to heighten the taste at all when all the intoxication needed was within its purple skin. These are the facts of life, she thought; the birth, death and regeneration in a garden, the gifts of the earth and how we accept them. They deserve respect, and so do we. In spite of the whiff of patchouli and New Age she was giddy for a moment and that helped her on to the next.

Linda was hopping mad as she burst into the library. She would dance on those bitches' graves yet. The crashing through the doors managed to create a breath of wind in the interior doldrum. Carol looked up and put her finger to her lips to shush the intruder. Her face could not hide surprise.

'Don't you start, I'm in no mood,' Linda snarled. 'Where's the author index?'

Carol was genuinely taken aback. Linda never expressed an interest in any publication that wasn't weekly, glossy and needlessly expensive. Carol pointed at a computer nearby. Her friend's nails raked across the keypad clicking out a name: Treacy, Ruth. No match in the Kilbrody repository, so she searched further, and further, glowing with each no show. Oh, the sweetness of the technological age.

'I'm doing this for you,' she assured Carol, who stood over her shoulder, perplexed. 'In fact, I don't know what's taken me so long.'

The Woman on the Bus

The computer screen reflected Linda's face in a portrait of misanthropy. Carol was uncomfortable with the image and wondered might it be time to find other friends in the neighbourhood. She needn't be shackled to Linda for ever. She thought about Charlie Finn, who would be great company and a catch to boot. It was time to redouble her efforts in that camp but, if she was honest, she'd have to admit that they had no chemistry. There was another in town who would be most acceptable, if she could make a little more progress. She'd bedded him, but would she wed him? Her mind wandered over the naked body of Bert Folan.

The Youth Project group sat on the wall enjoying a break. Each had a glow looking at the churchyard with its neat verges and trimmed grass. Miss Cahill explained that they would chronicle the gravestones next and enter the details in a special register. She even had a plan to mount an exhibition of photographs, before and after, and montages of information gleaned from the work.

'What about the very old stones?' Cathy asked.

'We'll do rubbings of those and see what turns up. And hopefully we'll be able to connect families in the area with our findings. It'll make quite a stir and you should all be proud to be part of the most significant piece of detective work in the region for years.'

Cathy felt a tingle in her bones at the prospect of meeting and greeting her ancestors. She would unearth the families from which she came. She might make some new friends amongst the noble dead. It would be interesting to know where they came from, and might give a pointer to where she was off to. She said as much to Peter.

'You're getting soft in your old age,' he remarked.

Cathy paid no mind to the note of cynicism. She allowed herself to feel good about life and death and all the people involved in between. Her dad was safe where he could get help, her mother and herself could look after anything else; invincibles against adversity. There was hope. I might be getting soft, she thought. Well, whatever, she'd give it a try for now.

She felt eyes on her back and looked to find the woman off the bus staring at her. Oh no, now she was speaking to her, low, like she didn't want anyone else to hear.

'Hi there, Cathy. I know this is going to sound a bit mad, but is there any chance that I could have seen you on the evening I arrived?'

Cathy shot her a speciality blank face but the woman was determined to be persistent.

'It's just that I think I remember seeing you from the bus and, I know this'll sound totally off the wall, but I thought you were, well, barking as we went by.'

Cathy laughed in spite of herself and therefore felt

obliged to tell the truth. 'Our dog, Dennis, used to salute the bus on its way in and out of town and after he died I kept it up. Dunno why.'

'A testament to his memory.'

If Ruth Treacy had detached herself to look around she would have seen the layers of testimony, living and dead, that surrounded and included them. The signs were always there to be seen or interpreted as required. The only question, how much could ever be believed?

'Where will any of this get us?' Carol implored Linda.

'It'll expose that jumped-up little arriviste for the fake that she is.'

'All it'll do is cause bad feeling. And for all we know she writes under a pseudonym.'

Linda's eyes narrowed at the possible fissure in her masterplan.

'It's common in the book world,' Carol insisted, seeing the chink in her friend's armour.

Linda's nails drummed the desktop like a raptor weighing up the pros and cons of the hunt. She was not happy to hear doubts. She just *knew* Ruth Treacy was a liar and false, through and through. It would be a pleasure to tell the world. For now, she would merely toy with the blow-in, gathering further details, but her time would come and she would see the nuisance off. It wouldn't take long. And that would teach her and her poxy sister to cross Linda Meehan. Carol, to the side still, could have sworn that Linda's eyes turned red briefly and, scarily, they suited her like that.

Ozzy was hoping for a breather, relief from the grief of his domestic scene, or scenes to be more accurate. Fiona was in a strop over her incarceration in Surf 'n' Turf, even though she was on a wage, and her mother wanted to go shopping for a weekend, to Paris of all places. When Ozzy pitched for Cork, and then Dublin, he was mocked like a halfwit applying to join Mensa. It also became clear that Ozzy was not required on the journey. To cap it all, the O'Briens had restarted their campaign for the new bungalow, no matter that he'd told them it was never going to happen. He needed the calm of watching the town from afar. It was often good to know that others were worse off.

He roamed like a mobile phone on holiday. Tom Long was banged up in the drink tank so his wife was run off her feet. Linda Meehan was in a snit over something judging by the speed she travelled over to the library in her (very) high heels. She must have a powerful sense of balance, Ozzy thought, like a circus acrobat. The Treacy girl and her sister were wandering like two lost souls. And Bert Fahy was still up to something but Ozzy couldn't get a good look at what. It involved a member of the opposite sex; that was all Ozzy could make out. Opposite sex? Impossible sex, Ozzy decided. He lay in the shade of the old chestnut tree in the churchyard and allowed himself forty winks, with his binoculars cradled like a precious offspring and the distant yells of the Youth Project lulling him to sleep.

Twenty-Three

Cathy wasn't happy to see Peter's dad planted in their kitchen when she got home for tea. In fact, she was furious. Her father was hardly warm in his clinic bed and this guy waltzed in and got his feet under the table.

'Harry, this is my daughter Cathy.'

'Hi there, good to meet you,' the man said, extending a hand.

As if, you creep. Cathy ignored him and his scummy mitt. And anyway what ancient and out-of-date custom was that to offer her? The 'adults' exchanged one of their supposedly adult looks, the one that read 'she's going through an awkward phase'. Her face boiled with the sheer presumption of them. Peter coughed lightly and asked if she wanted to go play some music or a computer game. She had forgotten he was with her.

'No. I want to know how my father is.' She pointed

the question directly at her mother but it was clearly meant for Harry too.

'He's fine, sleeping a lot. We might be able to see him in a few days.'

'I miss him.'

'I know, so do I.'

She couldn't bear her mother's long-suffering tone. 'Oh really?' she sneered.

'Cathy . . .' But she had stormed out of the room before her mother got a second word out.

'Do you ever have live music in the pub?' Kate was asking.

'Ah, that's what makes Finn's unique,' Charlie explained. 'No diddly-aye. It's a haven of peace and quiet. Besides, all the trad lads want mileage allowances now and breaks and extra-filtered air and their grapes peeled; I could go on and on.'

Ruth was lying on a sofa cooling herself with a makeshift fan folded from the local gazette. She wasn't feeling the best and put it down to the murderously close weather. It sapped her energy and left her open to brooding. She felt her life fester in her veins. Her shirt stuck to her back and her armpits oozed. She was short-tempered but trying to ignore it.

Kate sat on a high stool by the breakfast bar that divided the main living area from the kitchen. 'What about pub quizzes and the like?'

'O-ho, no, made that mistake and I couldn't believe

the fallout. There was war. I've never seen the natives so het up. It was worse than Armageddon. Feuds, schisms and near manslaughter is what the quizzes caused. I even had to bar the retelling of victories and defeats, the bad feeling ran so deep. No way, never again.' He looked shaken to remember those dark times.

'It can't have been that bad,' Ruth said, trying to make an effort to join in.

'Are you kidding? I still get oddballs coming in with an encyclopaedia to prove they were robbed of some crucial point and due a prize. Round here the winning is everything, doesn't matter if it's beating a speeding fine or making sure your kid collects the most at Halloween.'

Charlie peeled cloves of garlic and pounded them into a paste with cumin and coriander and a range of other mysteries. He'd announced a night of Indian cuisine and universal chat. Did he have another romantic adventure relating to that? Ruth wondered. She shifted uncomfortably on the couch. While the many dishes cooked, he'd relieve Deborah for a break, then she'd go back on duty for the night. He was whistling again, which even he noticed this time. He was aware of a silly grin on his face too and he really didn't care who saw it.

'Is it not costing you a fortune having us around?' Ruth worried.

'It makes a pleasant change. Besides, Deborah tells

me she needs the extra cash but she's very circumspect as to why. I can't wait to find out.'

The meal was interminable. It riled Cathy to hear her mother fawn all over this smoothie, and she didn't care who knew it, including Peter. He was a good guy, but his dad was a lowlife. And a chancer. What sort of man rushed in and put the moves on a sick man's family? Here he was, eating their food, telling tall tales about his work while her mother took it all in, impressed by this . . . this bullshit. Cathy nearly choked on her lasagne. If she hadn't been so famished after the hard day at the project, she'd have gone on hunger strike.

'Joyce tells me your birthday is soon. What age will you be?'

'If you know it's my birthday, then I'd say you know what age I'll be too.'

'Cathy, if you can't keep a civil tongue in your head, you should go to your room.'

'I will,' she shouted. 'I can't stand any more of this crap anyhow.' She ran from the kitchen, indignation and tears fighting for control. She threw herself onto her bed and the tears won.

The kitchen heard the sound of a hi-fi cranked to deafening proportions and the house shook. The racket stopped after one unidentifiable track, the point having been made.

* * *

Charlie had laid on some beer for the Treacys and it made Kate come over all philosophical. She chewed on a lamb biriani and wondered, 'Are we defined by our names?'

'Have you added something hallucinogenic to this?' Ruth asked.

'Not that one. The mushrooms are in the vegetable korma.'

'Take Charlie for instance.'

Charlie groaned. 'How did I know we would?'

'It conjures up dodgy car dealers or prats who'd pull a girl's hair and run off.'

'Let's hope we're not defined by a name, then,' he suggested. 'Though there's also the druggie connection. I believe I'm expensive but buzzy.'

'In that context,' Ruth teased.

He indulged her with an amazing display of eyebrow work. A girl could fall, she knew.

'Of course, a surname is a different yoke. It comes with all the "are you one of the Ballydehob Treacys?" And suchlike.'

'*Suchlike?* You're definitely trolleyed, or out of it,' Ruth said.

'I'll give you the surname point,' Charlie agreed. 'I'm known and judged in Clare long before I'm met, with the name Finn. It's the way of things. That's not to say that people don't change, they do, and maybe that's our little legacy to the family name, to have introduced a blip in the characteristics along the lineage.'

'People can change, can't they, break out?' Ruth posited, quietly.

'Of course,' Charlie said. 'It would be a sorry state of affairs if we couldn't.'

'Kate,' Ruth mused. 'It says to me fiery, like in *The Taming of the Shrew*, and straightforward.'

'Mmn, but not boring, like, or too steady or steadfast?'

'Ah no.'

'Ruth, now, what's all that about?'

'I think it sounds euphonic,' Charlie ventured.

Ruth liked the sound of that, which was entirely the point of the word and it made her smile to return to thinking this way, to play with the tools of her trade.

'Do you remember the time we looked you up in the dictionary, wondering if you were an abbreviation of something else?'

While her sister wittered on, the words sank coldly into Ruth's mind: 'an abbreviation'. Was that how best to describe her, an abbreviation of the woman she was expected to be?

'Very interesting,' Kate said, mouth full. 'We found Ruthenium, which is a metallic element used to increase hardness, and the symbol is Ru, which is my name for little sis. Gives a whole new meaning to ru-ful.'

'No it doesn't,' Ruth mocked. 'It just means you can't spell.'

❈ ❈ ❈

Cathy heard the guests leave and waited for her mother's footsteps to make their way to her room. Instead she was left to wait till the kitchen was cleared and the dishwasher loaded. Then her mother obviously went to check on the poultry and tidy around the yard. It was an agonising delay and one that she knew her mother was deliberately inflicting. Cathy was up to high doh by the time the gentle knock came on the door. Two could play this game. She didn't answer.

'Cathy,' her mother called, entering to sit on the edge of the bed.

Cathy buried her face further into the pillow, aware that her eyes were like golf balls and her face blotched with crying.

'I hope you're feeling a bit more reasonable now.'

Cathy balled her fists at her mother's sheer cheek. Reasonable, my arse. I'm not the one who needs to be reasonable. I'm not the one flaunting myself around the parish.

'I think you jumped to a wrong conclusion earlier. Adults can have friends that are just that, friends. Harry is someone to talk to and have a bit of a laugh with, that's all. It so happens that he's a man, and a fine one. But he's not trying to be your dad or to take your dad's place. Nor would I want him to.'

Cathy was now close to apoplectic. Her mother had actually taken time out to tell her this, as if she was a child that needed placating. She was ruffled all right, but with right on her side, even if no one else could see it. She hated Harry for what he'd caused. She would never speak to him again, not even if she was paid to. And she didn't care whose father he was.

Her mother left but Cathy's rage was unabated. She wanted to lash out. She thumped her pillow in frustration and screamed into its absorbent heart. It felt good, so she repeated herself until she was spent. She was asleep before the last blow met its target.

'Thinking alert, thinking alert,' Kate said, pointing at the sombre Ruth. 'Brood incoming.'

'I'm tired,' Ruth insisted. 'This hot weather is very sapping.'

Charlie took her side and waylaid Kate with a question about nature versus nurture with respect to hairdressers. It was way too silly to be taken seriously and they delved into a kooky spiel of total rubbish. Ruth took her opportunity to escape to the loo.

She listened to the merry sounds at the dining table. She wanted to be lifted by them, but she was still uneasy at the chemistry between her sister and Charlie and distrustful of the comfortable situation she had landed in. Her face stared back from the bathroom mirror. It was a more relaxed and bronzed one than had arrived on the bus with her, but the eyes still had a look of darkness about them and a wariness, waiting to be pulled up.

We are defined by our actions too, she thought. And if that was so, she wasn't very prettily represented by her back catalogue. She had brought shame on herself and her family, whose name identified her and her tribe. She was a disgrace. She had lied and, therefore, cheated. Byron said a lie was 'the truth in masquerade' and she wished it could be passed off so easily; precocious wit counteracting the wrong involved. In Shakespearean parlance she was responsible for 'the lie with circumstance' and 'the lie direct', a number of times over. None of it was the stuff of valour and pride. Trust her profession to fire up these gems. Deserved, too, as she never stopped badgering her students to apply what they learned in class.

'Stupid, stupid, stupid,' she told the reflection.

It didn't answer back. Worse, it didn't contradict her.

Linda was holding as much court as Deborah would allow. No doubt about it, the woman could cast a shadow on the brightest scene. Deborah was unsure if she had the power to throw the shrew out. She had barred a few, young latchikos from Ballyvaughan, once, but that was an exceptional case and wouldn't wash as an example to be followed. Nor was Deborah blind or heedless of the action between Charlie and Linda, bad cess to it. She was busy serving a tidy crowd and couldn't halt all of scold's assaults on the absent Ruth.

'I'm simply asking has anyone ever heard of her as a

writer or, better again, read one of her books?' She sipped her vodka tonic daintily. 'That's if these books exist at all.' She gazed around, innocently. 'I can't seem to locate one, and no bookseller seems to have heard of her.'

'She has a notebook,' Old Mikey offered in mitigation.

Deborah wanted to say 'hear hear' but thought it inappropriate.

'It's just very, very strange,' Linda purred. 'Don't you think?'

Twenty-Four

Tom Long pushed through the treacle of sleep to an unfamiliar room. He was sure he'd heard the clanking and hum of voices before; it was the sound of working corridors.

'Welcome to Parklands,' said a cheery voice.

It belonged to a young man in a white coat standing by the bed.

'Hello,' Tom croaked, trying to sit upright. He was parched and reached for a glass of water. His mouth was so tight and dry he could only sip the contents.

'You've been out for a day, but it's good to have you back. I'll just check your blood pressure and so on, then you can head to the dining room for breakfast. Take it easy on the solids today, you haven't had any for a while.'

Longer than you know, Tom thought.

When the medical business was done Tom pulled a light robe over his pyjamas and hobbled out. He stopped every few steps to stem nausea and faintness. His head throbbed and his knees buckled. His hands shook as they reached out to lean on the shiny cream wall. They looked thin and bony, the veins standing blue-proud against the parchment-yellow skin. He needed more water, and something sweet. He craved sugar.

The dining area was bright, noisy and very warm. It housed a large communal table, at which various inmates sat and talked. There was a minuscule frisson of interest as he entered, but not enough to stop the breakfast activity. Tom poured tea and put one triangle of bread on a plate. He chose a chair at the quiet end of the table facing the window, and sat to spoon three sugars into his mug and slather his bread with butter and jam. The sweetness made him close his eyes with pleasure. He sipped his tea steadily and waited a while before repeating the bread routine, trying to mind the warning about too much too soon. No one bothered him with questions. They had time, he knew, he wasn't going anywhere for a while. Outside in the gardens a yellow Rose of Sharon waved to him. He smiled weakly back.

Ruth wakened to a time warp. Charlie and Kate were still talking in the living room below her. She checked the clock. Surely they hadn't stayed up all night? If not, why was she always the last to get going of a morning? She felt a hundred years old and lay for ten minutes allowing her eyes to close and switch off at will, until the rest of her body protested that it needed to be seen to.

She purged herself in a hot shower, scrubbed teeth and splashed cold water on her face. She consulted her reflection. It was looking happier than last night. Her hair was getting longer and she could see some dark root taking hold. It pleased her. Time was passing and her body was regenerating. She treated it to a general pamper with some body lotion Kate had brought. It had a citrus waft and she felt zingy as she chose a bright turquoise top and white capri pants. Blue shoes with white polka dots called to her and she didn't ignore them. She even added a blue scrunchy to her hair and bounded out to meet the folks.

Charlie and Kate had changed clothes, so chances were they had slept too, rather than pull an all-nighter discussing the meaning of life. She dismissed the horror that they might have shared the same bed.

'The last little orphan emerges for breakfast,' Kate announced.

'Has the mocking started already?'

'Said mocking has been hurtling along at a healthy pace for an hour, my little dormouse. But nothing that can't be recapped swiftly. We three are orphans, all alone in this world.'

'Phew. When I heard "we three" I thought of the witches in *Macbeth*, which is bad luck to quote. But as we're three wretches, the curse is altogether different. Orphans, I'll give you.'

'She's taking it well,' Kate said, suspicious of the

equanimity of tone and the seeming acceptance of the orphan tag.

'I'll get used to it. After all, I've got you, babe.'

'Again with Cher. Be very, very careful,' her sister warned.

Ruth chortled, sipping an orange juice. 'You should treat Charlie to your Hubba Bubba theory.'

'The mockery baton has been passed on,' Kate commented. 'Well, it's just that I think it was invented by a chewing gum magnate with a penchant for Shakespeare, especially *The Scottish Play*. And that Hubba Bubba is a direct reference to the first few lines of the three witches.'

Charlie was stumped for a comment.

'I have to do something with my brain all day, besides talking about where other people are going for their holidays.'

Ruth considered the oddness of the morning: here they were, three people thrown together by some mad accident of fate, forming bonds and talking rawmaish. They could have been anywhere, she thought: Clare, Dublin, New York. Charlie's eyrie was an entity in itself. She said as much, using the words haven and sanctuary to tart up her theory.

'Asylum,' Charlie added to the list.

Cathy's clothes were stuck to her from yesterday's work at the churchyard and from having been slept in. She was in a foul temper and convinced that she hadn't slept well because she hadn't been under the bedcovers, or in her nightie. Her teeth were furry and her eyes felt bloated. She had a premonition that this was a bad hair day.

She snuck to the bathroom on winged heels, unwilling to draw attention before she was clean, clear-headed and decked out in fresh gear. Her mother was singing along with the radio in the kitchen. Parents didn't have the same levels of embarrassment about themselves as teenagers, but they should, she decided. Weirdly, her mum knew the words to the current chart topper. Megastrange.

'Cathy,' she heard. 'Will I pop on an egg for you?'

The woman must have ears on the doors now. And here was another aspect of the oldies, they were always 'popping'. Her mum would 'pop the kettle on' or 'pop out to the shops'. Once they popped, they couldn't stop. Thank you, I'm here all week, as Peter might say. She sagged to think of him. The plan would be not to mention last night, at all. That way it might go away. She got into her favourite jeans and a T-shirt that said 'No Problem'. It was an up move and she hoped everyone would follow the direction.

Her mother 'popped' a boiled egg in front of her.

'I didn't ask for that,' she pointed out.

'No, but I'm a mind reader and I knew you'd want it.'

Cathy did, and decided to eat it without further comment. No Problem.

'I phoned Parklands and your dad had a light break-fast today and they say he's in good spirits. I wasn't talk-ing to him, but I'll call in there later if I'm let. I'll give him your love.'

'Do, please.' No Problem.

'Peter said to tell you he'd call on the way to the proj-ect as usual.'

Cathy held her breath, waiting for more, like full match analysis of her behaviour last night. When none came, she breathed freely again. Her hair might be like a gorse bush, but the T-shirt was a winner.

'No problem,' she said.

Charlie re-read Deborah's note. She had thrust it into his hand while he was locking up the previous night. So, Linda had her claws out. He should have seen this coming a long way off. He thought he'd mention it to Kate, but not to Ruth just yet. He opened the windows and checked the stock. The elder sister appeared.

'It's still a bit smoky in here,' she commented.

'No ventilation system can deal with the dilettantes of Kilbrody when they get into their stride. And there are decades of smoking to be counteracted by that poor machine. Actually, I fitted it before the ban and nearly everybody in the town took time to slyly tell me that it was a great idea but, with the law changing, I seemed to have wasted my money. They were basically calling me a fucking eejit to my face.'

'Your feet of clay.'

'God forbid I should get ahead of myself.'

Kate ambled along the bar. She pointed and asked, 'Why the baby monitor?'

'It was for Ruth, when she arrived, so we could hear her if she woke. Deborah suggested it.'

'What a woman. The more I hear of Deborah, the more I'm convinced she's a genius. I hope you've turned it off.'

'Yes, but unfortunately not till after I got a round of applause for my life story.'

'Ooh, cringe-making.'

'There wasn't anything new in it but apparently the telling was an award winner.'

Charlie handed her the note.

'Ah.'

'She's not a writer, is she?'

'Not yet.'

'Why did she tell a lie?'

'She wanted to escape herself, even for a short time.'

'Good for her. I like the way she was thinking.'

'Foxy.'

'But now it may have come back to roost. We'd better tell her the good news.'

'She'll be devastated if you think less of her because of this.'

'I don't. It's another fascinating layer.'

❖   ❖   ❖

Cathy's toes curled at the prospect of the walk into town with Peter. She was deeply embarrassed by her actions, but only because she was misunderstood. She told herself this was everyone else's problem. They were wrong and she was, clearly, right. Like all martyrs to a cause, she would have to bear the ridicule and slights of the ignorant. She sat on the gate and watched his approach. His stroll was untroubled and she had hopes of not discussing the incident. He raised a hand in greeting and she gave one back. So far, so good. Mind you, he was far enough away for her to need a megaphone to speak to him.

'I like your hair,' he said, when he was close enough to be heard.

She searched his tone for irony, but couldn't pin any down. Her head was an explosion of curls and there was nothing she could do with it, aside from lying under a steam roller. Could he be freak enough to think it was OK? Guys were from a different planet to girls, after all.

'I prefer it straight,' she said.

'You must be mad.'

I sometimes think I am, she thought.

'How are you today?'

Uh-oh, here it comes. 'Fine. Why?'

'No reason, Cathy. It's a polite question from one friend to another.'

'My dad's doing well,' she blurted.

'So's mine, in case you're wondering.'

He gave her a light push and she half stumbled into the ditch.

'You are in such trouble,' she shouted, chasing his dust along the road.

So, Ruth Treacy had finally caught up with the woman on the bus. She read Deborah's note and sighed. 'I got a good run out of it,' she acknowledged.

'Still are getting a good run,' Charlie pointed out. 'And all you have to do now is write a book, or a poem, or make a few research notes and we can see off the begrudgers.'

She looked him square in the eye. 'Lovely Linda?'

Kate could see their expressions but didn't know their meaning. She kept out of the exchange. The gladiators paused.

'The very woman.'

'I sometimes think you might be as deranged as I am, Charlie Finn.'

'Oh, I hope so, Ruth Treacy.'

'Of all the bars in all the world . . .' Kate intoned.

'Why don't you two get out of town for the day and frustrate the literary gumshoes a little?' Charlie suggested.

'I'd like a drive around the Burren,' Kate admitted. 'It's my last day here.'

The silence was broken by Ruth's footsteps when she walked quickly from the room.

❖   ❖   ❖

Cathy's luck could only last so long. At mid-morning break Peter launched his theme. 'Dad didn't mean to upset you last night.' Bald as that.

'Right.' She wasn't going to help him along. His father's behaviour had been appalling. Putting moves on a woman in her family home, really, the nerve.

'I suppose he gets a bit lonely sometimes. But he doesn't have designs on your mum, I checked that.'

Something in his voice reminded Cathy that his mother was dead and maybe he wasn't too gone on the idea of a replacement, even one as splendid as Joyce Long.

'I had a chat with him about it.'

'They're nearly more trouble than they're worth,' Cathy said.

'Yeah.'

'He might meet someone else some day.'

'We'll deal with that if it happens.'

She'll have to be pretty damn good, Cathy realised.

'Would you let him?'

'I suppose I'd have to. And it'd probably be better if he got settled before I go into all that malarkey too.' He rubbed the inside edges of his shoes together. 'It's complicated, isn't it?'

'You don't hear me arguing, do you?'

Ruth surprised herself by avoiding a sulk. In a mood of (what she was willing to call) cheery maturity she went into McGrath's Medical Hall to buy a disposable camera 'for fun, as it says on the label'.

'Did Charlie tell you about the wicked witch?' Deborah asked.

'Yeah. Hump her and the dog she rode into town on.' She was suddenly puckish. Better to Good on the dial.

'Fair play to you. Don't forget to take lots of photos of her and maybe it'll take her soul away like the Native Americans think.'

'That'll be one dark roll of film.'

'With glowing red eyes from the poke of a Preparation H applicator.'

'I love you, Deborah.'

'I know. Sure, how could you not?' She spotted a mother and child at the sunglasses carousel. 'Be careful of the wee lad,' she warned. 'If he catches his hand in that, he could lose a finger or have his arm ripped off.'

She returned her attention to Ruth, with the look of a saint who dealt with mentally challenged simpletons all day.

Kate and Charlie were at the pub door when Ruth returned, waving her purchase. She found their worried faces gratifying.

'Hi there. Didn't bother throwing myself into the river. I bought this instead to record our adventures and to have pictures to cheer us through the lonely winter evenings back home.'

It was her first mention of leavetaking. Charlie's heart skidded and lurched. Was she going with Kate the following day? He heard a click and realised she'd taken a photo at the very moment his face had fallen. He felt ridiculous. He knew she'd leave sometime. All it involved on his end was returning to a regular routine, and there was nothing wrong with that. Was there?

Twenty-Five

Visiting Parklands had to be like visiting prisoners in jail, Joyce thought. There were rules. She couldn't bring sharp objects, for obvious reasons regarding their lethal properties. No aftershave, which had a surprising amount of alcohol in its ingredients, she discovered, and was therefore also harmful. Mouthwash was suspect and belts were frowned on and, until they could be proved innocent of charges, they stayed outside too. She did take some of the poached plums and if Tom ate them soon, the sugar wouldn't get a chance to ferment into any of its stronger cousins.

It was an 'us' and 'them' situation and she was 'them'. She was one of the untarnished, the uninfected. There was almost an air of superiority about the inmates, as if their addiction had given them a nobler suffering. She wanted to laugh in their faces for that. I've suffered too, she could tell them, just as much as the alcoholic. With every suspicious glance she felt like yelling, 'It's no great elevation to admit that you're an alcy.' She was surprised at how uptight she was by the time she got into the garden for a walk with Tom. She was resentful too.

'They don't mean it,' he told her. 'It's a way of getting by. We grasp at anything we can.'

'So you're in the "us" camp too.'

'Of course I am,' he said. 'I'm here to be treated.'

The statement lacked complete honesty but, after denial for so long, they would take this in baby steps. She bit her tongue and remembered Charlie's achingly slow progress. It had the feeling of being slapped hard and kissed lovingly all at once. To rush it would be to ruin it, and walk a road littered with relapse.

Tom was thin and sprouting a rugged stubble. It would be a beard before he was trusted with shaving equipment. His clothes hung loosely from his wasted muscles. She resisted hugging him and taking him away to feed him up. It would be so easy to kill someone with kindness. She was an amateur and must take a back seat. It was good to give the burden to others, people who knew what they were about. She couldn't quite reach a guilt-free zone though, and felt the knots of worry tie her innards tighter.

'You'll have your turn to tell everyone what you think of them, especially me,' he told her. 'There are group sessions with the families.' He let out a short, strangled breath. 'Christ, I'm not looking forward to that.'

They sat on a wooden bench worn smooth by legions of the afflicted.

'Everything going OK at home? On the farm?'

'Yes to both, sir. All is going to the well-oiled emergency plan. But we want you better and back as soon as possible. Even Winnie misses you.'

He crinkled his eyes, remembering their prize layer, Winnie the pooh-pooh, shittiest hen south of Sligo.

'Me and my birds.'

'We'll all be waiting for you.' She shivered, remembering Cathy and her suspicions. Had she paid too much attention to Harry? Was she taking advantage of her husband's confinement?

'Someone walked over your grave?' Tom said.

'Nah. Itchy back.'

'Here, let me scratch it. I'm still good for the odd thing.'

Joyce allowed herself to relax with her husband for the first time in months.

The sisters lay in the long grass by a ruin in Killinaboy. They had posed with the last Sheela-na-Gig in situ in the church. She was a brazen hussy of a carving, legs and pudenda spread, her presence fading with the centuries and votive touching.

'She's a symbol of fertility and wards off evil spirits,' Ruth told Kate. 'Double whammy.'

'I'd be wary of her on a dark night,' Kate admitted.

'Poor lady is nearly worn away to nothing now.'

'So would you be if you'd spent centuries in that

position. She must be a yoga genius to stay like that and not get cramp.'

'She looks happy enough.'

'It's amazing what you can get used to.'

'I miss Mammy and Daddy. I don't think that'll be easy to get used to.'

'No.'

They lay in silence, listening to the grass sway gratefully in a welcome breeze. Ruth closed her eyes and tried to picture her parents. Already their image was waning, like music disappearing into air as it's played. It worried her. Their essence was here but their physical manifestation was disappearing into ghostly shadow, a faded photograph decipherable only to those who'd seen the original print. They were evanescing. So many people and places would never know them now.

'They will through us,' Kate said. 'Or at least I think that's the general idea.'

'Jaysus.'

'Exactly.'

'I can't get my head around the thought that I will never see or meet them ever again. I keep thinking there's a chance they could come round the corner, and if they did I wouldn't be that surprised. That's how little it seems to have sunk in, in a way. It's too big a concept, too much to fathom.'

'I find it hard in the most unexpected of ways. Like

what you just said, not actually seeing them in the flesh again.'

'How long do you think the hurting will continue?'

'Ah now, Ruth, you know as well as I do, that's like asking how long is a piece of string.'

'You seem to be managing much better than me.'

It sounded like an accusation.

'Don't be ridiculous, or uppity. You know I'm devastated. I'm just not roaming the roads of Ireland howling like a banshee. I have my moments. And I never know when they'll be. It can be the strangest thing that sets me off. For instance, do you know what I think was the saddest thing about the funeral? Mind you, I'll probably choose something else next week.'

'What?'

'We didn't carry the coffin. It's mad, I know, we wouldn't have been able and we didn't want to. Lar was playing so he couldn't. I think now that there was something sad in the fact that it was distant cousins and not a brace of sons who took them out down the aisle. It's irrational and stupid and it's breaking my heart.'

Tears rolled freely along her face. Crying didn't come easily to Kate, a trait that her sister more than made up for. All through their early years Ruth was the cry-baby, as her sister was ever behind the door telling her. Now the tables were turned, but it brought no satisfaction. Ruth reached out and they held hands, tight.

❀　❀　❀

Charlie couldn't settle. It made no sense to him that in less than a fortnight his world had been turned arse over heels by an act of kindness. It was like inviting a vampire into his home, in that he was directly responsible for the fallout of the action. A stupid analogy, he knew, but he wasn't too rational in the face of current events. Ruth Treacy was leaving. She's been leaving since the day she arrived, he reminded himself. His mood darkened as Linda's shadow fell over the door.

'Dearest,' she smiled, with such a lack of genuine feeling it was difficult not to gasp. What an operator. 'I missed you last night. I had a treat lined up. I suppose I could let you have it now.' She raised a well-plucked brow as she closed the door, purposefully.

In spite of all his better urges, Charlie wanted to know what it was. She took his hand and held it between her legs. She was naked beneath her white crossover skirt.

'I started without you earlier.' She was breathing heavily now, kissing his neck and writhing on his hand. Charlie pushed her up against the bar counter. She began to laugh.

'You are so out of control,' she told him.

The effect was instantaneous. He immediately went limp. She had told the truth and he wasn't ready for it.

'Get out,' he rasped.

'My, you have got selfish. Time was when you'd make sure a girl had a happy ending. You've lost even that.'

Linda walked to the door, then stopped to deliver her

denouement. 'I'm sure you know by now that your new beloved is no writer, just some cheap fraud doing you out of the little dignity you had left.'

The echoed clacking of her heels mocked him long after she'd gone.

The Burren shone sharp in the hard, bright sunlight. It was a surrealistic image of nature bleached, seeming barren with its cloak of grey stone. But Ruth knew that just kneeling would reveal vast worlds of flora and fauna. This miracle should not host these precious visitors from other climates, but here they were, native now and feral. The impossible bloomed, exulted, in unexpected nooks. Even the bleakest of futures held rich surprises, tumbling through the cracks of missed opportunity, waiting for someone to look, notice, savour. Ruth tried to fix these thoughts for hard times when she needed succour and courage. Then, as she noticed a shapely wisp of cloud on her periphery, she turned and they vapourised. The journey continued, whether she wanted it to or not. Might as well hitch a ride.

Joyce had a special place she visited regularly. She was not the only one in town who came to this spot to pay tribute and remember. When Cathy took up her job at the cemetery, she stopped going as often, not wanting to upset her daughter, initially, then hoping Cathy would find the town secret without her intervention. Today, she didn't care so much. She carried a small bunch of flowers to the side of the old cemetery wall. Others had left floral offerings, she saw; some fresh and recent, some wilted and browning, waiting to be replaced at the next visit of a family member. And someone had once organised an unobtrusive stone sculpture to mark the patch yet avoid emphasis.

This was the plot of the little angels, the stillborn and miscarried who were not allowed interment on hallowed ground. Joyce had a sister and a son there. Every family in the parish had representatives. These were the ones the Church didn't get in time and didn't want as a result. They were the hidden, the disappeared of the generations. She laid her flowers and chatted to Bernadette and Rory. When they were up to date, she turned to leave.

Cathy was at the wall. It was time to explain.

Kate and Ruth walked the pier at Doolin.

'Am I shy?' Ruth wanted to know, thinking that might go a-ways to explaining how she was, apparently, something of a loner.

'You're reserved. When you trust someone you open up. It can be hard to shut you up then.'

'So, I'm not an utter oddball.'

'Odd, but not utterly,' Kate agreed.

'When I got here, I didn't have to worry about any of that. It was a lot more elemental, like was I in danger, what was my next move? I just let me emerge, and it doesn't seem to be the same Ruth as Dublin sees most of the time. I can't help thinking that's a positive thing.'

'And you're away from that man.'

'Greg, yes. Jeez, what was I thinking of?'

'You were flattered and lonely. It's a fairly potent combo.'

'Do I tell many lies?' Another concern, as her facility to improvise was immediate once she'd hit Kilbrody.

'You'd prefer to please people than disappoint them.'

'Oh.'

It made perfect sense, of course. She had acceded to Greg Deegan's requests, even though she hadn't agreed with all of them. She had changed, rather than disappoint him, and then let him hide her away. She was an easy conquest, pleasing him and at what a price. She didn't want to take the thoughts further, to wonder why a mature, educated woman would let this happen. That was for another day. She was still not yet ready. But she knew it was coming.

They sat at the end of the pier and watched the water try to whip up some decent waves.

Ruth pulled at her top to create a draught, redistributing the heat instead. 'It's like the whole county is becalmed,' she complained. 'It's stifling. We need a great, big, dirty storm of wind and rain. Flush out this stagnant fug.'

If she had looked to her right, she would have seen her sister's enigmatic smile.

Charlie tried to lose himself in the hot lashes of the shower. He wanted to scour off any vestige of Linda and her taunts. The phrase 'out of control' echoed in his mind, whipping him with its truth. He was towelling briskly and feeling purged when he thought of Ruth and wondered what she was washing away.

He was at the bar and still thinking of her, feeling the verge of truth beneath his skin, when Joyce Long stepped in. The day was going from bad to worse in a series of unwelcome intrusions. Great. A brigand had come in the stealth of night and branded him with the words 'welcome mat', and he was the last to notice.

As he adjusted to Joyce's presence he saw that she had company, a tall man with a weathered face. She introduced him as Harry to Charlie and Old Mikey. In keeping with the potency of local information, they knew who he was without asking for details; this had been transmitted weeks ago on bush telegraph. Charlie was beyond more than a resigned grunt as greeting. What might once have had potential as jealousy now passed into weariness at the constant battering doled out by the years and their cruel legacies.

They made a peculiar little ensemble, uneasy with their mutual company. Charlie saw a woman half-widowed by alcohol, two men who'd lost wives to life's inevitable outcome and a man cheated by himself, alcohol and love's caprice. They ordered a round of lemonade and dry-roasted peanuts.

'This is where it gets difficult,' Charlie explained, holding up a selection of bottles. 'We have a choice of white or red, slimline or regular.'

'Dammit,' Old Mikey said. 'I'm tired of watching my weight. I'll have full fat everything.'

'Good choice. I'm all out of the low-calorie peanuts.'

Harry looked puzzled.

'Joke,' Charlie told him, without the warmth.

Joyce rushed to rescue the situation. 'You're keeping your figure beautifully, for a man of your age,' she said to her father.

'I am, but it's hard work and let no one tell you otherwise.' He rolled his pot belly left and right. 'It's not easy being a babe magnet.'

'Cathy keeps him up to date with the lingo,' Joyce confirmed for Harry.

Cathy had also tried to teach her grandfather to rap but from his mouth it sounded like he was 'bustin' nursery rhymes' instead of 'hangin' with his homies'. He confessed to being a little confused about that phrase too and there wasn't a dry seat in the house when he'd finished.

When the main topic of interest could be ignored no longer, Old Mikey asked, 'How's the patient?'

Joyce felt odd discussing Tom. She wondered if it was

wrong to talk about him, and his treatment, with other people. She wondered if it would upset him. There was no ignoring the question, though. 'He's admitting he has a problem and he seems determined to change,' she managed, feeling like a traitor.

'That's great news.'

'We have a long way to go yet, but fingers crossed,' Joyce said.

She could not look Charlie in the eye, nor he her. Harry could feel the white heat between them sparking static and danger for meddlers. He guessed the rest.

The Treacy sisters stood on top of the Cliffs of Moher, taking in the enormity of the vista before them: a haze of misty-whites, abstract purples and blue vapours that had once been sea and land. The earth was a suggestion against the sky, and they were infinitesimal human dots in the ether. On a clear day you couldn't see forever, or New York, but they were out there.

'You have to hand it to me,' Ruth insisted. 'I picked one fabulous place to run away to.'

'No argument. These cliffs have got to be one of Ireland's seven wonders.'

'I'd say the country has more than seven surely.'

'But not all are as beauteous. Take Saint Patrick, who may well have been a fine thing, but he was also a Welshman, so I never count him. And we can't have the potato because it's South American, strictly speaking.'

Ruth scoffed. 'You are holding perfectly useful brain cells hostage by remembering crappy trivia like that.'

'So you say, but when you're floundering some night at a quiz, I'll be charging you for that sort of solid-gold fact.'

'Yes, Einstein.'

'Did you know that Mam and Dad came here on their first anniversary?'

'You're kidding.'

'No, it's the truth. Did you never hear them say they'd made a plan to visit a different Irish county for each wedding anniversary?'

Ruth chuckled, deep. 'Didn't they stop after they thought they'd been to all the good ones?'

'Yeah, and they wouldn't say which ones those were.'

'Diplomatic to the end. We should hope to be so gracious.'

'I think it was more that you'd never know when you'd be insulting a big Cavan lad and get a thump.'

'There's a practical streak in you, Treacy.'

'What will we do without them?'

'We'll manage, kiddo. We'll make them proud.'

Ruth's gut cramped to think of the future; it was too imperfect a tense. 'We have to decide a few things, don't we?'

'There's no rush to do anything with the house, unless you have a devilishly brilliant plan that requires immediate action?'

'Me? The one who plans to keep breathing and see what comes of that?'

'There's that practical side again. Let's not rush things. I'm happy with that.'

'Are you really going tomorrow?'

'Yes. Are you coming with me?'

The words, loaded like a gun, hovered in the stillness. Ruth was measured when she replied.

'School doesn't start for a couple of weeks yet. I may as well bide my time. The longer I'm away, the bigger the chance of growing up a bit.'

It was not lost on her that while her sister was here, she could talk out her problems and fears. She still compartmentalised, not willing to share everything, unwilling to face it all. When Kate left she would again be at the mercy of her memories and nightmares. She would be alone with herself, to face trials of her own making, and tackle the past as well as the future. The now was a limbo crunched between what was and what might be. It was a world of personal demons and unnamed fears. If she avoided it she would never go forward, but standing still was out of the question. It was time for bravery and a little spunk. She would be a Sheela-na-Gig, her wide smile welcoming all while warding off harm. She would be bold.

'At least you'll have a handy bar work reference in case you chuck the teaching.'

Ruth harrumphed. 'I'm a writer now, I don't need anything more than a Biro.'

Twenty-Six

The afternoon grew heavy and dead, thanks to the weather as well as his company, so when the lemonade party broke up, Charlie heaved relief. He saw the revellers to the door to be sure of their leaving and glanced at the sky to see why it was as moody as he was. Dark clouds matched him and he retreated, somewhat gratified that nature was feeling the same way. He wanted to be automatic again and that was difficult with Joyce in the room. He was better able to deal with the fact of her now, but it was still easier in the abstract. So, when she left, he breathed freely and treated his nearest customer to a pint.

'How did you know it's my birthday?' a bemused Whinge asked.

'I smelled a new aftershave and put two and two together,' Charlie lied.

The Whinge was not one to put a man right if it meant cutting off a nose to spite a face, particularly his own.

He allowed the ruse and enjoyed his pint. It was, after all, his special day.

'I'm celebrating by taking herself to the bingo tonight,' he confessed.

'May your luck be in,' Charlie said.

The Whinge agreed. 'That we may win the jackpot and not let it out to those hoors in Ennistymon.'

'Again.'

'Again.'

Charlie raised his Diet Coke, the Whinge his stout. The ancient foe must be vanquished. There were enemies within us, as well as at large against us, Charlie knew, often of our own encouraging. We humans were our own worst friends.

His heart gave a familiar tug as the Treacy sisters came through the door. They were flying high from their day out, chattering happily and lugging booty. It was hard to credit that the scrap who'd got off the Dublin to Limerick bus was now this happy, colourful beauty. Charlie's spirits were buoyed. So was Ruth's hair, which stood on end electrically. She rubbed it down but it sprang up again.

'It's magic,' she said.

'Ladies, you are in for a treat this evening,' Charlie announced. 'It's bingo night at the school hall.'

'Just when you think it can't get any better, it does,' Kate declared.

'Correct. Not only do you stand to win riches well

within your wildest dreams, you also carry the honour of Kilbrody with you.'

They rolled with this and accepted their mission.

'Happy birthday, Mr O'Brien,' Ruth said to the Whinge.

Charlie's forehead crinkled, the Whinge glowed. Then they heard the first rumble.

'What have you been up to out there?' Charlie asked.

Cathy was lost in thoughts of the small, unhonoured plot outside the wall when the sky began to complain. 'Sounds like it's hungry,' she said to Peter.

'Me and all.'

'Wouldn't it be great if it rained? Then I wouldn't have to kill anyone in a rage from this heat. I saw that in a movie once, an over-fifteens one.'

'Lightning would be cool too, with us in a graveyard.'

'Wild good.'

They waited for more action but it was slow to materialise. The sky was a grey blanket sucking the oxygen from the air. Cathy felt sweat roll down her back and into the crack of her bum. She didn't like that. It was clammy enough to have clothes on without reservoirs of spare liquid starting up. Bodies were mysterious and badly designed. Her feet felt moist in her trainers and she was sure there were damp patches under her arms, she could smell as much. Her hairline was drenched and she couldn't straighten up, her energy sapped by the day. All in all, murder was not a tall order.

'Are you feeling OK?' Peter asked. 'You're a bit off colour.'

'I'm fine,' she said brusquely.

Peter took his cue and closed the subject.

The sky lit up and the group held its breath, counting the miles between them and the storm centre. They got to eight by the time the thunder growled. Cathy and Peter clapped their hands as the first, fat raindrop splashed on the gravestones.

'Do you fancy taking on a mission?' she asked him.

'Sure.'

'Come with me, I want to show you something.'

Tom Long gazed at the brooding sky and waited for the inevitable. He wondered if a storm would affect this building of alcoholics like it would a madhouse? He trained his ears for howling but heard nothing beyond the usual clatter of inmates and trolleys. He sipped a heavily sugared tea and savoured the cloying sweetness. Lightning flashed. He waited. Counted to four. If the storm was headed in the direction of Parklands they were in for a good show. Joyce was terrified of thunder and lightning and usually sat in the hall cupboard with Dennis and the vacuum cleaner. She would only have the Hoover now. He might have phoned her if he'd had a mobile, but he did not. He was weary and selfish and reasoned that she could look after herself. Cathy might even be home from the Youth Project to sit with her. He moved close to the window, mindful of the danger if the storm hit. He even considered sitting under a tree in the garden. He could go down in a blaze of glory then drink his head off in that great, hereafter bar or perhaps the fiery, underworld lounge. He continued to sip his tea, slowly, waiting for nature to come and get him. He had all the time in the world.

Joyce Long was not at home. She was with Harry. He held her trembling body and whispered comfort into her ear. She leaned into his chest and breathed in his protection. He smelled of salt and lemons. It had been so long since she'd let someone care for her that she was rigid with guilt as well as fright. Harry took it to be simple terror at the impending storm. He stroked her hair and rocked them a little.

'It's OK,' he whispered. 'Everything's going to be OK.'

He loved being close to her. If Joyce had not been trembling, she might have noticed his surreptitious kisses. As it was she wanted the darkness of his embrace and the safety it offered. This was temporary, she said to herself. She would deal with any awkwardness later, when the pyrotechnics were done and her status quo was returned. She could imagine Cathy's horror and disgust at her behaviour, but she was frightened and didn't know what else to do. She blocked Tom from her mind, unable to let even the haziest of images take hold. She was a bad person. Her tremors doubled their efforts.

'Don't worry, Joyce. Everything is going to be fine.'

The storm began to roar.

Old Mikey ducked back through the door with the news that they were, in his opinion, 'in for a good one'. He propped himself up on a stool and rubbed his hands together. 'I could feel it in me joints all day. It won't last long by the look of it, but it'll be just what the doctor ordered.'

The pub phone rang and when Charlie answered, Ruth's voice said, 'Heaven to Charlie, heaven to Charlie, come in, Charlie.'

'I can't believe you're so lazy you wouldn't come down the stairs.'

'I'd only have to come back up again,' she said, 'and my legs are fecked after our travels.'

'What can I do for you?'

'I bought a Sheela-na-Gig and I was wondering if I could hang it up in the garden?'

'So it's witchcraft now. I'd better come up.'

Charlie served enough booze to keep the clientele calm, locked the till and went to see the latest woman in his household. He found himself taking two steps at a time and only just resisted the urge to whistle. He had a grin as wide as the little flat sculpture when he met her on the rooftop.

'Isn't she fab?' Ruth asked.

The first shudder issued from the clouds.

'She certainly is. I presume she's to ward off evil.' He had a vision of Linda, beautiful on the eye, poison to taste.

'I thought she could do that from up here. If we put her over the main door she might scare off customers.'

'We', she had said. His heart skipped skittishly. The weather groaned again.

'Can I put her in the Albertine over the arch there?' Ruth was indicating the access doorway.

'Sure. She'll be perfect. You know, of course, that she's a symbol of fertility too?'

'I'll take my chances.'

A bright flash lit up the sky and Ruth's face. She was smiling broadly and Charlie stopped breathing. There was a magic at work, tingling the air and his heartstrings. Eight beats later thunder cracked and Ruth laughed. She held her arms out at right angles and twirled.

'Rain, Charlie. We're finally getting rain.'

The heavy drops splashed down as he took her hands and moved close. She blinked the moisture away and pushed her wet hair from her eyes.

'What?' she asked, perplexed.

He reached to smooth the vertical lines between her eyes. 'Ruth,' he began.

Kate's voice interrupted with a jolly, 'There you both are. Isn't this exciting?' She lifted her face to the cooling sky.

But that didn't stop Charlie falling under a spell. Sheela grinned from the wall and Charlie winked at her. He gave a whoop and joined the pagan rejoicing. We have rain and I have Ruth, for now, and the storm is right over Ennistymon.

At Parklands the excitement was tangible. Recovering patients danced and shouted on the lawn and grateful staff relished the longed-for rain. Tom Long laughed and wondered why no one was trying to stop the roaring of someone in the unit. High whines and animal howls filled the corridors. They invaded his room. Why was no one doing anything? At last a white-coated doctor entered and said, 'It's all right, Tom, it's only a storm. Nothing to worry about. Hush now. It's OK.'

His was the voice crying aloud. The screams were his own.

He felt her lift his sleeve and then a slight prick as the needle broke skin. Soon he was falling into darkness. As he succumbed he said, 'Who will look after Joyce? She'll be afraid of the storm.'

'Don't worry, Tom,' the voice soothed. 'Everything's going to be all right now. Everything's going to be OK.'

Twenty-Seven

Kilbrody was filled with an hysterical relief. The damp streets glistened with residual water. Windows glittered as crystals ran along newly showered glass. Cars swished through puddles and drains led the mud, hatched of a month of dust, away to the river and on to the sea. The cascades swelled and rushed on, busy and self-important, no time to chat to the onlookers bent over the town bridge. The little river passed fields of lush greenery, exhausted with drinking and emitting pungency almost impossible to breathe.

Joyce hurried home, keeping her head down and her thoughts reined in. She was still shaky after the storm. Her nerves were tight and her mind bent on self-recrimination but she shut them out. She had done nothing wrong. A friend had consoled her when she needed it. Anything else was overactive imagination, dishing out needless guilt, and she had plenty to worry about without that. The fact that she had gone out of her way bothered her, but she had needed company and hadn't wanted to worry her father. There were gaps in this logic as wide as a nuclear crater, and about as comforting. She seemed to spend her time making excuses for everyone, including herself, and it was seriously getting her down. She ached from the tiredness of having to do everything now that Tom was in treatment. Her patience was running thin. She wanted rest. It was a lot to ask under the circumstances and that fuelled her anger. I've been faithful to others all my life, she thought, and it feels like servility. And now I'm paying the price.

Harry watched Joyce go, regretful that they parted on difficult terms. He sighed, feeling his loneliness more keenly than usual. He had grown inured to it but it still managed to sneak up on him and ambush. Life had a way of showing him what he was missing, just when he wanted to see all that he had. At least he hadn't lost a friend. He hoped. He was sorry he'd taken time off. He would go back to work tomorrow and throw himself into chasing the secrets of the sea. He wasn't doing too well on land, and maybe it was time to admit that. He wanted shepherd's pie for dinner, but Peter knew it was his comfort food so he began to prepare salad and an omelette. Another ruse, another little cheat to get by; the politics of living.

Ozzy, Father Kilcullen and Miss Cahill set up the school hall cum gymnasium for the bingo session. The ancients of Kilbrody came out of the woodwork for the event and each had their vagaries when it came to seating. Some could only have luck if they sat on a wooden chair, others favoured orange plastic, and each had a lucky table, which had to have its usual number and be placed in the correct spot in relation to the bingo caller. The configurations had to be perfect. It was a black art of a science and they dared not get it wrong or they'd have a riot on their hands.

'God willing, we'll have the jackpot home tonight,' Ozzy said.

'I have no doubt but Patch Collerane himself will be at the Lord's side this evening, encouraging Him to deliver it to us,' the priest intoned.

'He was a great man for the bingo,' Ozzy said.

'And a good Christian, may he rest in peace.'

The three crossed themselves and muttered, 'Amen.'

'And sure, what with us getting the rain and all, our luck must be in,' Miss Cahill said.

'God willing.'

They crossed themselves again and Ozzy went in search of Mrs Whinge O'Brien's lucky red cushion. He had tried to convince her to take it home for safety but as it had originated in a school nativity play she felt it would be wrong to remove it from the building and its work there. Every time he saw it used for other productions or simply to adorn a staff chair, he blanched. Today it was wedged behind a radiator in the head's office.

The Sergeant stuck his head in to say, 'Keep it clean this evening. I don't want any trouble.'

Ozzy calmed him. 'Sure everyone'll be in great form after the rain. They'll take it as a lucky sign. Are you coming along yourself?'

'I might, I might.'

Might, my rocks. Ozzy knew the man hadn't missed a session since the famine ended. He could see him now, swigging from his hip flask and sweating over the two books he liked to play simultaneously. The rookie McGowan would patrol the empty streets of the town, then collect his boss from the pub, much later, and drive him home in the squad car. It was a big night out.

Kate soaked in a lavender bubble bath and Ruth sat on the loo, top down, to chat to her.

'You should try this,' Kate said. 'It's really relaxing. My leg muscles may even unknot after all the walking. Will I leave the water in for you?'

'Nah. I'm a shower woman at the moment.' She trembled slightly, knowing that was a Deegan legacy. She felt anger rise too and took it to be a positive sign. She was fighting back. 'I'll miss you when you're gone,' she said, trying to keep bleating out of her voice.

'You'll see me again soon enough.'

'I was thinking I might move back into the house for a while, if that's OK with you. The flat has kind of lost its shine.'

310

'Not a bother.' Kate could have launched into what a shit idea she'd thought moving out in the first place was, and gone on from there, but what would be the point? She'd been caught out plenty of times expressing honest opinions and regretting them when the people on the receiving end went and did exactly what she'd been railing against. 'Will you be all right there by yourself?'

'I think so.'

'How will you manage at school?'

'You know, I have no idea. But I won't be driven out of my job just because of that bollocks Greg Deegan. It all seems hopelessly far away, though. I don't really care that much about the job or Dublin any more. It's probably because I've been away a while. I suppose I'll fall back into the groove once I get home.'

'There's no need to, Ruth. Don't throw away your new start if you want to keep it on.'

'I feel I have things to finish off. I think I have to go back.'

'Ruth, the fact is you don't have to do anything you don't want to. There's just you and me now.'

'And Lar.'

'Well, yeah, Lar, but he'll do and think what he's told.' Her sister waved a bubbly arm dismissively, then smiled. 'He's great.' She took a deep breath. 'No, what I'm saying is, in one way, maybe it's a freedom not having to think of Mammy and Daddy . . .'

Ruth was shocked. She stared at Kate, not believing what she'd heard.

'How could they not be important?' she exclaimed.

Kate sat up, bubbles snapping against her skin, water splashing onto the floor. 'No, no, don't misunderstand, they'll always be important. Always. But the person you have to worry about now is you. You don't have to prove anything to anyone but yourself. You only have to live your life for you. Do what you want, Ruth, and hang the consequences. It's what they'd want.'

Ruth gave the floor tiles a cursory wipe and left the room in a daze. She found her satchel and dug out the death certificates. She held her parents to her chest. 'Tell me what to do,' she whispered. 'Show me the way.'

Kate followed her and stood in a robe, dripping her bath on the carpet. 'Even Adam and Eve had to make a decision,' she said.

'Didn't turn out too well for them.'

'That's our faulted gift. We have a choice. We shape our own destiny.'

'You're wasted on hairdressing.'

'Au contraire, where else would I get a chance to spout my half-baked philosophies?'

'If you're experimenting on me again, I will kill you.'

'I suppose it's been a long time coming. I would point out that those home perm kits didn't come with any health warning, at that time, and I was sure the home-made moisturiser would be gentle.'

'It was a freaking, ballistic-strength exfoliator. I was flayed.'

'Oh, don't exaggerate. You were fine before the month was out.'

'Actually, I think I will kill you after all.'

Kate fled, squealing.

Ruth kissed her parents and put them back in her bag. 'We'll talk later,' she said. Then she had a thought. She opened the satchel flap and asked, 'Do you fancy a round of bingo?'

Crowds streamed across the bridge and up the slight incline to the school. It was a square concrete block, which failed to give off any discernible hint of knowledge or education. Ruth's heart sank a little, to admit she was part of this system. The building looked like a prison and in many ways it was. Tonight however it was the town mecca, and this was as good as it would ever look. Vague mutterings carried occasionally on the breeze but mostly silence was king. It gave off an odour of mystery and eeriness.

'It's like something from a zombie science fiction movie,' Kate whispered.

'That goes for term time too.'

'This is where I find out that you've been reprogrammed by aliens and you're not really my sister any more.'

They were both aware that half that statement could

be taken as true now and hoped they knew which half that was.

The queue at the entrance was moving slowly, as Ozzy took money and exchanged pleasantries with the punters. When it was their turn, he checked the numbers on the back of their books and said, 'If it's all the same to you, I'll hang on to one of these. Number ninety-four is Mrs O'Brien's favourite and it wouldn't do to upset her and her health in the state it's in.'

'That's fine, Mr O'Reilly,' Kate said.

'Oh, Ozzy, Kate,' he insisted, showing crimson dots on each cheek. 'May you both have luck.'

Ruth felt a sharp elbow in her side as a surprisingly robust Mrs Whinge pushed past and snaffled book number 94. She thrust a ten-euro note at Ozzy and was gone without an 'excuse me' into the maw of the hall. Already it was foggy with cigarette and pipe smoke.

'The Sergeant gives the place a smoking dispensation for the night. Same as mental hospitals have all year round.'

Sweet wrappers crackled and soft drinks were slurped. Pens were lined up on tables and clipboards produced by the businesslike gamblers of Kilbrody.

'They take it very seriously,' Ruth said, taking money from her satchel and paying for herself and Kate.

Ozzy nodded. 'Well, of course they do. It's bingo.' He turned to the next customers and the sisters stepped into the arena.

Every table seemed taken. They hovered close to the refreshment counter, wondering where to sit. Kate took the opportunity to buy two Cokes and a packet of Maltesers. Old Mikey materialised and ushered them to a table with Joyce and Cathy in situ. They heard a greeting and turned to see Harry and Peter arrive. Cathy growled lightly but didn't pursue it with any ardour. Mikey laid hands on another table out of nowhere and joined it to theirs for the newcomers. Cathy shifted to the point furthest from Harry and settled into a pre-teenage sulk. Peter plopped down beside her and stole some of her drink. She thumped him one and smiled. Ruth introduced herself and Kate.

'You're the woman on the bus,' Peter said.

'Well, formerly. I'm now staff at Finn's.'

'I'm slave labour at the old churchyard.'

'Pleased to meet you.'

Ruth wanted to have a good vantage point from which to observe Joyce. She tried not to stare, but it was hard when she took into account the history between her and Charlie. What made her tick for him? She was a good-looking woman, for sure, but what was she like? Tonight she was pale under the hall fluorescents and seemed a million miles away.

Linda and Carol made a late entrance and sailed past in a whiff of perfume and finery. Ruth didn't recognise the scent at first, it was new and thoroughly robust. Linda waggled her pincers in their direction and Ruth resisted giving her the bird, but only just. Instead she flamboyantly removed a large notebook and pen from her bag and made a big deal of writing some notes. Kate could see the word 'bitch' at least five times on the page and she tapped Ruth's hand. 'Now, now,' she chided. 'Play nice.'

Ruth added two more bitches and closed the book. 'The work's going very well,' she told her sister.

The crowd shushed itself as a man in a bad dress suit stood up on the stage behind the bingo machine. He tapped the microphone three times and said, 'One-two, one-two.'

'He can count higher than that,' Cathy revealed.

'Always handy for a bingo master,' her mother pointed out.

The man had a smooth twang and practised patter. He also had a bad case of dandruff and was snowing all over the shoulders of his suit. This was anomalous, as he appeared to have a total of five hairs on his shiny head.

'Welcome, ladies and gentlemen,' he began. 'It's always a pleasure to visit Kilbrody and tonight is no exception. I bring the good news that our jackpot was not won in Inagh last night, so it now stands at five thousand euro.'

There were low whistles and an excited smattering of applause.

'If it is not won this evening it will be carried over to tomorrow night's event in Ennistymon.'

A palpable boo greeted this.

'We will be selling our special jackpot sheet at the interval, during which time tea and coffee will be served by Miss Cahill and can be purchased at the competitive rate of one euro a mug. And so to our first game. First line wins ten euro, forty for the square. Eyes down.'

He flicked a switch and the machine cranked into action, spinning the coloured balls and finally sending them up a chute into the master's waiting hands. 'And we're off! Five and nine, fifty-nine. Two little ducks, twenty-two. All the threes, thirty-three.'

Bert Fahy and Deborah dashed by, marking their cards as they went. They sat with Carol and Linda, space being at a premium. Ruth looked long enough to see Deborah flinch at their enforced company, but the numbers were coming fast and even the barest of glances could throw a person off their marking stride. She felt the stirrings of a good night out and was surprised to realise that she might burst if she didn't win.

'Check,' shouted a voice behind them and won the first ten euro of the night.

On they went, with, 'Two fat ladies, eighty-eight.'

'Very un-pc,' Kate said and was waved down by the table.

'Key to the door, twenty-one. Clickety-click, sixty-six.'

The Whinge shouted, 'Check,' then changed his mind and received a wallop from his invalid wife. It appeared to hurt him and he rubbed his arm long after she had forgotten giving him the clout. The prize went to a large man across the room.

'Frank Marr,' Old Mikey muttered. 'God knows, he could do with a few bob.'

The games sped by and suddenly it was half-time. Old Mikey stretched his legs. 'I was waiting twice,' he told the company. 'I needed eleven once and then fourteen, but no go. Can I get tea for anyone?'

'I'll go and do that,' Ruth offered.

'Not at all you won't. Sure, you don't know the system and this mob'd eat you alive. They can smell the inexperience.'

It did look rough in the queue, so she gave in. Ozzy hove into view brandishing the special jackpot sheets. They set upon him with all the rest, locusts for the riches one of those pieces of paper offered.

'I can see why Charlie avoids this,' Ruth said. 'It's addictive.'

She thought she got a quizzical look from Joyce Long but decided that her imagination was overworked in that department and not to be trusted. She was eaten with curiosity, though, and could barely keep from asking questions like, 'How do you feel about Charlie now?' and, more worryingly, 'What's he like in bed?' If she was seriously interested in the answer to that she only had to ask Linda, but she didn't want to think of them together. Ruth could still see his expression as he touched her face before the first roll of thunder. She had felt a hot rush of passion then, but told herself it was lust, and that had got her into enough trouble already this year. She'd had a close call with Tom Long through sheer foolishness. Next time she might not be so lucky. She was not keen to repeat anything like the Greg Deegan incident. Men were off limits for the next while. It was safer that way.

Deborah came over with the news that Linda's perfume was so strong it would probably take paint off a gate.

'I think it's Poison,' Ruth stated.

'Certainly smells toxic.'

'No, really, I think it's a perfume called Poison.'

'Very apt,' Joyce Long interjected.

Ruth began to warm to her.

Twenty-Eight

Charlie's only customer was a very special person in his life. Hector Bradley was his AA sponsor and mentor. They both sat on the public side of the bar and munched peanuts, washed down with Diet 7-Up. Charlie explained what was happening in his life.

'I think she may well be right. You are out of control when it comes to women. You've never admitted that your sex life is a mess. You transfer everything to the booze problem but in fact you've somewhat replaced one problem with another, haven't you? Some people do it with gambling, with you it's women.'

'But I've been dry thirteen years now. It's not as if I'm in the first flushes of kicking the habit. I was careful not to form attachments then in case it jeopardised my recovery. Surely it should be fine now.'

'It would be if you weren't in denial about something. Has there been something all along that you haven't dealt with? A woman, perhaps?'

Hector knew him well. He was on to the Joyce problem, he just didn't have a name to play with. There was
no kidding a kidder, so Charlie capitulated. It was a
relief to come clean after so long, for him as much as
Hector.

'She's called Joyce,' he said.

'This is not the woman from the bus?'

'Oh, no, that's Ruth.'

'And then there's Linda. Three women. Most men
would envy you.'

'Oh no, no. Ruth is different. I'm not involved there.'

'No, or not yet?'

'She'll be leaving soon. Ruth won't be an issue. She's
not an issue.' Charlie's heart was sore to say it, but it
was a time for the truth, nothing else would save him.

'So Joyce is still in the mix.'

'Yes and no. I didn't see a lot of her over the years,
and that must have added to the myth. Her husband is
in Parklands drying out, so she's been around more. I
think my main problem is that I've invested so much in
her, and what we might have had, that I lost sight of
reality, and to be honest there isn't really anything there
any more. And I guess I'm dismayed at how much time
I wasted over nothing, a cipher.'

'Now we're getting somewhere. How do you think
you should proceed?'

'I think I'm going to have to try single life again. Get
myself sorted out without crutches.'

'It's really more a matter of identifying what you want from a relationship. Obviously, what you have at the moment isn't very healthy. You need to tackle that. You don't really have to turn into a monk. As a great doctor once said, "It is fun to have fun, but you have to know how".' Hector looked around the empty bar. 'I don't mean to go off on a downer, Charlie, but business is bad.'

'Bingo night at the school. It'll be animal in here later.'

Hector shook his head. 'It is a divine madness that you run a pub, Charlie. I'll never get used to that.'

'I'm a rich tapestry, complete with deliberate faults woven in.'

'The Kilbrody Masterpiece.'

A raffle was in full swing at the bingo hall.

'It's brilliant, really, they wring you for every cent you have,' Kate remarked.

Joyce laughed and said, 'There's more when it ends, because there'll be a chip van outside to relieve you of any shrapnel that might have survived the night in here.'

'Smooth.'

Ruth saw Mrs Whinge earwigging Ozzy. There was a lot of pointing and she assumed it was more grief over the road-front bungalow. Ozzy was keeping a healthy distance between him and the dangerous fingers. Finally, he pretended to wave to a customer in the distance and took off at a gallop.

Old Mikey arrived with refreshments, followed by Harry, who was playing sherpa and chatting animatedly with Carol, which pleased Deborah and discomfited Joyce.

A pink ticket, 'Seventeen, serial number F12889,' was announced from the stage.

Cathy shrieked, 'It's me!' and ran to collect her prize. She came back, laughing sardonically at the bottle of whiskey in her hands. She plonked it on the table and said, 'I think you should have this, Grandad. We have no room for it in our house now.'

'Someone up there has a weird sense of humour,' Joyce murmured. 'The gods are toying with us.'

'Hide it from the Sergeant,' Old Mikey said. 'I think you're a bit underage to be winning booze.'

'He'd be more interested in confiscating it for himself,' Cathy pointed out.

'From the mouths of babes,' Mikey said, shaking his head and grinning.

The bingo master called the hall to order for a resumption of the main business of the night. Prizes flew throughout the gathering. Mrs Whinge won a tenner for having the luckily numbered book, ninety-four.

'She owes us a fiver each,' Kate told Ruth.

'I'd like to see you tackle her for it. She packs a mean punch.'

The Sergeant scored a forty for a full square and seemed vaguely chuffed. It was always hard to tell under his perma-scowl. He was clad in an alarmingly shiny shirt tucked into a pair of slacks that had begun to bobble on the inside thigh area.

'I bet it's his pulling outfit,' Ruth said to Kate. 'Wouldn't want to be you later.'

Suddenly the jackpot game was upon them and Ruth was tempted to drop a safety pin to hear how loud its clang would be in the reverence swathing the hall. The lowered heads struck off ten, fifty-one, sixty-three, seventy-five, one number jumbling into and onto the next. Old Mikey shifted in his seat. He wiped his brow. He looked longingly at the whiskey. He shifted again. The numbers in this game were finite, hence the chance that the pot might not be won. The caller began to leave subtle gaps as the game moved to a close, each slightly longer than the last. Ruth could hear two hundred and fifty hearts hammering to the beat of the caller's voice. They sped from waltz to tango to jig.

'On its own, number five.'

'CHECK,' Mikey roared, jumping to his feet.

'No way,' Cathy shouted.

'Way,' her grandfather said, thrusting his sheet at a breathless Miss Cahill.

Calmly, she read out the numbers he had marked. The caller repeated them, checking against his cache, then paused before declaring, 'Winner all right. The jackpot goes to Michael Byrne of Kilbrody.' The joined tables rose, cheering and hugging Old Mikey.

'First the rain, now this,' he said, tears in his eyes. 'I can die happy.'

'You better bloody not,' Joyce told him.

'Which? Die, or die happy?'

'Neither,' she said, scandalised at both options.

'Not without making a new will to leave me your fortune,' Cathy added, jumping up and down. She punched the air. 'Eat dirt, Ennistymon.'

Kate looked at Ruth with raised eyebrows. 'There's a lot of history,' Ruth explained.

Old Mikey planted a kiss on her cheek. 'I think you brought me luck, from the day I backed Mysterious Stranger till now. You're the town charm.'

'And you are the town charmer,' Ruth said.

When the hordes arrived at Finn's, they burst through in a clamour of cheering. Ruth led the way. Charlie stood back and savoured the joy. This is what she's brought, he decided. This is what I've been missing for so long: joy. The crowd all spoke at once and he held up a hand to steady them.

'We've taken the jackpot home,' Old Mikey announced, proudly.

'He won it, he won it,' the Treacys were chanting, hanging off Mikey's arms.

'A round of your finest, Charlie,' the winner ordered.

The Sergeant slipped in behind him. 'You'll need protection with all that money on you.'

'It's a cheque,' Mikey said, then gave in to the inevitable. 'A pint for the Sergeant.'

Ruth joined her boss behind the counter and began to fill drinks. 'There's no way you'll manage this lot by yourself.'

Time was when I'd have had to, he thought, but now I don't. He was getting used to a habit he couldn't sustain. Ruth was leaving. He had to face facts and stay strong. For now he indulged himself. It was a harmless addiction. They fell into their rhythm and the till began to ching. Kate looked on and wondered, what if? It was time to make a wish.

Venom hissed in her ear. 'It's never going to happen.' Linda, the A to Z of bitchery rolled into one disgusting package.

'Thank you, now piss off,' Kate said, not caring any more.

Linda moved on, looking vindicated, as if she'd cracked Kate's veneer.

Charlie leaned forward. 'Did I hear you correctly?' he asked, hushed.

''Fraid so. Should I sling my hook?'

'No, it was a master class in the passive-aggressive. I'm only sorry I wasn't the one to display it. You won't put your hand in your pocket for drink tonight. It's all on the house.'

'The Treacy family is costing you a royal ransom.'

'Ye're worth every cent.'

'Break it up, you two,' Ruth said. 'It makes me nervous when you start whispering.'

Charlie laughed and squeezed her waist as he passed by to serve newcomers.

Kate crossed her fingers and tried to do her toes. What if?

The bar servers ignored Linda until she snapped. 'Will I have to wait as long for a drink as I will to read one of your books, Ruth?'

All activities ground to a standstill, waiting for the reply.

'I hope not,' Ruth replied, sweetly. 'I'm still waiting for my first book to hit the shelves. It's taking forever.'

Charlie put his arm round her shoulders and said, 'We're very proud of her.'

They got back to serving, but somehow forgot to give Linda her vodka tonic. Eventually, Carol took pity and bought her one. It nearly choked them both.

Cathy gazed at the moonlight on her ceiling, abstract shapes of trees moving slowly across the white expanse as the earth continued its endless journey. She thought of Rory, the brother she never knew. He had been conceived shortly after her own birth and stillborn ten weeks before his time, perfect to look at, hopelessly malformed inside. He now lay on the wrong side of the cemetery wall. Her grandfather had carried the tiny white coffin in his arms, while her parents held one another, annihilated. The priest said some unofficial prayers and Rory was consigned to oblivion. He was supposed to be forgotten. The burial plot was all but hidden by a large oak, but the access path was along the wall of the official graveyard, which was why her mother had stopped visiting so regularly during the project.

'I can't believe you didn't tell me before now,' Cathy said, hurt.

'We've never wanted you to be upset. And we were very protective of you, because you're so precious to us. I could never have any more babies. We felt like it might be bad luck to involve you.'

'Why did you put him there?'

'We weren't thinking altogether straight at the time. We could have buried him in the hospital grounds but we wanted him close by, and he had other relatives there. Your grandad goes to visit my sister too, and so do I.'

'How many babies?'

'I don't think any one person knows for sure. Rory was registered at the hospital, but that was only twelve years ago. For generations, no one took notes and these children were buried and forgotten. The families are probably the only ones who know who's there.'

'I'm going to make a list, a record.'

'I doubt that's possible, Cathy.'

'Didn't you once tell me that there are no problems, only solutions?'

Her mother sighed, but contentedly. 'Oh, I probably did, not realising where it'd get me.'

They both slept in Cathy's bed that night.

The air on the roof was rank with the luscious fragrance of the recent deluge, rich with moisture and the promise of new growth. Ruth wanted that to be apt to her situation, but all she felt was the damp as she pondered Kate's departure. Her life was filled with leavetaking and she wanted to halt the sadness it brought. On this occasion, the journey was nothing as long as eternity and, hey, that was an improvement, as Kate pointed out. Charlie agreed and cracked open a bottle of champagne in a spirit of celebration. He broke out a fizzy elderberry concoction for himself.

'I've had a great time,' Kate said. 'An accidental holiday. A bit like you, Ruth.'

'I beg to differ. I've been worked to the bone by that man there,' she said, pointing at Charlie.

'That's the thanks I get for taking her in,' he said, hanging his head. 'The ingrate.'

'Turf her out, it's the only solution.'

'Easier said than done. She has a taste for the high life now.'

'If she starts writing a book, you're totally fecked, you'll never be rid of her.'

Charlie adopted the pose of the suffering. 'What will be will be.'

'You used to love making up ditties and writing stories when you were a kid,' Kate told her.

'That was a long, long time ago. Besides, there's a world of difference between dabbling and being a writer,' Ruth pointed out.

'You've been teaching Shakespeare too long.'

'If you're going to do something, you might as well do it right.'

'Jeez, since when did you become such a perfectionist?'

'That would be more a fear of failure,' Ruth admitted. 'Perfection is a very tall order.'

'Hear, hear,' Charlie echoed.

Kate was not for thwarting. 'For God's sake, we're sitting on an inheritance that will allow you to do as you please. Why don't you?'

'I think it might be best to sort myself out first, then maybe I'll have something to share.'

'You have plenty now,' Charlie said.

'When did we all get so timid?' Kate wanted to know.

'It's not timidity, it's being careful,' Ruth said.

'Not much fun, though.' Kate knocked back her champs and glugged another.

Charlie thought of Hector's advice. 'We should lighten up. As some doctor once said, "It's fun to have fun, but you have to know how." Good, eh?'

Ruth and Kate laughed heartily. 'Everything that doctor said is good.'

'You know who it was?'

'Of course. It's Dr Seuss.'

'The Cat In The Hat.'

Charlie swore. 'Sweet Jesus, is it any wonder I'm the way I am?'

Twenty-Nine

It was like every special event in her life, it came and went too quickly. Ruth hadn't wanted to go to bed because as soon as her head hit the pillow she knew it would be morning, and the day that Kate left. She had given up on squeezing the last few hours out of the night when Kate passed out in her deckchair.

'You two make a great team,' Charlie said.

They watched the sleeping figure for a while, then he asked, 'Are you leaving with her? Have you decided yet?'

'I was wondering if it would be OK to stay.' Ruth faced the wall. 'I'll understand if I've outstayed my welcome and you'd prefer me to go.'

Charlie tried to look as grave as she sounded. 'I think I could stand having you around a bit longer. I've got used to you under my feet.'

Now she was frantically washing in the shower and thinking that maybe it was fine to be a little less than raw in every nook and hollow. When she got out, and presented herself, Charlie grinned.

'More of you today than other days,' he said.

'Yeah, I was worn out with the exercise.'

Kate was holding her head in her hands. 'I am never ever, ever, ever drinking again. Ever, ever. EVER.'

'So that would be never, then?'

'Aye. Agh, it hurts even to think. How is it you're not in this state?'

'I was working for most of last night,' Ruth explained, glad to be telling the truth.

Charlie arrived with aspirin, juice and liver salts. 'We'll see this suffering off.'

'And me out of town,' Kate begged. 'It must have been the bubbles.'

'Couldn't have been anything else,' Charlie confirmed, as he ministered to her prone figure. She had affected the pose of a tragic heroine about to suffer death by ignominy.

'I don't think I can move,' she bawled.

'I say we hose her down,' Ruth put in.

'I'll see to that myself, thanking you,' Kate said, slowly rising and teetering to the bathroom.

'Doctor Finn, will she make it?'

'I very much think so. The Treacy sisters are made of stern stuff.'

The sun was starting its antics again, shining down, toasting the earth and encouraging happiness. It was hard to resist the force of nature. Furthermore, it would be wrong to. Ruth stretched and purred.

'I'm glad you're not leaving,' Charlie said. He flashed her a genuine Finn special.

'Me too.'

'You're the best.' The statement was simple and unadorned.

'You too,' she returned in kind.

Joyce was surprised to wake up where she did, and without Cathy. She found her daughter at the kitchen table furiously scribbling names and addresses from the phone book.

'Let me guess,' her mother began. 'You are on a mission.'

'Yes. I want everyone to know and to remember.'

'Not everyone will want to.'

'We'll see.'

Joyce recognised the tone and knew there was no point in challenging it. She put out bowls of muesli and waited for the kettle to boil. Eventually she mentioned, 'It's half past five, Cathy. You might want to catch a snooze before you head to the project today.'

'I'd still be asleep except for you snoring.'

'I do not snore.'

'Do too.'

'You must have forced me onto my back.'

'Like a jackhammer, you were. I'm surprised you didn't wake yourself up with the noise.'

A knock rapped on the door and her grandfather appeared. 'Oh Lord,' he said, 'am I late for work?'

'No, Grandad, I'm early for it.'

'She's on a mission.'

'Uh-oh. I feel a hard time coming on.'

'Believe it,' his granddaughter said.

He sat at the table and regarded the cereal with all the enthusiasm of a rampant petrol spill meeting sand. 'I'll pass on the wood shavings and go for a rasher.'

'Daddy, you eat too much fat.'

'Lord God, can a man not enjoy a meal any more? How about a waffle?'

'Too many saturated fats,' Cathy affirmed.

'*Et tu*, Cathy?'

'I'll repeat myself, believe it.'

'There's no way I can eat that stuff,' he bleated. 'The least I can go is a few poached eggs.'

'Good man,' Joyce said.

'And a quare, big hape of toast,' he added, smiling to think of his feast.

'Grandad, don't be such a culchee bumpkin.'

'What are you up to there?' he asked her. When Cathy told him, he ate less, but promised to formulate strategy with her later. 'Bernadette deserves more friends,' he said.

Ruth sat on the bed in Charlie's room and swung her feet to and fro. 'I'm not sure he's had any significant number of nights sleeping here since we arrived,' she

336

said to Kate. 'Told me he doesn't mind, but he's too good to say otherwise really.'

'Well, he's not too good to be true, thank God,' Kate said, her head in a wheelie case. 'But close, like all the really good ones.'

'I was lucky to end up here.'

'Oh, yes,' Kate confirmed, emerging from behind a canvas flap. 'How did that happen?'

'That's one of the things I'll be needing to ask myself. Soon. Before I go back.'

'Are you sure you want to? Go back. Is that what's best?'

'I don't know. It seems like what I should do.'

'Tell you what I think, without any onus on you to listen, mind.' Kate sat beside her and held her hand. 'I think you should put the teaching on hold and pursue your adventure. It'll wait for you, you know that. This might not.'

An Aladdin's cave of hope threatened to open up. 'I'll think about it, how about that?'

Kate smirked. 'That'll have to do me.' She pressed Ruth's hand. 'Won't it?'

'That's all there is, for now.'

'When you're up to talking about what happened to send you here, let me know. It wasn't Mammy and Daddy that sent you over the edge. I was there for that and we weren't so deranged that I expected you to disappear and turn up in County Clare.'

Ruth smelled hot paint, a memory to unlock the puzzle, but said, 'Kismet, babe. Nothing more or less than fate.'

She wanted to believe it too.

Cathy sat with Fiona in Surf 'n' Turf. 'I need a good deal on these copies, there's a fair few of them.'

'God, I never knew that was what was there. I mean, sure, we knew it was a graveyard, but I always thought it was pets. Dogs and cats, you know?'

'They'd have been better signposted,' Cathy said. 'Can I have them at lunchtime?'

Fiona had never felt pride in her job before, but thrust out her chest and said, 'Give me an hour.'

'No, really, lunchtime will do,' Cathy assured her. 'I won't have the money to pay for them till then.'

Fiona scratched her back.

'Is the bra chafing you?'

'Yeah. I'm thinking of dumping it.'

'Fine by me. I'll have my own soon enough.'

Cathy left, practising her speech to Miss Cahill and Father Kilcullen. She didn't think they'd be easily persuaded. But what was a plan of action without risks? And there was a lot to gain.

Joyce scattered feed for the chickens and thought about the past week. Although she was bone weary, there was a spring in her step. It was as if a clearance was in progress. Tom was on the mend, she prayed. And at last the secret youth of Kilbrody might be commemorated. Even if they didn't succeed in providing more physical markers for the dead, at least they would be talked about and acknowledged. She felt happiness and found herself humming. Dammit, she would spoil her body and have a bath as well as a nap. She would rejoice in this sinful excess, then visit Tom with all the news. She danced to the kitchen door, attempted a pirouette and laughed her way into the house.

Ozzy watched and decided she'd finally flipped. He swung the binoculars and saw Cathy Long, her red hair flaming in the sunlight. Even without the magnification he'd have spotted her, shining like a beacon in the distance. Ozzy had courted a redhead from Kilrush once. The travelling was hell but, man oh man, she was a beauty. Lived in America now and was on her third husband, last he'd heard. He didn't think he'd have the energy for three wives.

Why were Cathy and her company at the Little Angels plot? Ozzy had a brother there: wee Lawrence. He'd missed him growing up, a lone boy in a family of strong women. It would have been great to have had an ally. His father didn't count, a man too fond of the fist, who never knowingly spared the rod to spoil the child. Maybe Lawrence was better off out of a world like that. He'd wheel by presently and see if he could get the story on this latest development.

❖   ❖   ❖

Kate stood at the door of her red Fiesta, gently postponing the act of leaving. They threw weather talk over and back, agreed on what a lovely drive it would be. Had Ruth enough money? Where would be good to stop for lunch on the way, or was it best to keep the foot to the floor? When they had exhausted their reservoir of inanity, Kate said, 'I'm useless at this goodbye lark, so I'm going to go now. I'll phone when I get home to let you know I've arrived, blah blah blah.' She hugged Charlie, then Ruth and said, 'See you all soon.' She fired up the engine and drove out of town.

'You are in for a rare treat,' Charlie told Ruth as they turned back in.

'Why does that sound like a warning or a threat?'

'I am going to make you a cup of Earl Grey, then I'm going to show you how to clean the beer pipes. It's mucky and very boring.'

'You spoil me,' Ruth said.

'I can't help myself, it's the way I am.'

'Lead on, I'm ripe for this one.'

'It'll make a scintillating chapter for your book.'

'I was thinking of calling it *Adventures of an Orphan: The Bar Years*. Wotcha think?'

'Catchy.'

Ruth noticed he didn't need to ask now, he poured milk in her tea but didn't add sugar. He probably knew lots more about her that she didn't even suspect. Strange, the way they'd fallen into each other's beat.

'How're you bearing up?'

'I'm fine. I know I can hop on a bus and see Kate within hours, so it's not as big a deal as I might make it.' She accepted a steamy mug. 'Thanks for letting me stay on.'

'It was very dull round here before you arrived, and it'll get back to that when you go, no doubt, so I think it's worth my while hanging on to you for as long as I can.'

He didn't mention that a lot had changed since she'd walked through his door. He was finally letting Joyce go, and Linda too, though that had always been on the cards. A different complexion was emerging on his life.

Cathy stood hand on hip, waiting for Father Kilcullen to come to the point. Miss Cahill had had her day in court, twitting about how this was not 'within the parameters of the project as set out in her mission statement'. Cathy wanted to give her a slap and tell her to shove her parameters. She rolled her eyes at Peter. The priest was droning on about privacy and old wounds and then, to her amazement, he said, 'But if you do this on your own time, I don't suppose any of us can stop you.'

Cathy didn't want to let him change his mind so ploughed in with, 'Are there any parish records relating to the plot?'

He rubbed his chin and said, 'We have some unofficial notes made over the years. That depended on who was in charge and how they felt about the situation. I suppose I could let you see those.'

Miss Cahill's voice was falsetto shrill. 'What do you plan to do with this information?'

'I'm going to make as full a record as I can of who's here.' Cathy gestured to the leafy knoll. 'And I think it would be nice to put up some railings and a little plaque.'

'Where will the money come from?' Miss Cahill asked. 'You can be sure I don't have it in my budget.'

'I'll organise that,' Cathy said, grandly. Her brain whirred, thinking of her grandad's windfall and her distant, rich uncle. 'When can I see the records?' she asked the priest.

'Give me a day or two to get them together and then you can have full access.'

Miss Cahill checked her watch and simpered, 'Father, we're eating into your lunch hour. Let me see you to your car.' She felled all interference with a poisonous look. As they walked away, the teacher all apologies and fawning, Father Kilcullen said, 'Let them be. They'll get nowhere when they contact the families. This will blow over.'

'He giveth and he taketh away,' Peter whispered, low.

'That's what he thinks,' Cathy said. 'I can't get over what an idiot that woman makes of herself over him.'

'Must be the uniform getting to her.'

'Let's collect the photocopies from Fiona. We have a lot to do.'

They shuffled down the hill to town, full of awkward shapes and street cred. They were riding high on their initial success. Their next break came at Surf 'n' Turf.

'Daddy says there's no charge for these,' Fiona said, referring to the pile of letters. 'We did up the labels and put them on envelopes for you. I was thinking I could deliver the ones out our way; that would save on postage.'

Cathy couldn't keep a foolish smile off her face. 'That'd be great, thanks.'

'And he left this for you,' Fiona said, handing over Cathy's first reply. It told the short story of Lawrence Patrick O'Reilly, 1950. 'Good luck with the search,' Ozzy had written. 'I'll help in any way I can.'

It was astonishing how quickly a mood could be shattered. Joyce was pacing the car park of the clinic raging against the world. Just one word had done it: 'enabler'. They were trying to make out that she had facilitated Tom's drinking. It was just short of suggesting she'd lifted the drinks to his mouth, to listen to the terminology. Jesus, next she'd get the blame for his being born in the first place. He'd sat like a lump of putty without sticking up for her. When she put this to him after the session he muttered, 'I had a bad day yesterday.'

'Mine was no picnic either,' she replied.

He looked so downcast she'd instantly regretted the

words. Now she was back to fury. She kicked the tyres on her car and eventually had to let loose a yowl of frustration and anger. How much more of this was she expected to take? And lying down, by the looks of things.

A burly woman with apple-blossom cheeks passed on her way in. 'You'll get used to it,' she said, without stopping. 'But it takes time and lots of patience.'

Even the advice sounded like a rebuke. Joyce kicked the tyres again, each in turn, got into the car and left with a squeal of rubber. She felt she could chew through iron bars or rip up the tarmac barehanded. That clinic should be running anger management classes for the families, she decided. She narrowly missed a passing tractor at the junction to the main road and slowed to a crawl. Getting killed wouldn't solve anything, or not much at any rate. A large sign read 'SLOW DOWN'.

'I'm trying,' she told it.

If this was going to get worse before it improved, as she suspected, it might be time to invest in a punch-bag.

Thirty

Ruth spread the contents of her satchel on the bedspread. It hadn't changed much since her arrival in Kilbrody, just the addition of a packet of tissues, a few new pens and the celebrated notebook. Something about the configuration bothered her but she couldn't put her finger on what it was. The detail would lead to others, and with it the reason for getting that particular bus on that particular day. She swam through her memory, eyes glazed to her present location, looking back.

The day had started with a hangover, as most had since the funerals.

She looked with loathing at the cage her flat now represented. Her head beat with the painful thuds preceding illness, her stomach keeping time and heaving, ready to blow. She looked at the clock and groaned as midday struck up on the dial. More time lost. The message light was blinking on her answering machine.

Greg's voice barked. 'Ruth, I'll only say this once. Never call me at home again.' Then the dead tone of disconnection.

She ran to the loo and vomited. She lay supine on the tiles until she began to shiver and her sweat turned to icy drops running down her body. She ran a bath and climbed in, dipping below the water for longer and longer periods, disgusted to find that she didn't have what it took to drown herself. She needed to apologise to Greg and to get him onside again. They were going through a tough phase and she had let her end get out of hand. If they could meet, civilly, she could put her case and make amends.

She towelled off and smeared his favourite body lotion all over. It smelled expensive, as well it should: it had cost her a small fortune. Then she dialled his mobile and left a message, short, sane and not too needy. He replied within the hour and they arranged to meet in a pub in Abbey Street, because it best suited him that afternoon. She was buoyed with optimism and the possibility of staving off this loneliness she felt was swallowing her up. She spent an hour fixing her hair just how he liked it and choosing an outfit that would meet with his approval but didn't seem too hell bent on impressing him.

She was early for the rendezvous and spent her time fidgeting nervously. Acid rolled through her stomach and veins, leaving her light-headed, but Greg would be here soon and hope flickered bravely. She clocked actors and actresses arriving, and leaving, after rehearsals at the Abbey Theatre across the road. Maeve Kelly was the most famous of the congregation and Ruth found it hard not to stare. She had seen her play Medea some months back and thought the woman walked on water. The actress smiled as she passed and Ruth's heart lifted a tad.

Greg was a further twenty minutes arriving. Ruth had just switched from water to lager to still her curdling nerves when he walked in. She caught her breath and swallowed hard. He spotted the drink and gave a theatrical sigh. She tried to ignore it.

'Ruth,' he acknowledged coldly. 'I see you've already looked after yourself, so I needn't buy you another.' He stressed the last word meanly, but Ruth knew this was her fault as she'd clearly overstepped the mark last night while drunk. She took it on the chin.

He sat opposite and waited for her to make a start. There were so many things to discuss, to clarify. She opened her mouth to start a few times then blurted, 'This is my first of the day,' defensively referring to the lager.

'Whatever you say.'

'Greg, I am so sorry about ringing you at home. I lost the run of myself. I haven't been great lately but I really do feel there's a light at the end of the tunnel now, and I'd like to make it all up to you.' She beamed a smile. 'It's up to you to choose a forfeit.'

'How about leaving me alone?'

She was shocked by the cruelty of the remark. It was also something she didn't feel she could promise. She sat back deep into the upholstered seat. What had gone so wrong here? She was still the Ruth he had pursued, albeit now under stress because of her parents' deaths. Why was he treating her so harshly?

'I know I haven't been easy lately, naturally.' She left a beat to remind him of her bereavement. 'But everything's going to change back to the way it was. We're good together and I don't think we should forsake that.'

'Ruth, get it into your thick skull, there is nothing left between us. It was fun while it lasted but it's gone.'

'Fun?'

'What else did you think it was? Love?' He spat out the word in a mockery of affection.

YES, she wanted to scream. 'Well, I suppose I thought there was genuine feeling there, at least I know I felt . . . passion and, yes, eh, love.'

'Don't make yourself totally ridiculous. I'm a happily married man with two beautiful children. Why would I throw that away, for a fling?'

Ruth was finding it hard to speak, her throat constricting in the agony of these revelations. 'But you wanted a place of our own. I left my home for you, to make a home with you.'

'You know, I can't decide whether you're plain stupid or so naive you need adult supervision when you're let out. What planet did you grow up on?'

Part of her was dying. She was reduced to small, pant-ing breaths to feed her body the oxygen it needed to survive, while her mind told her to give up, shut down.

'What do you have to offer that could possibly tempt me from my wife and children? You're thirty-eight years old with nothing to show for yourself, no husband, no kids, nothing. Just a pennyanny job in a washed-up school, with no prospect of going anywhere. You're a joke, Ruth. And we are so over it's hard to find words to express it.'

Ruth's brain began to keen in her head.

Greg held his face close to hers, his mouth spitting malice. 'If you ever contact me or my family again, you'll be very, very sorry. Do you hear me?'

She struggled into her jacket, onto her feet, somehow, and out the door into the street, blinded by hopeless-ness.

She was on her hands and knees by the bed in Kilbrody, desperately clinging to sanity and gulping back horror. She steadied her breathing and rose. Her hands shook and her teeth rattled as she shivered in spite of the day's heat. She felt cold and hollow. There was more.

Greg followed her, probably afraid that if she came to harm he'd have been the last person seen with her. He called for her to stop but she staggered on, bump-ing into walls, parked cars, a postbox. He finally caught her arm and steered her roughly into an underground car park.

'*Shut up, Ruth,*' he hissed. '*Shut the fuck up.*'

Ruth rifled through the contents of the satchel. Her purse was there, as it had been on the day the bag had been returned to her. But she had bought drink all that night and paid for a bus ticket. How?

Greg shoved her behind a parked van. 'If you don't shut up, I'll have to make you,' he threatened. Suddenly she was afraid and her voice rose another decibel. He put his hand over her mouth and pressed her face against the hood of the vehicle. She was fighting for breath now, her nose clogged from her earlier crying. She heard the engine still ticking from a recent journey and felt its heat burn through the metal on to her cheek. She lashed out with her fists but made no impact.

'This will keep you quiet,' he said, pulling down her trousers and thrusting himself into her. 'How is that?' he mocked. 'You don't have much to make a noise about now, do you?' Again and again he slammed into her. 'You like it rough, don't you, Ruth? You're a dirty bitch who likes a sound seeing-to.'

It seemed to go on for ever. She ceased to struggle or sob. When he came, he slapped her thigh and said, 'Clean yourself up now, you've had what you wanted.'

She was left abandoned and weeping across the bonnet of the van. She heard his footsteps move away, then he turned and came back. She swung around, terrified, trying to right her clothing. He thrust something into her pocket, said, 'Get yourself a treat,' and disappeared.

Ruth searched for the jacket she had been wearing. It was hanging on the back of the bedroom door, unused since she'd arrived. She put her hand into the pocket and brought out the loose change from the thirty pieces of silver he had used to pay her off.

The final, awful humiliation was complete. She could blame no one but herself. She lurched out of the dark underground and into the next pub she came to. She ordered a double brandy, then another and a third. She knocked them back, so quickly she could hardly taste them. The barman refused her a fourth, so she staggered next door and was served more. Her body throbbed with the rough treatment and shame, but each brandy eased her and, for the briefest of whispers, she felt she could take charge again.

She looked across the road at the bus station and all the people going places, sure of a welcome home or a fresh start. She crossed the road and boarded the first bus she came to. She didn't check the destination on the front and didn't notice the flirtatious glance of the driver. She went straight to the back row and sank. The bus pulled out of the station and Ruth's head began to bob. She smelled of Greg Deegan and wanted to scour him off. Later, she vowed. As the buildings on the Quays passed, grey upon grey, her eyes grew heavy. So heavy. She let them close and passed into another dimension. It was two days before she removed the last of Greg Deegan from her body.

'Don't cry, Ruth, I'm here,' Charlie said, wrapping his arms round her.

She howled, rocking them both with her anguish.

'I'm worthless,' she managed, finally, between gulps of tears. 'I let myself be humiliated and I deserve everything I got. I'm a waste of breath and space.'

He said nothing, trying to quell his desire to find the man who'd reduced her to this and kill him horribly with his bare hands.

'Look at me, Charlie. I have nothing. I'm a dried-up spinster with no hope of anything better.'

He held her till she fell into an exhausted sleep. He laid her on the bed and covered her with a light throw. He kissed her forehead and said, 'You can tell me all about it another time.' She looked at peace, and perhaps she was now. He cleared the bed and re-packed the satchel, then went to phone Kate.

Thirty-One

Ruth emerged bleary and trampled. She staggered towards the kettle and flipped the switch. She heard the crunch of a newspaper and wheeled round in fright.

'I forgot to bring this down,' Charlie said. 'It's quiet and I've finished that novel about Leonardo da Vinci. My head is full of theories and symbols. I thought this'd be the perfect antidote.'

'Tales from the real world should grind you back down,' Ruth agreed. 'It's outrageous, but I don't think I've read a paper front to back since I got here.'

'Good snooze?' Butterfly light.

'Mmm. Needed to shut down briefly. I remembered why I got the bus that Tuesday. It wasn't pretty. A nasty blend of cruelty and wilful self-destruction.'

'That good, huh?'

'You better believe it. Someday, if I can muster the strength, I might trot you through it. The only good thing is it's done and can now be consigned to history.' She gave a twisted grin.

'Result.'

'Hope so. I don't want to repeat the mistake. Not so much a learning curve as a vertical.'

She knew, when she did part with the details, the version would be sanitised. She would keep the whole truth within her, a hard kernel of experience, the touchstone by which she would keep strong. She would handle and polish it and protect it for herself. It would rest behind her mind's portcullis, shining and black and malevolent. She had pinpointed integrity and would never squander it again.

The theory was strong, but she was unsure how it translated into action. For the time being, she was content to sit back and wait for events to present opportunities for practice. She had rebuilding to do after a lesson hard learned.

'Better get back to work or the animals will take over the zoo,' Charlie said, exiting, calm that a corner was turned and Ruth Treacy was retaking her life.

Cathy was holding a council of war at the Long kitchen table. Joyce, Old Mikey and Harry were trying hard not to laugh at her stern behaviour. Peter was aide-de-camp and in tandem with her mood. Miss Cahill's talk of a mission statement had led Cathy to formally list the objectives of her satellite project and, if she said so herself (and she did), it beat the teacher's into the dark corner of oblivion.

'She's been reading a lot,' her mother said, explaining the purple prose.

Her daughter hushed her. 'Therefore, I propose that we make the library our centre of activities, as it has local records and it's in the middle of town. Now, Grandad, how do you feel about sponsoring some railings?'

Old Mikey chuckled. 'You mean, how do I feel about paying for them outright.'

'I don't think you've any choice,' Joyce whispered and was hushed a second time.

'Three strikes and you're out,' she was warned.

'I'm willing to stump up for the railings and the plaque,' the old man said.

'Good. We need volunteers to deliver the letters. Mum, you can do around the Rock Road and Peter and me will take care of the River Walk and Lahinch Road area.'

Joyce leaned in to her father. 'Shame she couldn't rustle up a map and a pointer,' she giggled. 'She'll have us in uniform next.'

Harry put up his hand. 'I'm a member of the library but Peter isn't yet, so we'll need to sign him up.'

He received a curt nod of approval and reckoned that was as much as he could ever hope for from Cathy Long. She looked at the clock on the mantelpiece and said, 'If you go now, you'll make the library before it closes today. We have no time to lose.'

Old Mikey smiled. After such long inaction, suddenly everything was urgent and needed to be done yesterday. He watched Cathy's red curls bounce as she issued orders and felt a warm stir of pride at being her grandfather. The wilderness years were about to end for the tiny bundles of bone and coffin buried in the ground.

Harry and Peter were still seated. 'What are you waiting for?' Cathy asked, amazed at them. 'Go now.'

They scurried out.

'If you two would be so good as to reply to me, I would have three answers.' She thrust pens and paper across the table at Joyce and Old Mikey and, obediently, they began to write.

Ruth bounded downstairs and into the pub. She found the charity box on the counter and slotted in the coins she'd found in her jacket pocket. 'Ill-gotten gains,' she told Charlie. She felt a ton lighter as the last euro disappeared on its way to help the local football team. 'Tonight is lemon roasted chicken night, with seasonal vegetables and a mixed leaf salad. Served at six thirty when Deborah goes on duty. Dress, casual.' She was gone before 'get out'.

'You'd hardly credit that's the same woman wound up here off the bus,' the Whinge opined.

Charlie nodded in agreement. 'Our good air suits her.'

'I think you might too,' his customer slyly lobbed in.

Charlie pretended not to hear, but his ears burned.

Cathy Long appeared. Had they been in the open she

would have stopped traffic, so unlikely was this occurrence now that her dad was in therapy. Charlie opened his mouth to welcome her but she stanched him with a hand. She flicked through a pile of envelopes and selected a range for distribution amongst the bar folk. She was out the door again before they could ask questions. In the wake of Ruth's appearance and disappearance, it seemed the order of the day was a smash-and-grab style arrangement. Slick, whatever the reasons.

'Lord God Almighty,' the Whinge gasped, reading his delivery. 'Someone's finally doing something.' He reached for a pen and made some notes. 'Do you have anyone in there?' he asked Charlie.

'No. There've never been many of us in the town and we all made it past birth.' He felt the label of blow-in-without-adequate-roots acutely.

The library's afternoon visitors astounded Carol. 'Harry, isn't it?' she chirped, wishing she'd replenished her lippy after lunch and didn't sound like a chipmunk. She ran a hand through her hair and got caught in a knot on the right-hand side. She left her hand there, for the time being, leaning onto it casually. 'We met at the bingo.'

'Yes, I remember, Carol. This is my son, Peter, and he needs to sign up as a member.'

They processed the necessary paperwork and Carol was alarmed at how oily her hands became under pressure. She prayed her shine-control face powder was

357

doing the job it had promised on the packet. Her perfume was working overtime.

'Can we assume we'll see more of you from now on?' she enquired, hoping no one would ask who else was part of the 'we' she had found herself referring to. God, silly and presumptuous all in one.

'Peter is part of a new venture, which I'll allow him to explain, and it'll involve library work.'

'Should we sign up your wife too?' Carol tried, shamelessly fishing. She felt a line of perspiration break out above her upper lip and prayed her last wax had lasted. She didn't think she had a shadow there last time she'd looked, but when you weren't checking for something specific you tended to miss a lot.

'I don't think there's any need for that. She died a number of years ago.' He said it with kindness and Carol, shredded by her stupidity, knew he would not hold the faux pas against her. As for the son, who knew?

And Linda would certainly have mentioned a moustache if she'd grown one.

Ruth was nervously fixing napkins for the fourth time when Charlie appeared.

'Sorry,' he apologised. 'Deborah was late 'cos she has some sort of tummy bug. As you can imagine, she felt obliged to give me full details of her "ring of fire" and multiple gawks. She says it's amazing the amount that comes out of a person no matter how little goes in.'

'You'll be ravenous after that,' Ruth guessed, lashing on the irony.

'I might go a short breather before tucking in, unless that would ruin the chef's meal.'

'No, it's a one-oven wonder, turned way down low till we decide we're hungry.'

'Brilliantly thought through, Miss Treacy.'

'Don't get too excited, you're an experiment. I'm not sure it'll be much, even with the "Chicken for Dummies" recipe I'm using. The blurb says it's foolproof, and all I know is that we have the fool and the proof.'

'It smells wonderful.'

'You've probably done this dish a hundred times. I bet you were holed up in outer Mongolia once with a chicken and a few lemons.'

'That matter is still with the courts and, as such, I can't discuss it,' he said, gravely. 'I will admit to "angel dust" and "a lot of", in mitigation, and best leave it at that. A drink on the terrace, ma'am?'

They leaned on the parapet and watched Kilbrody go by. A late flurry of sunshine was melting the Albertine over the doorway and Sheela was smiling broadly. Honeysuckle gently scented the air. Every breath was an expression of the beauty of the moment, and the day, and being alive in time.

'I'm surprised you never had children,' Ruth broached.

'I spent so long compromising, because I didn't get the girl, that it never really was an issue. I suppose there's an outside chance I have kids from my travels. It's not something that's altogether engaged me over the years. Being an alcoholic can be a very selfish way of life. Same with recovery. You have to look out for number one in many ways, especially initially. And after that it can be hard to make room for someone else.'

'Do you think you ever could?'

'I hope so. It'll be a lonely old life otherwise. Now that I think I may have freed myself from . . . you know . . . the past.'

'Joyce?'

'Yes. Although I can't blame her. I put her on an impossible pedestal. And I think, deep down, I loved the fact that she was unavailable to me and it gave me every excuse not to try with anyone else. Broken-hearted and disappointed as I was, and all that baloney. It was a perverse way of carrying on.'

'You're harsh on yourself.'

'I have to be realistic. Otherwise the chinks start to appear and the temptations will come. The wrong sort. I wouldn't mind some of the right ones, of course.'

They saw Ozzy lock up his premises. He had a binoculars case hanging from his shoulder.

'Does he birdwatch?' Ruth asked. 'Is he a twitcher?'

'Sort of. You might say Ozzy is a people watcher too. He's the local anthropologist.'

'You mean a peeping Tom?' Ruth was shocked. 'That's got to be against the law.'

'He practises the art gently. The day he oversteps the mark we'll stop him. All it really is, when you think of it, is an inquisitiveness that he's gone professional on. He's handy if people are looking for missing animals and he can spot traffic problems a mile off, literally. If you call with a query, he supposes you think he's on a computer, but we all know it's the binoculars.'

'I'm flabbergasted, truly. I don't know how I feel about him now.' She had a memory of her encounter with Tom Long in open country the day she'd taken the bicycle out. How might that have looked to a far-off observer? Did the scene seem a lot more than the sum of its parts? She was uncomfortable to recall how closely she had courted disaster, with very little reason other than the attraction of two damaged people willing to help each other self-destruct.

'It's an idiosyncrasy, and he's never done any harm. Live and let live.'

She thought of Ozzy's little face with its small features and kind eyes. Maybe he'd seen enough of humanity to know the value of compassion.

'This is one bizarre town.'

'Ah, now, we're no odder than any other. We're more concentrated than Dublin, say, that's all.'

'A microcosm?'

'Now you have it.' He sniffed the air. 'I adore the way the plants give off such lovely scents in the evening. It's magical.' He turned. 'How about you and kids?'

She frowned. This was back to the hurtful territory Greg Deegan had dragged her through, but it couldn't be swept away indefinitely.

'Would you like to have some?'

'I don't know. I hadn't felt the lack till recently. Then someone told me I had nothing to show for my life without them. Is that true, do you think?'

'I think how you deal with people is important too. That's a legacy. We remember individuals and what they stood for, not just because they were a mother or a father. You don't have to repopulate the earth to leave something behind.'

'It got me at a bad time. I had buried my parents and didn't have a partner of my own. And I'm not getting any younger. To say that I felt inadequate would be the understatement of the year.'

'Greg Deegan is the pig of a man who did that, isn't he?'

'Ah, you know his name. Kate, I assume. Yes, he was a big mistake. I'm coming to terms with that.'

'We could form a club.'

'Why not? We're already a mini support unit.'

'What must we seem like? Two decent human beings struggling to find the way.'

'We're late starters. We'll get there.'

Thirty-Two

The dinner passed off without any indication that a hospital visit would be required in the near future. In fact, it could be argued that the meal was a success. The vegetables were crisper than intended, sure, but extra sweet from their extended stay in the oven and the chicken was melt-in-the-mouth.

'Mammy had me spoiled,' Ruth admitted. 'The dinner was on the table every evening when I got home. There was no need to learn much in the culinary line . . . until this year.'

A by-product was that she bought a lot of lingerie. Fact is, you can't have sexy underwear if your mother is doing the laundry, as Rita had always insisted on doing. Ruth squirmed in her recently delivered lacies, thinking of it. She didn't mention the detail to Charlie.

'How long were you with Greg?'

The name sounded ugly and Ruth shivered. 'We were never truly together, because . . . he's married. All told,

the débâcle stretched over six months. I think he was
bored after the Christmas break and I was handy.' She
crunched through some lettuce. 'Actually, as I think of
it, he might go by school terms, because he took up with
the Dumbestic Science lassie after Easter, but I was too
thick to pay attention and give up on the whole sordid
mess.' She waved her fork viciously. 'If Brian Cook next
door hadn't turned out to be an insane nerd I might
have been saved all this.'

'Was he the childhood sweetheart?'

'Eeyoo, no. All I'm saying is, if he'd been halfway
decent I wouldn't have had to cast my net any further.'

Charlie had a mono-brow figuring out the logic.

'Yeah, yeah, the theory mightn't stand up to scrutiny,
but you know what I mean.'

'You must have had other boyfriends.'

'On and off. No one too special. I guess that's just
how it goes.'

'You're remarkably sanguine about it all.'

She grinned. 'I am now, or getting there. I wasn't
when I arrived, was I?'

'Mmn, no.'

She thought of what she'd been through during the
year and wondered that she was so uncynical. Her parents
had been through lean times in their lives with belt-tight-
ening and redundancy, and scrimping to make ends meet.
And all the time they'd faced adversity with good humour.
There was an innate happiness to them, as a couple and

as parents. They were solid people with an easy smile and a pleasant outlook, with no facility for the long-term whine. Not saints, no, but they believed that bad thoughts brought others, and multiplied, inviting a vast network of cousins to the mean, never-ending party. They wanted nothing of that. She had inherited a gene that precluded prolonged self-pity and she had used up her quota this year. But it was no harm to keep a gritty memory system simmering gently under her skin to maintain a defence system.

She would never forget the hurts of the last months but she would move on. She was the one with the power to choose between wallowing or change. One road was boring and the other a terror. So, moving on it was. The worst was over. Hell, even if it was about to begin again, she was in better shape for it now. Her jaw set gently to survival.

'Will you show me how to make a hollandaise?'

'We might have to spend a month in Tuscany.'

Cathy could not eat. She gazed at the pile of paper before her.

'I've got thirteen replies and we only started delivering today.' She read the names aloud. 'O'Reilly, Byrne, Long, Cronin, Phelan, Flynn, Farrelly, O'Brien, Broderick, Gilfeehan, Staunton, Finch and Marr.'

'Darlin', people are ready. I only hope you are.'

Her daughter gave a pointy chin her way.

'Have you had any more thoughts on what should go on the plaque?'

'Not really.'

'All in good time. Broccoli?'

Cathy's nose curled up and around itself. She was prepared to consume the vile brassica in solidarity with her mum during the hard times, but this was beyond the call. 'You must be joking.'

'I might have known it wouldn't last.'

'That's life.'

'Don't I know it.'

'Mam, something's been bothering me.'

'Yes?' Joyce's voice gave an upward inflection that was both encouragement to her daughter and the wariness of a person not wanting to hear an unpalatable.

'Does Daddy drink because Rory died?'

'No, darling. Daddy drinks because he's an alcoholic. Nothing happened to make him one. It's a disease.'

'Right. So, will he never drink again after this?'

'That's what we're hoping. I'm told there's a saying that for the alcoholic, one is too many and a thousand is not enough. We have to hope he can be strong enough to stay off it.'

'Mam, there's another thing.'

'Shoot.'

'Why did no one ever do anything about the Little Angels?'

'That's a hard question to answer. When I think of ourselves, your father and me, we were so shell-shocked and mixed up when Rory died that we couldn't see beyond the next day for a long time. As well as that, we didn't want to make others uncomfortable with our loss. It all compounded the confusion, and eventually we fell into the natural order of things. And that was just to visit the grave and not rock the boat. So many other people had been through it that we felt it must be the thing to do. It's not that we didn't love our children and want them to live, it was more a matter of getting on with the gifts we'd all been given and making the best of our lot.'

'I hope Grandad doesn't mind that I've tried to make off with his winnings.'

'Are you joking? He'd take the stars out of the heavens and lay them at your feet if that's what you wanted.'

'He mightn't have to anyhow. I didn't mention it before but there's been money in all of the envelopes too, to pay for the memorial.'

Charlie brewed coffee while Ruth talked to Kate on the phone. It was a conversation of silly pleasantries and needlessly coded messages about how well things were working out both sides of the River Shannon. Kate passed the phone to Lar, who sounded slurred.

'Are you stoned?' Ruth asked.

'Ruth, Ruth, Ruth. You're getting too much pure oxygen in the air down there. Think about it. I'm heading out to the Saturday night session in the Pit, of course I'm having a few spliffs.'

She could picture his happy, bendy face.

'Have you jumped this Charlie fella's bones yet?'

'What?' Ruth squeaked higher than usual, or intended. 'No way.' She was sharply aware of Charlie's proximity and worried about voices leaking beyond the phone or saying too much to alert him to the topic of conversation. 'You have the wrong impression, Lar.' She thought that sounded noncommittal, on any subject, but detested how primly it emerged.

'That's not what I hear from my lovely wife. She says neither of you can take your eyes off each other.'

Ruth's aforementioned eyes felt as if they were bulging for Ireland and she noticed that she and Charlie were staring at one another, as if on cue. She deflected him by signalling a half cup, then moved her gaze and stuck it firmly to the kitchen tiles. 'I don't think that's the case,' she murmured pleasantly. It bought her time to regain composure and reduce the temperature raging in her cheeks. 'Could you put me back on to Kate?' she chattered, again as carelessly as possible.

'Sure, but you know she's an expert on people, Ruth. It's her job.'

'She's a hairdresser,' Ruth pointed out, exasperated.

'There's more to hairdressing than cutting hair,' her maddingly calm and happy sister said taking over the phone. 'I give counselling, holiday advice, and the confidence to face the day afresh. I'm a one-stop, feel-good shop. A magician, really.' She gave a contented sigh, from the safety of her south Dublin home.

'You are precariously close to dying young-ish, Maestra,' her sister warned, keeping her volume low so as not to tip her Kilbrody audience off.

'I hadn't meant for Lar to spill the beans so soon, but as it's done, you might as well face the truth. You and Charlie should get into some hot bed action soon or the air will crack asunder with sexual tension in that little house.'

Charlie handed her coffee and sat on the main sofa, his bed for the period of Kate's visit. He was watching her with amusement or some expression from the land of Sardonia. Could he hear?

'I have to go now,' Ruth said. 'I have a lot to do.'

'Ooh, he's still there, isn't he? I knew you'd see sense. Go get him, sis. The ride would do you a world of good.'

'I'll deal with you later.'

Her reply was merry laughter and the sound of a hang-up on the other end.

Charlie was smirking. Had he heard? They were all in this together: let's make a gom out of Ruth. His mouth was drawn into a grin. Then he leaned forward and gasped. 'Fuck, that coffee's boiling.'

Peter and Cathy settled in front of the television, surfing channels. They complained loudly about how there was nothing on worth watching.

'Are you absolutely sure it's OK for him to stay over?' Harry asked.

'Completely. They have tactics to talk and badness to hatch. Leave and don't give it another thought.'

'Thanks, Joyce.'

'There's nothing to thank me for. I intend this to be a quid pro quo. I'm storing up my credits.' She smiled to convince him of her sincerity.

They walked to the front door and stood, not knowing what to say or do next. Joyce wrapped her arms round her body, defensively.

'I've been wanting to talk to you,' Harry said. 'I hope you didn't think I was trying to take advantage, the day of the storm.'

'Of course not. Anyway, I was the scaredy cat turned up on your turf looking for attention. I'm useless around thunder and lightning. Ridiculous carry-on for a farmer's wife, but there you go. In fact, I'll bet I was so preoccupied I didn't thank you properly.'

'Don't mention it. It was a pleasure and a little bit of an ego boost.'

They had smoothed over the cracks. And even gone far enough to suggest that things might have been different, that they were human, but in the wrong situation. Another time, another place, Joyce thought, but not on this round of the wheel. Then again, she hadn't had sex in months and it could be making her fanciful.

'You're looking especially dapper this evening,' she remarked.

'Oh, this old thing,' Harry said, to make her smile and to be self-effacing.

'You have a date, admit it.'

'I'm just meeting someone for a few drinks. I'd hardly call that a date.'

'If she asks if you want to be buried with her people, consider yourself pulled. Enjoy.'

She watched him walk off towards town, his long back bouncing with each energetic step, as dusk began to paint the sky in broad stripes of orange and indigo. The lights of Kilbrody sparked on and twinkled. Stars peeped through millions of light years. Cathy and Peter cackled in the house. Joyce made a silent and predictable wish and went back inside.

Charlie had displayed an ability to read her mind before, so Ruth was uneasy as she sat down in an armchair opposite him.

'Those two are smashed and not making much sense,' she said, casually.

'Why the porky about having lots to do?'

'They were beginning to ramble.'

Her fingers were resting on the velvet of the chair, pressing forward and back on the tactile elegance. She had spent so long feeling what someone else dictated, it was great to call text and texture, action and reaction. It was horny. Lar and Kate smiled, knowingly, in her mind. She shook them off. Of all the things she could do, falling for someone, and especially falling into someone's bed, was the tip-top To Be Avoided thing. Time to switch tracks.

'I was thinking it would be good to let Deborah go home if she's got a bug. I don't mind working. The television is shit tonight. Always is during the summer.' Was she prattling? Covering up too much, trying to distract him from Kate and Lar and the possibility that he knew what they'd said? It was ridiculous to say they couldn't take their eyes off each other. For God's sake, there was nowhere else to look. It would be plain rude to ignore him. Kate was well off beam with her latest theory.

Charlie was boring a hole in her skull. She refused to let her imagination run away with itself and consequently her night. There was usually a prosaic reason for most things. Run with it.

'Did you want more milk to cool your coffee?' she asked.

'No.'

Her plan to ground mental aberrations and the evil workings of the new enemy agents (Kate, Lar, Charlie) went belly up. Now they had a nasty hiatus as Ruth boiled and squirmed and Charlie let her. He must have heard the phone conversation. Desperate action was required; time to get out.

'So, will I?'

'Will you what?'

He loved toying with her to make her flip, but she

was not for turning. Here was the benefit of learning from experience, in its most nascent form. She would heed her lessons and refuse history its repetitious clichés. Florid thinking, but righteous.

'Will I take over from Deborah?'

'Yes, if you'd like. That'd be a very nice thing to do.'

She really couldn't read his mood or tone. That finally settled it. She got up, rinsed her cup and made for the door.

'I'll be down to give you a dig-out later,' Charlie said.

She spun round. 'Why?'

'Ruth, quit acting so skittish. It's Saturday night. We're likely to be busy.'

She gave herself a mental kicking and fled.

Tom Long doused the light in his room, grateful to be shot of the cruel fluorescence. He gazed at the sky, trying to name the few early stars that sparkled against the brightness of the extended summer day. His head raged as poisons left his system, but he avoided asking for a painkiller, saving it until he needed to sleep. His mouth tasted of flint and his tongue was fuzzy, his eyes were red and scratchy. A beard was growing longer by the second and it itched too. It had an orange tinge and he remembered telling Cathy once it was from eating carrots.

'Is that why my hair is red?' she wanted to know, before refusing any ginger-coloured foods for a month.

He was growing stronger with each day, but finding the battle to think of anything but drink a very difficult one. He obsessed about alcohol, craving it, loving it still. The better his body, the more he felt he could handle a pint. He knew this was false confidence. He could never drink again. He hated that finality, the tyranny of the idea. Didn't want to believe it. Whatever happened to control, free and informed choice? He was fair game for everyone in the place now, too, and this was getting right up his nose. Accusation heaped on accusation. People called him names, mostly coward. These were strangers, and yet they felt they could poke into his life and make cruel observations, when most of them were even worse off than he was.

If he could have one drink, the guilt would ease and he could make some constructive changes. Joyce and Cathy had suffered. He had to make that up to them. How was he to do all of these things without a crutch? He could see no light, no way forward. He rocked and tried to chant to take his mind off that one glorious shot of whiskey, its amber warmth relaxing his pain-racked frame and clearing his thoughts. He poured water from the litre jug beside his bed and drank some to slake his thirst. Amazing that something so good could be so bland. A terrible shame, really.

Deborah took time out from belching to greet Carol. 'Where's Tweedledee?' she asked, astonished.

'Linda's given up on Finn's, says she needs pastures new. So she's gone off to Paris with Angie O'Reilly for the weekend. After that, who knows where they'll fetch up.'

Deborah sucked in air. 'That'll cost Ozzy a pretty penny.' She put a vodka and tonic in front of Carol. 'I'm assuming you still drink this stuff.'

'Oh, yes. I'm gang of one now but the signature tipple remains the same. Anyhow, I'm meeting someone.' She couldn't keep it in.

Deborah looked through slitted eyes. 'Bert, is it?'

'No, Harry Finan.'

Deborah whizzed through her files. 'Ah yes, the new lad. Buys the expensive vitamins and sunscreen. Verruca on his left foot but it's shifting.'

'Thanks for that,' Carol said, trying to sound sarcastic, but her excitement got in the way. She paid for the drink and set her good side towards the entrance.

Deborah belched again and clutched her stomach. 'God, I hope that sandwich stays put. I sprayed the bath products section next door earlier with a banana that went down wrong. Honestly, I'm just a big barf bag at the moment. I'll wither to nothing with the dehydration if I'm not careful.'

'A flat Seven-Up is what you need,' Ruth said, appearing at the bar. 'Sit yourself out there and I'll get it for you. And then you can go home and have a rest. I'll finish off the shift.'

'Did the dinner not go well?' Deborah asked, pity-ingly.

'It was fine,' Ruth said, in a tight voice. Was there no such thing as a secret round these parts? 'I thought it'd be good to let you go if you're not well.'

'We'll have to get used to that for a while.'

Both other women stared, antennae twitching, wondering if they'd heard properly and had reached the correct conclusion.

Deborah nodded. 'I'm not that far gone, and I'm having terrible morning sickness. Don't know why it's called that when it's all day long sickness in my case.'

'And who . . . ?' Carol petered off.

'I won't be announcing that till I get the fecker to agree to marry me, or at least to part with a ring. It'll kill the mammy otherwise. Though not till after she's had skin and hair flying all over the house. Ah well.' She broke wind again, thought short and hard, and rushed to the ladies.

Harry walked through the door and smiled so widely his face looked like a gurn. Carol was a mirror image. Deborah made up a pale rear as she returned.

Love is in the air, Ruth thought. She prepared to sit back and enjoy the show.

Thirty-Three

Old Mikey was granted an audience with his granddaughter. He brought two replies from neighbours and was eager to know how the work was going.

'The Gilhooleys can't help because they're doctors and have an oath not to share patient information,' Cathy said. 'Still, they were very nice and seemed to think that most people would be keen on the scheme.'

Joyce brought tea and Jaffa Cakes.

'Do you remember Patch Collerane that died this week?' Old Mikey asked Cathy.

'Yeah, he lived over the Inagh direction. Bit of a mad lad.'

'Patch was married when he was in his teens. His wife had a stillborn baby boy and then died herself two days later. They buried them together in the graveyard you're clearing out. I was thinking that we should include that wee lad on our list. His name was Patrick Joseph Collerane. Poor aul Patch never got over it and spent the rest of his days praying for death, I think. He didn't get to be buried with them either because the old graveyard is closed to funerals now. He's above in the new place. And he was the last of that branch of the Colleranes. There's no more of them left round these parts.'

Cathy added the name. 'I always thought he was odd, now I know why.'

'Another thing. How do you feel about a bouncy castle?'

'I don't think that's very appropriate,' Joyce said.

Mikey frowned, then twigged. 'Ah no, not for the Angels. For Cathy's birthday.'

'Grandad, I'm going to be thirteen. I'm not a kid any more.' She wanted to disappear through the floor. What would Peter think?

'Did you ever have a go of one?' her grandfather asked.

'No.'

'Me neither. I'd love to.' He gave a smile that told her he would be hard to dissuade. Was someone putting something in the water to drive the oldies mad?

'Oh God, this means I'm having a party,' Cathy groaned.

'And a bouncy castle,' Peter whispered.

Ozzy had the sorrows of the world on his slender shoulders. He was valiantly trying to drown them in a vat of porter.

'She cleared the bill on the credit card before she

went. That's bad news.' He shook his head. 'The woman won't be satisfied till I haven't an arse left in me trousers,' he declared. 'She won't rest till I'm beyond in Parklands like Tom Long. Or sectioned.'

'And, sure, isn't that what women are for?' Charlie said, egging him on. 'To vex a man and spend his money.'

Ruth gave him a quick dig in the ribs. He was pleased with the attention, but had the decency to give a pained yelp.

'God bless all here,' Old Mikey trilled as a greeting.

'Enter a free man,' Ozzy said, bitterly.

'A pint, Charles. Does anyone know where I might lay hands on a bouncy castle? I have the notion to hire one for Cathy's birthday.'

'Is she not a bit old for one of them?' Ruth asked.

'No one's too old for a bouncy castle,' Old Mikey pronounced.

'When is the do?' Ruth wanted to know.

'This day week. It's the day after the Youth Project finishes, so we thought we'd have it to celebrate the whole shooting match. Will you be here?'

'Don't know,' Ruth stammered. Her heart bounced around in her chest and refused to slow down. The school term was nearly upon her, and if she wanted to take up her post again she should get back to Dublin the following weekend to prepare.

Charlie rested his hand on her shoulder. 'Relax, Ruth,' he urged, softly. 'We have a whole week.'

What did he mean by that? She searched his face and got a Finn dazzler. Her knees began to knock. Ridiculous. Kate had infected her brain with nonsense and it was beginning to get to her. Charlie Finn was no more interested in her than the man in the moon. He was an inveterate smoothie and treated all women like this.

Bert Fahy joined Deborah and was immediately plunged into the saga of her excessive health. The scene unfolded in dumbshow from Ruth's point of view and she was glad of the distraction. Bert was stunned, silenced, elated. He threw his arms round Deborah and kissed her exuberantly. She finally held him back, put her hand to her mouth and spewed gently through her fingers, onto his shirt. He reached for a handkerchief and wiped them both down. He dropped to one knee and asked a question. When the answer was clearly 'Yes', he stood and tapped his glass for attention.

'Ladies and gentlemen, I am the happiest man in the room. Miss Deborah A. Dunne has agreed to be my wife.'

Loud applause filled the bar.

'And we are looking forward to the birth of our first child in . . .' He looked for information.

'April,' Deborah supplied.

A cheer threatened to raise the roof and tears lined every eye.

'Finn's, where love stories begin,' Charlie intoned.

Ruth repeated the dig in the ribs. This time he grabbed her and kissed her cheek. She was left gasping for breath and wondering what time the bus went through the following day. Escape might be just the thing. She was living in dangerous times.

She looked around at the smiling faces. Carol and Harry were in the first throes of exchanging life stories and preferences, and whooping to confess their naff record choices. Deborah was snoozing on Bert's shoulder. His face could not have been marked with more happiness.

'You know, Ruth,' Mikey said. 'We're only here the once. It's a terrible sin to waste time.'

Great, now everyone was a savant and knew what she should be doing. She decided to ignore the proffered wisdom. Charlie winked. She was the victim of a widespread conspiracy, initiated by her sister and perpetuated by every last wretch in Kilbrody.

'Cathy is nearly out the door with the response to her appeal for the Little Angels plot,' Mikey told his audience.

'What does she plan to do?' Ruth asked, glad of a change of tune.

'She'll compile a register to be kept in the library and we'll fence the plot and put up a nice plaque.'

'Suffer the little children to come unto me.'

'Exactly, Ruth. Do you know, I think that would make a great dedication.' Mikey raised his glass. 'Thank you.'

The clock said nine thirty. Ruth saw eternity stretching ahead and felt vulnerable. The night was a mixture of fancy and the strange spell she was under, reinvented and included in the epicentre of the new world in which she now lived, however temporarily. She prayed for fresh troops to the beer trough to pass the time as quickly and uneventfully as possible. And she wanted Charlie gone. He was brushing past and playing havoc, a giant mistake waiting to ambush her, and to be avoided. When her mid-session break came she rushed to the shower and let ice-cold water bring her back to scabby, inadequate earth. It cleared her head and introduced a note of sober reflection that reminded her she was leaving soon and might never return. One time round on the carousel or not. Sorry, Mikey.

She was feeling safe as she prepared to re-enter the bar. She had inured herself against foolishness, she thought. Then, as she carelessly slung her used towel on the rail in the bathroom, she took in her surroundings. She had made an automatic gesture. She knew where everything was. Charlie's discarded shirt lay on the tiles waiting to move to the wash pile. She was at home. *Home*.

Cautiously, she went to the main living room. It spoke to her of Charlie and of Ruth, now. Her bag was by the chair, her notebook on the coffee table. The daily paper was flung on the floor. The place smelled familiar and happy. The hum of the bar below was the soundtrack she knew, and loved. And in that midst was Charlie. She trembled as she moved towards the stairs.

As she returned to work, doubt set in and began to beat her up. Charlie was paying her no more and no less attention than she deserved as a co-worker. He smiled when smiled at and returned jokes. She became microscopically strict in dissecting his reactions to her and finally admitted that she had jumped the gun like a smitten teenager. Stupid. And so pathetic she could hardly hold her head up. The evening dragged, like moving through a pillow. She was detached from her body and movements, waiting for work to end and sleep to begin, and the days to move on till her departure. She could go sooner than Saturday, there was nothing to hold her.

Deborah and Bert left to break the news to her mother. 'Say a prayer she doesn't have a conniption and keel over. They won't send the ambulance for her any more, not after the last time.'

It was best not to delve.

Harry and Carol slipped away and the Whinge slipped in, in time to say goodnight to Old Mikey, who was leaving relatively early, and only half cut, because he was still helping Joyce out in the mornings. He tucked a sodden Ozzy under his arm and promised to see him home. He pooh-poohed the idea of calling the hackney. 'Sure, he's only a wee scrap of a thing. I can carry him if the walking gets too much.'

When the last of the night's revellers passed into the

darkness, Charlie turned and said, 'You were wearing that outfit the night you arrived.'

She thought of the rag that had arrived. She had little to lose.

'Why did you let me stay?'

'You needed somewhere but you didn't have any money, and after you got naked I didn't have the heart to throw you out onto the street.'

'I what?' Her face was a masterclass in surprise and Charlie could barely keep from smiling.

'You misunderstood what I meant by working off your debt.' He paused. 'For what it's worth, you looked fantastic.'

Ruth hesitated, unsure of what was going on between them now. There was only one way to find out. 'Then what happened?'

'I draped as much as I could over you and led you upstairs.'

Ruth moved ahead of him as she had on the night. She could scarcely draw breath. 'Like this?'

Her muscles quaked, trying to climb the stairs calmly and without falling.

'When we got to the main room, you began to stagger a lot, so I lifted you, like so.' He hoisted her into his arms and she rested her head against his chest. His heart tapped at her ear. 'I brought you here to my bedroom, laid you on the bed, where you passed out for two days.'

Ruth, lying on the duvet, said, 'So, like this, but naked.'

'Butt naked, yes.'

Fortune favours the brave. She squeezed her doubts shut. 'Would you kiss me, Charlie?'

'I thought you'd never ask.'

'I didn't think I'd have to.'

He leaned in and whispered, 'You're my miracle.'

Before she could respond, his lips were on hers and she misplaced reality. Her body tingled and her mind lost focus on anything but Charlie. *I can't feel my toes any more,* she thought. *Why were they ever important?* His tongue slipped over hers, caressing, then teasing. He moved to her neck, slowly tracing a graceful curve. It felt amazing but she stopped him. 'Can we take this slowly?'

'We'll do whatever you want, Ruth.'

'It's not that I don't want to. It's just that I had a bad experience recently and I need time to get over it.'

'I understand.' He kissed her forehead. 'I'll be here when you're ready for me.'

Ruth groaned. 'We've still got to clean the pub.'

'Leave it to me. I've got a lot of spare energy to work off.'

'Ten more minutes asleep on that bus and I'd have ended up in Limerick.'

'It doesn't bear thinking about.'

Charlie skipped downstairs humming while Ruth hugged her knees to her chest in delight. An image from her journey returned. She was paying the bus driver for her ticket. 'One way,' she had said. 'All the way.'

Thirty-Four

Ruth woke ridiculously early and could not lie still. She had a quick shower, chose her trendiest clothes and dabbed on a little lip gloss. She went in search of breakfast. It was still only eight o'clock. She took a cup of coffee to the garden and deadheaded the roses. At nine, Charlie appeared, freshly washed and looking as giddy as she felt.

'Good morning,' she trilled, knowing that a foolish grin was spreading across her face.

Charlie kissed her. She put her arms around his neck and he held her tight, breathing her in. She wanted to stay like this for ever. Instead, they rustled up some cereal and sat on the roof wondering how to proceed.

'First things first,' Charlie said gravely. 'Where are the Sunday papers? You were first up and should have taken care of those.'

'Fair point,' she conceded. 'But I don't think I can

be fired from my post as we haven't yet defined it, so any aberrations might stem from the lack of job description.'

They were lightly drawing up their new boundaries, with ease that showed them both how different this relationship was to anything they had known previously. They trusted each other. Charlie was first to take the plunge.

'Well, girlfriend, lover, partner, you choose.'

Ruth accepted with, 'I'll take them all, thanks.'

Cathy and Joyce were silent for the journey. Joyce hated the trips to Parklands, being made to feel an outsider, and not seeing the improvement she hoped for in Tom. Cathy didn't know what to expect, but had a feeling it would be no cakewalk.

'You got a great reception after Mass,' her mother said. Don't expect the same at this place, she wanted to add.

'Yeah, even Father Kilcullen didn't seem to mind and he likes to be the centre of attention on a Sunday. He's giving me a look at the priests' records this afternoon, so I can compare it with what I have already.'

'I'm really proud of you, Cathy. And I know your dad is too. He might not get the chance to say that today, because of the big session and all, but I know he wants to.'

The car paused at the turn-off, waiting for a break in

the traffic. The indicator clicked soothingly and the Long ladies tried to relax. It was impossible, of course.

Other cars delivered their human cargo on to the tarmac in front of the clinic. The noise was muted but for one small girl who wailed her protest. No one minded; she was voicing the mood of all. Cathy and Joyce walked reluctantly forward, following the crowd to a big assembly hall. They took a seat in the front row because they were told they had to. Both would have preferred to hide in row four or languish at the back. Tom appeared a few minutes later and came to kiss them.

'You're like a yeti,' Cathy told him.

'Do you not like it?' he asked with mock surprise.

'It's totally heinous.'

'Not for very much longer,' he assured her. 'One of the lads is going to lend me his electric shaver and I'll get rid of it all.' He sat between them and held their hands. 'Thanks for coming. I need the support today of all days.'

'You seem better in yourself,' Joyce said.

'Yeah, I'm getting more sleep and that helps the positive thinking. But it's hard, I'd be lying if I said otherwise.'

A woman in a white coat called attention and said, 'Today is family day and we're happy so many of you could make it. Some of our newer guests will speak today. We'll kick off with Tom Long.' She signalled to him and he rose, trembling.

He turned to the hall, in front of his wife and child, closed his eyes to focus on the job in hand, breathed deep, opened his eyes again and said, 'My name is Tom Long. I'm an alcoholic.'

Cathy and Joyce clutched each other's hands. They wanted to clap. Instead they smiled and nodded. This was a small sentence for a man but a huge statement for Tom Long.

Ruth closed her eyes. She wanted this to work so badly she could taste the hope. 'Do you believe in fate, Charlie?'

'I do now.'

'What else do you believe in?'

'I believe in making the best of what we've got. But I also know there's no need to rush.'

'I can't help feeling my timing is still out. I have a life back in Dublin that needs sorting.'

'Ruth, if you decide to go back, you'll still only be up the road. I won't panic just yet. But that is not to say that I'm taking you for granted either.'

Her face hurt from smiling. 'Of course, I could always write that book. I was thinking of a story about a woman who turns up drunk in a small country town and stays on to get her life back to right.'

'Is there a love interest?'

'Several,' she teased.

'Sounds implausible to me.'

'Back to the teaching then.'

'We'll see.'

Ruth thought of the opportunity opening up for her. All her life her parents had lived the ideal. She craved the stability they had maintained, and their security of love. It was a rosy picture but, surely, it was right to aim high. She had gone the low road and found it wanting. It diminished all around it. Now was the time for chance, after the accident of turning up in the right place at all, let alone at something approaching the right time.

She was afraid, no point in denying it. A rip tide of conflicting emotions fought inside her. Was she expecting too much? Loading the new arrangement with too much baggage? Her assumptions were big, and included a man who had proved fallible before. This was his humanity. And she was no pin-up in the love department. Panic brewed gently beneath her senses, but she had to face reality head on. The next week would be for exploration and, hopefully, consolidation.

'Do you expect good things?' she asked.

'Always. And it's nice when they turn out that way too.'

Cathy and Joyce regaled Old Mikey with news of their visit to Parklands.

'There are some seriously messed-up people there,' Cathy said, awed. 'And those were just the visitors.

Daddy is really normal by comparison. There was one woman who was completely orange.'

'Fake tan left on too long, we think.'

'She looked like she'd been Tangoed.'

'Her husband's recovery was set back a month when he saw her.'

'When can we expect Tom to get out?' The question was for Joyce. Cathy wondered too.

'He'll need another week, at least. That's just to get him fit enough to start the process out this side. It'll be with him for ever.'

'Isn't that why they say one day at a time?'

'We have to go to more sessions this week. I'm going to be an expert on madsers by the end of it. And I am never ever going to drink, that's for sure.'

'Everything in moderation, Cathy.' Mikey put a glossy brochure on the table. 'Railings,' he announced. 'You'd be surprised at the variety there is to choose from.'

The customers in Finn's had second sight. Everyone knew of the new situation before Charlie and Ruth got a chance to flaunt it.

'Ah, that's been coming like a jail on wheels,' was one romantic comment.

Old Mikey was jubilant. 'I knew something good was afoot when Father Kilcullen cut his sermon in half today. The last time he did that, Clare won the All Ireland final.'

'Looks like we've been added to the annals of great sporting moments,' Ruth told Charlie. He looked suitably impressed.

Joyce sat with her diary and marshalled the week. She listed her farm work, pencilling her father in to help, and marked the Parklands sessions she needed to go to. She booked Cathy for shopping in Ennis on the Friday to get her birthday presents. When she was done she allowed herself to think of love. I will have my husband back and well and good, thank you, she wrote. Joyce thought shared love the ultimate goal and she wasn't about to let that go now. She loved Tom, and was in love with him, still and notwithstanding. They had made Cathy and she loved her unconditionally. He will return to me. We were meant to be together for ever. She stuck with the purity of her notion and vowed to endure and win.

Her daughter appeared. 'Anything I can do?' she enquired.

'Just be, Cathy.'

She screwed up her face. 'I think I can manage that.'

Charlie and Ruth had worked with one another long enough to have a shorthand. They were already a team behind the bar, so it was no trouble to add another layer to the mix. Now, she didn't have to avoid bumping into him, or taking his arm. Her pulse raced to enjoy the nearness. But as time moved on she worried about the growing physical aspect of their new status.

Although she desired Charlie, her ordeal at the hands of Greg Deegan had soured thoughts of sexual contact. She didn't know how she would react when the time came for them to sleep together, as she was sure it would. She wanted to believe that everything would be fine, but couldn't help dreading the moment. She felt somehow spoiled for Charlie. As Sunday wore on she grew more reserved.

'Don't worry about a thing,' he whispered, more than once.

But she did.

Deborah and Bert arrived to tell the world that her mother would recover from the news that she was going to be a grandmother and gaining a son-in-law.

'She's started knitting,' Deborah said.

Everyone cooed.

'Ah, not so fast. The booties are for Bert. God only knows what the baby'll end up with.'

'I suppose as long as she doesn't try to do you a wedding dress too, you'll be grand,' Old Mikey threw in.

Deborah blanched and made a dash for the ladies.

'There's always one person that goes too far,' Mikey admitted.

Closing time came and went without acknowledgement, and they eventually got everyone out of the door by half past one. Ruth was visibly shaking by then. Charlie made her tea and asked what the problem was.

'I'm not sure I can talk about it properly, but something bad happened between me and Greg the day I got the bus, and I haven't dealt with it yet.'

'He hurt you?'

'Yes.'

Charlie took her hands. 'Ruth, that's not something I'll ever do. I can't believe I'm the lucky man whose door you walked through and I'll cherish that till the day I die. I won't make demands and I won't tell you what to do. And I'll wait as long as I have to for you.'

'I'm the lucky one,' she said as she reached up to kiss him. With each moment she was erasing Greg Deegan.

Charlie saw her to her room and left for his own. She lay on her bed, her mind racing with romance and the sheer wonder of him. When she slept it was only briefly. Charlie, for his part, thrashed fitfully, listening for sounds of Ruth. In the morning they both felt cheated that sleep had robbed them of time together. The week would be a quick one.

Thirty-Five

Charlie was stunned to realise how narrow his world had been without Ruth. He had existed in a limbo between work and AA meetings. Now, it contained so much more detail and excitement. They took drives, went swimming, climbed hills. He laughed a lot. And he would never tire of kissing her. Each encounter was more intense than the last. Both were mindful of an invisible line in the sand and pulled away when needed. This was more and more difficult as the days wore on.

It was Wednesday night and the bar cleared earlier than usual. They were in the garden, talking, unwilling to let the day go.

'I really think I should drive you back to Dublin,' Charlie said.

'And I really think I should get the bus. I can't reason it properly but it's like the bus is lucky for me. I arrived on it and it'll be good luck to leave on it too.'

'I'm being selfish,' he admitted. 'I want the extra time with you.'

'Look at me, why do you think I'm still up at this hour? Can't bear to be without you.'

They both knew they needn't be, but it was Ruth's call to make.

'I love you, Ruth.' Charlie felt liberated to say it at last. He wanted to keep on and he did. 'I love you, I love you, I love you.' He was shouting it now.

Ruth threw her head back and hooted. 'I love you too,' she said.

Charlie put his arms around her and kissed her passionately, again and again. When they drew breath, Ruth whispered, 'Let's go to bed.'

At first they were tentative, Charlie wary of rushing, Ruth of hesitating, but when they found their pace and let the inevitable take them, it was all they'd hoped for and more.

'This love business is great,' Charlie said, afterwards. 'It's certainly worth waiting for.'

The Youth Project posed by the graveyard wall. Miss Cahill tore about making sure the tallest were at the back and everybody knew that this was a vitally important shot. 'In years to come, people will study this photograph along with the gathered information, and they'll want to be able to identify you all.' When she was satisfied that they were sufficiently marshalled, she sat in her special seat, front row, middle, and the shot was duly dispatched to celluloid.

Cathy was in the second row with Peter and Rachel, the girl they'd been paired with initially. She now stumped them by saying, 'I had a marvellous time.'

Cathy had almost forgotten that Rachel could speak.

'I hope I wasn't too much of a pain.'

'No.' It would have been difficult, seeing as she never expressed much of an opinion on anything. God, Cathy thought, we're probably as close as she's got to friends. 'Would you like to come to my place tomorrow?' she asked. 'It's my birthday, and we're having a cake and that. And I know it's goofy and all, but we're having a bouncy castle too.' She rolled her eyes. 'My grandad is mad into them. We can ignore it.'

'I've never had a go on one of those. I'd love to come along, if you really mean it.'

'I do. Ask Peter. I mean everything I say.'

'It's scary,' Peter warned.

Joyce tooted the car horn and Cathy raced off to join her for the Ennis shopping trip. She checked her list as they drove off. 'Let's get the railings and plaque out of the way first, then we can let loose.'

'Yes, ma'am.'

Ruth and Charlie took half of Friday off. They had stolen every moment to make love but Ruth wanted to keep her last night in Kilbrody as normal as possible.

They lay in Charlie's bed and discussed the following day.

'It's no big deal. I have to go back and settle up there. I want to help Kate sort out our parents' house, and I have to decide what to do about my job. I don't want unfinished business hanging over us.'

'I understand. I'll miss you.'

They listened to the sparse soundscape of early evening.

'Will you be back?'

She kissed him. 'I think you know the answer to that.'

He got out of bed. 'A shower for the lazy lovers and work,' he ordered.

'It would be a waste of water not to share.'

Parklands had its usual full complement of cars and people for the weekend. Cathy checked her reflection in the dark paintwork of a gleaming Mercedes. Her new T-shirt said 'Princess' in diamanté and she'd matched it with deadly black jeans. They went straight to the garden where she could see her father under an oak tree. He had his back to them and was talking to himself. Cathy's heart sank. Had he had a setback? Joyce called ahead and he turned awkwardly, hiding something behind his back. He had obviously got hold of a bottle. Cathy wanted to jump on him and claw. She fell in behind her mother and retreated within herself.

He began to sing 'Happy Birthday', hands still behind

his back. Did he think they were so stupid they wouldn't notice what he was up to? Then he produced it. Cathy did a double take. The bottle was a puppy, a little golden bundle of fluff and yipping. It wriggled to be free.

'She's a frisky one,' Tom said.

'Oh, Daddy, is she for me?'

'If she'll have you, yes. Happy birthday, Princess.'

She took the puppy and let her lick her face all over, washing her with her baby breath. Tom and Joyce embraced and kissed, holding on to each other afterwards. Cathy turned away, not wanting to cry in public, especially as she was now a teenager and had a new ultra-hard front to maintain. 'I'll call her Bella,' she said. 'Because she's so beautiful.'

Joyce Long was less gobsmacked to see Charlie on this visit. She welcomed him and Ruth and showed them round to where Old Mikey was supervising the erection of the bouncy castle.

'You'd think he knew something about it to hear him go on,' Joyce said.

Ruth bent to pet the puppy.

'That's Bella. She's Tom's present to the birthday girl.'

'How is he doing?' Ruth asked. The moment was surreal for her. Tom Long had scrambled her hormones when she'd arrived, but that seemed like a century ago and a world away. She looked at Charlie and let her heart soar as it did each time she caught sight of him.

'He's getting there, inch by inch. Thanks for asking.'

Old Mikey waved and got back to issuing orders, which were duly ignored by the two men pumping air into the castle. Cathy joined the fray and a mild argument erupted. Ruth went to intervene.

'I'm hearing good news,' Joyce said, smiling at Charlie.

'About me and Ruth? Yes. I'm happy to say it's all true.'

'At long last.'

'You know me,' he said. 'I'm a fussy bugger.'

They gathered around a small table in the garden and sipped Coke and ate early birthday cake. Ruth and Charlie presented Cathy with a basket of soaps and bathing foam from McGrath's.

'Deborah recommended these,' Ruth told her.

'I bet that was worth hearing,' Old Mikey said.

Charlie agreed. 'There was mention of avoiding ulcers and the plague. Very enlightening.'

The guests began to arrive and with them the excitement of gifts and greetings. The Sergeant had a large parcel under his arm and a frighteningly happy expression on his face.

'I'm sorry to miss the party,' Ruth said to Cathy. 'I have to get the bus and it leaves at exactly the wrong time.'

'It always does,' Cathy snorted. 'You could nearly set your watch by it.'

'I still don't know why you won't let me drive you.'

'I'm tired telling you it's lucky for me to go on the

bus,' Ruth said. 'I don't know how I know it, but I do. It's symmetry.'

Charlie shook his head, indulgently. 'So long as it's not a full stop.'

'You great eejit. It's a beginning. I love you and I want to be with you, and I will when I sort out the other Ruth.'

'I'll be in Dublin next week for that vintners' thing.'

'Charlie, you've told me that on the hour, every hour, for the last twelve hours. Yes, I'll see you then. Yes, you'll stay with me. Stay as long as you like. And yes, I'll phone you when I get there later today. I want to. I want to hear your voice all the time. I'll probably phone from every stop along the route.'

''Course there's no guarantee this bus'll ever turn up,' he said, cheerily. 'It's already fifteen minutes late. Told you before, it's a terrible service.'

Ruth squinted into the distance but saw nothing. 'Maybe I should call Ozzy to check.' She turned threateningly to Charlie. 'Are you sure there is an afternoon service?'

'I don't want you to leave, even for a short while, but I did promise never to lie to you. So, yes, during the summer there's an extra service on a Saturday.'

They heard a rumble of metal and diesel and saw a plume of dirt rise as the bus came into view.

'I don't believe it,' Charlie exclaimed, checking his watch. 'I didn't think it'd be here for another hour at least.'

A young scarecrow was at the wheel. He opened the

doors and stepped out to supervise the loading of the baggage. The hold was already bulging with backpacks. He looked at Ruth's satchel. 'You can take that on with you,' he said, magnanimously. 'You don't look like you're going for long.'

'She's not,' Charlie said.

'Bit of shoppin' for the missus in the Big Smoke,' the driver said, winking.

Charlie didn't contradict him.

'Where's the other lad?' Ruth asked.

'Ah, Jack couldn't take the long runs. His temperament was all wrong. He's switched to Dublin Bus now and does the short hops around the town. I'm delighted. I always had me eye on this route. I nearly have it running on time, you know.'

He boarded and began to sell tickets. Ruth hung back till last. Finally she found courage, kissed Charlie and said, 'Talk to you later.'

She sat in the back row, to leave in a reflection of her arrival, but on the correct side of the looking glass. She placed her bag beside her on the seat. She blew a kiss and they were away. Her heart lifted with affection as she whispered her goodbyes to the town. I'll see you all again soon. It felt good to breathe, to simply be alive, but mostly to be in love.

Ozzy scanned the countryside. There was no way that bus would make any more time over the journey, especially with the snarl-up at the Inagh junction. Looked like Mrs Gilhooley Senior had mashed the fender on another Volvo; tough work and them built like tanks. Deborah and Bert were sunning themselves at his place. The banns would be read from the pulpit tomorrow and he knew the bride wanted to get the wedding over with before she was as big as a house. The town had a good do to look forward to there. Carol, the librarian, was walking along the road with the scientist fellow and his son. They were headed to the Long place. He might go down there later himself and have a try of the inflatable yoke in the garden. Old Mikey hadn't been off it since it went up two hours ago. First he'd swing by and say hello to wee Lawrence and let him know that the Angels would have their new railings and commemoration the following weekend, according to Cathy.

The bus made slow progress, which gave Ruth ample time to take in the surroundings she'd missed on her previous journey. The Long house appeared with the huge bouncy castle on the lawn. It was going ten to the new time. The driver honked the bus horn at it and Old Mikey emerged, tousled and red-faced from his workout. He waved happily. Ruth was convinced she could see the Sergeant's head pop up and down above the parapet.

Cathy ran past her grandfather to the wall, with the

yelping puppy on a leash, four legs to Cathy's two but so short she lagged behind still. Her skin rolled over her little bones, too much of it to be filled just yet by her tiny frame. Cathy pulled at her new T-shirt and its precious bra beneath. She felt important in them. She placed the pup on the wall, settling her safely under her arm. As the bus passed, Cathy waved to Ruth and Bella gave three short barks, to signal another safe departure.

You can by any of these other **Review** titles
from your bookshop or *direct from the publisher.*

FREE P&P AND UK DELIVERY
(Overseas and Ireland £3.50 per book)

Fame and Honour	Jincy Willett	£6.99
Jaded	Lucy Hawking	£6.99
Spit Against the Wind	Anna Smith	£6.99
All is Vanity	Christina Schwarz	£7.99
The Distance Between Us	Maggie O'Farrell	£7.99
Sorting Out Billy	Jo Brand	£6.99
The Bad News Bible	Anna Blundy	£6.99
The Secret Life of Bees	Sue Monk Kidd	£7.99
Sitting Practice	Caroline Adderson	£6.99
Small Island	Andrea Levy	£7.99
Dancing in a Distant Place	Isla Dewar	£7.99

TO ORDER SIMPLY CALL THIS NUMBER

01235 400 414

or visit our website: www.madaboutbooks.com

Prices and availability subject to change without notice.